The Love We All Wait For

by Lee Doyle

KOMENAR
publishing

Disclaimer: This novel is a work of fiction. The events and characters described are products of the author's imagination.

Cover design by KOMENAR Publishing
Interior design by BookMatters

THE LOVE WE ALL WAIT FOR.
Copyright © 2008 by Lee Doyle.

Special book excerpts or customized printings can be created to fit specific needs.

For information, address KOMENAR Publishing, 1756 Lacassie Avenue, Suite 202, Walnut Creek, California 94596-7002.

Library of Congress Cataloging-in-Publication Data available

ISBN 978-0-9817271-0-3

First Edition

10 9 8 7 6 5 4 3 2 1

Printed in the United States of America

For Tim and Lily.
I love you this *much,*
and then some.

Acknowledgements

I'm grateful to the many dear friends and family members who willingly read early drafts of this novel and encouraged me to stay on the path, and particularly to past and current members of the Women's Group. I'm also grateful to Clive Matson, Tom Jenks, and my other writing teachers for their guidance over the years. Countless thanks go to Elizabeth Banning, Annie Robinson, and Mary Reynolds Thompson who cheered me on during the final revision of the manuscript.

My heartfelt appreciation goes to Charlotte Cook at KOMENAR Publishing for her instinctive ability to make a good story great and for her precision editing. Special thanks to Jasmine Nakagawa for a gorgeous cover and for her exemplary marketing of this book, and to Julia Tanner and Madelen Lontiong for their support.

I'm grateful to my mom and dad for transplanting us from the City to the Salinas Valley, and for teaching me discipline and compassion. I'm also thankful to my sister Mary Lynn Korn whose optimism and creative talents have saved me on more than one occasion. My husband Tim Burby has been there every step of the way and I'm deeply grateful to him.

The Love We All Wait For

One

I stuck my bare feet on the dash of my mother's ten-year-old 1965 VW Bug. The metal was hotter than I'd bargained for. I let the heat sink in and felt the relief of its intensity. My brother Josh just chewed his thumb while he used his elbow to hold the steering wheel.

We were camped in the gas line at Qwik Gas. A quarter of a mile of pearly low riders, rusted out Pintos, and pickups outfitted with roll bars and rifle racks stretched out behind us. Josh eased the VW up to the bumper of the Mustang with "Wash me, asshole" across the back window. I wiped sweat from the back of my knees.

"This sucks." Josh spat out a piece of thumbnail and tossed a wedge of blond hair from his eyes. "I can't wait to get to the coast."

I glared at him. He blinked his swimming-pool-blue eyes at me several times. In a week, he would leave for Imperial Beach for basic training. He had dropped this bomb at breakfast this morning. Mom had taken the news surprisingly well. The Vietnam War was over, and more importantly, she was in love. My little sister Annie worried only about King, our feeble black Lab, who'd favored Josh since Daddy had died. I was pissed off, which Josh had expected. And why shouldn't I be?

"I can't believe you're doing this," I said.

"Come on, Sheila. It's not like I'm going into combat." He fingered the keys dangling from the ignition. "It's a good time to serve."

"Serve?" I punched his leg below the fringe of his cut-off Levi's, a sure bruise he deserved. "They've brainwashed you already."

"Shut up, Shee," he said, wincing as he rubbed his leg. "You sound like Dad."

"Someone in this family needs to talk sense," I said.

I wished I'd hit him harder. I wished Daddy was still around to straighten him out. Daddy would get him to see the light.

Across from the filling station, the *shuk shuk* of the sprinklers in the fields seemed cheap relief from the heat. A braver girl than me would scale the fence and run through those sprinklers.

"They'll shave your head," I said, trying another angle.

He shrugged and ran his fingers through his hair. He'd quit competitive swimming the previous fall, and now his hair was shoulder length and sun-streaked. My mother called it his lion's mane.

"Dad hates you doing this," I said.

Daddy had detested the military and the CIA. Richard Nixon and his cronies were demons, Vietnam their infernal playground.

Daddy was the only person in town who had thought this way. Except for Tall Larry, the black janitor at Tristes High School.

"Dad's dead," Josh said, rolling his eyes. "In case you didn't notice."

I swallowed the dusty lump in my throat. I was suddenly dying of thirst.

"Do you have any change?" I asked.

I smiled at him with mock sweetness. To my surprise, he reached into his pocket and dropped two quarters into my hand. He was typically tight with his money.

"You owe me," he said.

"Consider it payment for your stupidity," I said.

The soles of my flip-flops seemed soft when they made contact with the pavement. The air was dense, resistant to movement. We had another hour of one hundred-degree temps to endure before the wind passed through to wash away the dust, the metallic odor of pesticides, and woodsy, shivering smell of Fat City, the steer ranch in the Gabilan Foothills, just east of town.

"That's cold, Shee," Josh called.

I turned around and stuck out my tongue. "You want a soda or not?"

The soda machine ate the quarters. I looked around for Ramon Ramirez, the attendant. He was busy filling the Fratti Farms truck at the pump. Fumes shimmered from the metal gas nozzle. Ramon had to stand on his tiptoes to squeegee the truck's windshield, flicking the toothpick in the corner of his mouth as he worked.

One night, under the influence of tequila sunrises at a roadside keg party, Ramon had professed his love for me. Since I'd turned him down, he'd pretty much steered clear of me. My best friend Ingrid kidded that we'd make a great couple. Ramon was four foot eight. At nearly seventeen, I was a towering five-eight. Ingrid had strange ideas about romance.

When I got back in the car, Josh was spinning the radio dial. He looked at me blankly. His forehead glistened with sweat.

"No soda?" he asked.

"The machine's out of order," I said.

"It figures." He frowned at the pulsing Spanish music coming from the radio.

Tristes got three stations. KHTS Top 40, for the thirty-five-and-unders. KPSA with its campy Spanish ballads. And KJAZ broadcast out of fog-choked Monterey on the other side of the Santa Lucia Mountains. KJAZ only came in during rainstorms.

My father had died on a stormy February night. He had been a Miles Davis fan. I was only eleven years old at the time. A few weeks after the accident, I had called KJAZ and asked the DJ what they'd been playing at 1:48 A.M., when the train barreled into Daddy's stalled pickup. Miles Davis. Daddy's timing was impeccable.

Josh switched off the radio and went to work on his thumbnail again. I watched Ramon toss the squeegee into a tub, sending soap suds flying. He mopped his hand across his forehead and surveyed the line of cars.

"Poor guy," Josh said. He was scrutinizing Ramon too. "See what I mean? There's nothing here for me."

"You could always work for George," I said. "If you could stand it."

George Fratti owned most of the land around Tristes, along with the only produce packing company in town. He'd been lusting after my mother for years. That meant he would do anything for us.

After Daddy had been killed, George had waited a while. Then he made his move. My mother eventually gave him the signal, and they went on a first date. Roses and a candlelit dinner on Fisherman's Wharf in Monterey. A year later, the proposal. The wedding was set for this October.

"George is all right. I just don't want to work for him," Josh said. He let out a deep sigh. "I'll be fifty by the time we get gas. I thought the oil embargo was over."

"Mom will probably get a new car now," I said.

"It's about time," Josh said. "Look at it."

The bent metal seam on the VW's hood threw out a blade of sunlight. The deer had come out of nowhere one night after my mother's shift at the Steak Pit. Chief Rodriquez was out patrolling for drunks and found my mother in the middle of the road hunched over the doe. My mother refused to leave the deer's side. She said she owed it to the doe to stick around.

"I love this car," I said.

The Fratti Farms truck at the pump pulled out of the station and headed south into town. A bearded collie darted across the truck bed. Another hot passenger on this miserable day. Josh moved up a car length.

"I wish Annie would shut up about the pony George is going to buy her," I said.

Annie had been an infant when Daddy was killed. Josh's and my memories were all she had. Poor Daddy had even less than that. A plain pine box and the *Winnie the Pooh* book Annie had given to my mother to put in the ground with him.

"Annie needs a dad, Shee," Josh said.

"She has a dad," I said.

"You're unbelievable." The sharp blue of his eyes held muted exasperation.

"That makes two of us," I said.

I glanced in the rearview mirror. Betty Rodriquez was sitting in her pristine white Buick. Her candy-red lips were moving, counting the pearl rosary beads she kept in her purse. Betty was Ing's mom and therefore always praying.

Her suspicions about Ing's promiscuity were warranted. Ing had lost her virginity when she was twelve to Billy Rollins. She later referred to Billy's penis as a Vienna sausage. He had tried to make up for it by grinding Ing's butt against the pitcher's mound. The scrapes were still healing a week later. By the end of our sophomore year, Ing's interludes had totaled eleven to my zero.

The only guy I had ever considered dating was Jimmy Emmons. But Ing had snagged him the previous summer. Betty was convinced Jesus had brought Ing and Jimmy together. He would do the right thing if Ing "got in trouble." It was true,

Jimmy adored her. And she loved his adoration. Ing called this love.

"Have you been to the cemetery?" Josh asked.

"What?" I was a million miles away.

"Have you been to see Dad?"

Daddy's plain tombstone was tucked among the marble crosses and pink granite headstones of well-to-do Swiss Italians. I had tried to get my mother to bury Daddy closer to the migrant workers' graves whose anonymous wood crosses Daddy would have found solace in, given his political leanings. But Mom had insisted that he have a burial that befitted a father and a high school teacher.

"Not for a while," I said. "But the last time I went, he talked to me."

"Dad never talks to me," he said. He ripped a stray thread from the fringe of his cutoffs.

"That's because he loved me more." I grinned at him, and he cracked a smile.

Truth was, I would rather have had Daddy talking to both of us in the flesh. His voice didn't make up for him dying. I would never stop missing him. But it kept me from losing him completely. Sometimes this seemed like enough.

We were at the pump now. Ramon approached the driver's-side window with his hands tucked in the greasy pockets of his uniform trousers. He looked in at my bare legs.

"Fill it, would you?" Josh said. When Ramon was out of earshot, he added, "You're too picky. He's crazy about you."

"Look who's talking about being picky," I said.

"At least I took a chance." He turned on the radio again and immediately switched it off.

Josh was referring to Violet from Hollister, his only girlfriend really. He'd fooled around with Ing's cousin Lorna once or twice, but then he decided she liked him too much. Violet lived a safe distance. Hollister was fifty miles away on the eastern side of the Gabilan Mountains. The drive there was a good hour plus.

Josh and Violet had met at the first football game of the season. They wrote letters, met at games to make out. Then around Christmas, Violet's letters stopped. Her phone had been disconnected. Josh had chewed his thumbnails down to the cuticles and, after three days, driven to Hollister. Her parents' ranch house was empty.

"You think you would've married her?" I asked.

He stared out at the dry field beyond the sprinklers. Workers spilled out of a migrant bus to pick a late crop of strawberries. They dispersed amid the rows slowly, ignoring the shouting foreman.

"Probably," he said in a low voice.

The gas pump clicked in the tank. Ramon took a ten-dollar bill from Josh. He fingered the bill and rocked on his heels.

"I hear you enlisted," he said. He glanced at me and then settled his gaze on Josh. "I've been thinking of doing the same. Maybe I'll see you down there."

"Yeah, man," Josh said. "That would be great."

"See you around, Sheila." Ramon flicked the toothpick.

"Stay cool," I said.

Josh pulled out of the station. He threw on the blinker and waited for a truck hauling a trailer of irrigation pipes to pass. The pipes clattered as the trailer wheels bounced over twin potholes. Road maintenance was not a priority for the City of Tristes.

"Ramon will never leave," he said.

"I know," I said.

The Santa Lucia Mountains panned down the west side of the valley. Their creases, carved by rain and wind, seemed dark today, the mountain tips blunted where they met the sky. Across the valley, the Gabilan Mountains shone a quiet gold. The folds in the hills always reminded me of a giant's fists. The giant clung to the edge of the earth, too shy to show his face.

On Main Street, early drinkers had already parked their cars in front of El Ranchero. The bar had been unofficially renamed the Hero when the E and R-A-N-C burned out, leaving L——H-E-R-O. The owner had had the sign fixed, but the name had stuck.

Josh turned down C Street. It consisted of mostly ranch-style homes and the occasional unkempt bungalow, ours being one of them. A crow departed from one mailbox, cawing as it flew to another. A nearby pepper tree shimmied. Breeze, finally.

"You forgot Mom's smokes," I said.

"I thought she quit," he said.

"Not exactly." I snorted. "But George wants her to quit."

Josh sighed. A purist about his health due to years of swimming, he had little patience for my mother's smoking. But no one got Mom to do what they wanted her to do, even for herself.

Josh turned into the Beckmans' driveway to turn around. The Beckmans' Doberman gnashed at the chain-link fence. Mrs. Beckman was standing on a ladder on the porch, wadding up newspaper.

"Use your own damn driveway," she yelled.

"Old bag," Josh muttered.

"Bet you'll miss her," I said.

"No." He shifted into second, gunned the engine to the corner, and stopped. He turned to me. "But I'll miss you guys."

I counted his cinnamon freckles to keep from crying. Five on each side of his nose, just like always. I wanted to say something brave. But all I could think of was how stupid he was, joining the Marines.

⌒

The VW's tires hit the curb in front of Kim's Grocery. I smelled rotting meat. On hot days, the stench coming from Kim's was nauseating. The produce was bad too, either peppered with fruit flies or rock hard. My mother only bought cigarettes from Kim and a carton of milk or loaf of bread on the rare holiday Friendly Market closed.

Josh shoved his hands into the pockets of his cutoffs and went in. He shook his hair from his eyes and reached up to touch the hem of the Dole Pineapple banner hanging from the store ceiling just inside the entrance. I tried to imagine Tristes without him.

Down the street, smoke billowed from the Steak Pit stacks and curled around the year-round plastic reindeer and Santa faded to a Valentine pink. My mother would quit the Pit soon. She was sick of her boss nagging her and the other waitresses. And with the wedding coming, she wouldn't have to work. George would take care of her, of us. My mother said I should be happy. Our lives would change for the better.

Chief Rodriquez lumbered out of the police station. I watched him fold his burly frame into his patrol car. He thought I was a good influence on Ing. "Mi hija, my daughter, my Ingrita would be lost without you," he'd say. His wife Betty prayed, and he counted on me. I'd just nod, allowing him this small comfort.

The Chief had been the one to come to our house that night to report the accident. His heavy footsteps on the porch had woken Josh and me. His voice had been thick with emotion. "He misjudged the train's distance. Lo siento, I'm sorry, Alicia. May his soul find peace." From the doorway where Josh and me watched the Chief cradle my mother, all I could think of was how small his tears were for such a large man.

The wind was starting to kick up, rustling the pepper trees along Main. A stranger came out of El Ranchero. He brushed the burnt-orange hair from his eyes and squinted at the daylight, as if trying to figure out where to go next. He lit a cigarette and headed towards Kim's. A green duffel bag slung over his shoulder bumped his lean frame.

When he passed in front of me, my heart thumped. His T-shirt was damp with sweat, his skin weathered and the color of wet leather. Tristes got few strangers. And never like this one.

God knew what possessed me. I called out to him, asked if he needed help finding someone or something. He turned around and flashed a smile.

"Been told there's work at the packing shed," he said.

"You met Will Fratti," I said.

"Know him?"

He slid the duffel bag off his shoulder. A patch of an American flag was stitched to the pocket of the duffel. Wincing, he rubbed his shoulder. I imagined both shoulders T-shirtless and me rubbing them, and my breath quickened.

"My mother's engaged to his brother." I sounded remarkably calm.

"One of those complicated situations." He gave me a little wink.

"It's boring, really," I said.

"How can anything that happens in Tristes be boring?"

His eyes were white-green, like sea foam. He dropped the burning cigarette and twisted the sole of his boot over it. I held his gaze.

"Easy for you to say," I said.

"Who you waiting for?" he asked.

"My brother," I said with a shrug. "Where'd you hitch from?"

"You're a curious one," he said, reaching for my hand. "What's your name?"

"Sheila."

His calloused fingers curled around mine. My heart was beating like a hard rain on an aluminum roof. When he let go of my hand, his touch lingered. The sensation was both cool and warm.

"I'm Buck Hanson," he said.

Josh came out of Kim's with the cigarettes. He looked from Buck Hanson to me. Buck nodded.

"This is Buck," I said. "He's looking for George."

They shook hands. Briefly. They stood almost toe-to-toe, and nearly the same height. Josh gestured at the duffel on the ground.

"You were in Nam?" he asked.

"Yeah." Buck cleared his throat and looked up the street. "Haven't been able to sit still since."

"I leave for Basic next week," Josh said.

"Why are you going to do a thing like that, kid?" Buck's eyes probed my brother's. "War's not a TV show, man."

"We're not at war." Josh looked away.

"You think so?" Buck picked up the duffel. "I wouldn't put it past those bastards in Washington to get us into another one."

He gave us a mock salute and turned away. His hips shifted under his faded Levi's as he walked up the street. I inhaled. It felt like I was breathing him into me.

"Did you see his face?" Josh said. "Those are wrinkles."

"That's from the sunshine," I said. I couldn't take my eyes off of Buck. "And there's no harm in looking."

He stared at me and folded his body into the VW. He tossed the pack of cigarettes into the glove box. He checked the rearview mirror, then waved to the Chief in his patrol car.

"I got a weird feeling about Buck," he said, backing the car out of the parking space.

The wind was blowing full force now. Buck Hanson crossed the street, eyes locked on Fratti Farms Produce and hair tossing about like a flame. I resisted the urge to tap the horn.

Two

I sat on the edge of the tub, watching my mother get ready. Down the hall, King's toenails tapped the hardwood floor in rapid fire. He'd been scratching for a good five minutes and still hadn't gotten any relief. We'd tried various ointments, but the eczema persisted, a rare form Dr. Wong the vet had only seen in one other black Labrador.

My mother's long fingers, her nails polished a frosted pink, roamed the top drawer of the bathroom vanity for the missing silver hoop earring. Its mate shone against her garden-tanned cheek. She held up a brush choked with my hair and hers and probably several of Annie's brunette curls that had been tugged loose this morning when she and my mother had their daily battle trying to braid Annie's fine, flyaway hair.

"Here it is," my mother cried. The missing earring dangled precariously from a strand of my blond hair. She fastened the hoop to her right ear. "I'm only going by the shed, honey. George left some work papers here last night. You really want to come?"

I had spent the morning trying to figure out how I would "run into" Buck, and now I had my chance. The day before, I had overheard Sally Fratti, George and Will's sister and my mother's best friend, telling my mother that George had hired a new guy, "a handsome southerner with heartbreaker written all over him."

"I need to get out of the house," I said. "I can't stand watching Josh pack anymore."

She seemed to buy my reason for wanting to accompany her. She fluffed her auburn hair, which she'd recently started curling. Prior to falling in love with George, my mother had never so much as picked up a blow dryer. Now she'd gotten even prettier and looked ten years younger.

"You're being very brave about this." She smiled at me in the mirror.

"As if I had a choice," I said.

"I suppose neither of us do," she said. "Mind you, Josh will be fine. The structure will do him good."

This morning, Josh had packed his books, clothes, and swimming trophies, meticulously labeling the boxes. He had tried to pass along the jar of pennies we had set on the railroad tracks when we were little. Annie had refused them. She said faceless pennies couldn't be spent and were therefore worthless. I think it had more to do with the tracks and with what she knew in her heart about Daddy's death.

I dabbed some of my mother's rose-scented body lotion into my hands. Outside, the chimes under the pomegranate tree tinkled. Through the open window, I heard the gentle *thunk* of a blossom hitting the ground. The tree had never born fruit. Daddy had once explained the tree was male, and every summer the bright red-orange blossoms in their tight casings on the ground proved him right.

King appeared in the bathroom doorway. He circled his tail twice and settled on the threshold. Patches and scabs showed through his thinning black coat. He looked at my mother with a long face and grunted.

"Poor thing," she said.

"Do you think he knows?" I asked. "Will Josh leaving do him in?"

"King will survive," she said briskly. "It's good for Josh to take a stand like this. You know how your father could be."

The vanity drawer jammed when she tried to close it. She gave the handle a hard yank and carried the drawer over to the wastebasket. Jars of cold cream, several combs, and a tangled nest of bobby pins and hair tumbled into the wastebasket. King's skinny, long black tail slapped the floor as if to punctuate my mother's summer cleaning effort. She gave the overflowing wastebasket a satisfied nod.

"I've been meaning to do that for a long time," she said, sliding the drawer back into the vanity.

"Dad was right, Mom," I said. "About the war, I mean."

"And now the war's over, thank God. Anyway, you two always agreed."

I watched her apply a satiny pink lipstick. My mother's toiletry had previously consisted of lotion for her parched hands and

Vaseline for her lips, which were always dry from all the time she spent in the garden and wind. People always said she was a natural beauty and didn't require dolling herself up like most women. But now she matched the shade of nail polish with her lipstick. I still wasn't quite used to how feminine she looked. Or that she cared about things she didn't use to give two cents about.

"Mom, I was only a kid," I said.

"It wouldn't have mattered," she said, blotting her lips with a tissue. "You and your father are cut from the same cloth. Glass always half empty."

"You're mixing your metaphors," I said.

"I do love you, Sheila Lorraine." She pressed her cool hands to my cheeks. "Even if you're a pessimist. Fortunately, a sweet one and smart beyond your years. Shall we go?"

Hearing the word "go," King scrambled to his feet.

"You stay," my mother said, pointing to him. "We don't want you wilting in the backseat."

He padded after her down the hallway, looking disgruntled. His tail bounced from wall to wall like a metronome. I followed. After all of this, I hoped Buck would still be there working.

⌒

A blast of cold hit us when we entered the packing shed. The conveyor belts squeaked and groaned under the weight of harvested broccoli. Women in print dresses and sweatpants stuffed into rubber boots were yelling in Spanish over the noise of the spray.

They looked up from their work as my mother and I passed. One of the women smiled and waved, her lips closing shyly over her silver front teeth, Mexican dentistry at its finest. I kept an eye out for Buck.

"That's Rudy's wife, Estella," my mother said, beaming from the good turn she had done the couple. "This is her second day. Now they'll be able to pay their mortgage."

Rudy was the dishwasher at the Pit. My mother had been sneaking doggy bags of leftover prime rib and baked potatoes to him for years. They had six kids. When my mother had first broached the subject of George hiring Estella, George had said he didn't want his workers to think he was doing favors for his fiancée.

"George would do anything for you," I said.

She raised an eyebrow. "Isn't that how it's supposed to be?" she asked.

"I don't know, Mom."

"You're not very tolerant of George," she said, rolling in her lips.

"I'm trying," I said. With Buck hopefully close by and about to show his gorgeous face, I couldn't have cared less about getting along with George.

A forklift whipped around a corner, the lifting blades stopping inches from my mother's sandaled feet. She jumped backwards. I grabbed her arm to steady her.

"Goodness," she said, straightening.

"Hi," I breathed.

It was Buck. His eyes were velvet green in the dim light of the packing shed. Fortunately, my mother was too busy recovering from being nearly run over to hear me say hello.

"Sorry, ma'am." He tipped his Fratti Farms cap at my mother and turned to me as if he'd been expecting me. "Hello, Sheila."

"You've met?" my mother asked, her mouth tight.

"I was a little lost the other day," Buck explained. "But Sheila and her brother—Joe, is it?—set me on the right path."

"Josh," I said, correcting him. I turned to my mother and forced myself to look her in the eye. "It was when we were buying cigarettes at Kim's."

"I'm Alice O'Connor," she said in a businesslike tone I'd never heard before. The princess-cut diamond on her engagement ring twinkled. "Mr. Fratti's fiancée."

"I figured," Buck said, climbing out of the forklift. He gave her a little bow. "Mrs. O'Connor, it's a pleasure."

Over at the sprayers, a woman with a braid the color of a moonless night whispered in Estella's ear. They smiled behind their hands. Buck could have anyone he wanted. And it wouldn't be me, not with my mother hanging around.

"Sorry again for the scare," Buck said and hopped back into the forklift.

The forklift whirred down an aisle of boxes. My mother shot me her "I'm-on-to-you" look and steered me towards the office. I felt the pull of Buck from across the shed. Two minutes of him had only made me want him more.

"Now I know why you wanted to come," she said. "Let's pray he's not interested in you."

"You're making a big deal out of nothing," I said. "And we don't pray in our family."

"It's an expression, honey," she said, giving her wrap-around skirt a smart tug.

~

George was on the phone with a fertilizer sales rep. He pointed at the receiver and flapped his fingers like a duck's bill opening and closing. He motioned for us to take a seat on the vinyl baby-shit-brown couch. The glasses he wore in the office made him look studious.

Daddy had distrusted men like George. One night after fetching my mother from work at the Pit, he had called George and his dice-throwing buddies Republican phonies. There was no worse an insult from my father.

Framed photographs covered the wall over George's desk. His sister Sally on horseback, brother Will bronco-riding, George and Will in matching cowboy outfits. George stood straight and tall, and Will was slumped, his mouth a knot of dissatisfaction. In a very faded photo of George Sr. and his wife Dottie, Dottie's hair was pulled into a severe bun, accentuating the same high cheekbones and brooding eyes that Will had.

George picked up a crystal tractor paperweight, re-positioning it on a stack of paper. He covered the receiver.

"This guy's a motor-mouth," he said to my mother.

"No rush." She smiled and set a folder of his papers on the desk. "I almost forgot."

"Fine." George spoke into the phone. "Bring us some to try on the pinto crops."

In his hand, he turned the pencil-and-pen holder he kept on his desk. Annie had glued on the cup pictures of horses cut from an equestrian magazine. George had claimed it was the nicest gift he'd ever received. I didn't know who had who wrapped around their finger.

Bored, I got up to look at the map of California above the couch. Someone had circled Tristes and drawn an arrow to the words "Home Sweet Home," written in the margin. I followed the Sierra Nevadas with my index finger, touched the blue dot of Lake Tahoe, and moved west and down the coast to Imperial Beach, where Josh would do basic training. He wasn't even gone yet, and already I missed him.

George hung up. He came out from behind the desk, combing his fingers through his coarse black hair to cover his receding hairline. My mother lifted her face to meet his kiss.

George leaned against the front of the desk and crossed his ankles. He was wearing bumblebee laces on his work boots. They looked ridiculous.

"We just ran into Buck Hanson," my mother said. "Rather, he almost ran into us."

"Damn hard worker." George polished the crystal paperweight against his shirt. "I'll talk to him about the driving. He gets working and forgets other people are around."

"Sheila has a little crush on him," my mother said. She crossed her legs and straightened the front flap of her denim wrap-around skirt over her knees.

"Stop it, Mom." I felt my face go scarlet.

"I'm sure he'd be flattered," George said. He nudged my mother's sandal with his boot. "We still on for dinner? We have 8:30 reservations at the Grove Inn."

"If I can find something to wear," she said.

"You look fine the way you are," George said. He picked up Annie's pencil jar again and chuckled. He looked at me, glanced at my mother, and cleared his throat. "Just so you know, Sheila, Buck Hanson is twenty-six."

"That's nice," I said.

"I'm only looking out for you, Sheila," he said.

"I don't need looking out for," I said.

I wanted to scream. George uncrossed his ankles and stood up to his full six foot two.

"Well, I don't know," he said slowly. "Alice, what do you think?"

"I think we all need looking out for," she said. She smoothed her skirt. "I'd better see how Josh's packing is progressing. Come on, Sheila."

"Three more days," George said. "Time's flying." He held the door open for us. "Less chance of getting run over if you use the back entrance." He patted my shoulder. "Bye, now."

"Hardy har har," I muttered.

My mother shot me a look.

The wind was blowing so hard it snapped open the back door

of the shed and nearly carried us to the car. When we got into the VW, my mother wiped the wind-tears and mascara from her eyes.

"George is trying," she said.

"I don't care," I said, fighting tears. "My life is none of his business."

She took my chin firmly in her hand. When I pulled away, she sighed.

"You're wrong, Sheila Lorraine," she said. "Your life is his business." She repositioned the rearview mirror for driving. Her voice softened. "It will be soon, anyway."

Three

My mother, Josh, Annie, and me, along with Jimmy's mom Mrs. Emmons, the waitress, were the only occupants of the Depot Café that Sunday morning. We had been sitting at the table by the window eating breakfast for at least an hour. Josh was to be the only passenger to get on the southbound Greyhound this morning. The bus was scheduled to arrive in Imperial Beach at ten that night, a thirteen-hour trip. Outside, Main Street was quiet except for an occasional empty migrant bus.

The Greyhound Bus, like the train in Tristes, had never been on time. In the time we'd been waiting, Josh had read the Tristes Gazette cover to cover while devouring a stack of pancakes and three scrambled eggs. Now he was on his second order of bacon. Annie was still picking at what remained of the pancakes she'd drowned in strawberry syrup. I wasn't one bit hungry. Big good-byes stole my appetite. Still, I'd managed to swallow most of the toasted English muffin Jimmy's mother had brought me.

My mother, who for years had lectured us on the importance

of eating a healthy breakfast, was chain-smoking and drinking coffee. The yolk of the untouched sunny-side-up eggs on the plate next to her elbow had a congealed sheen. She looked at the Depot Café clock over the food pickup counter and asked Josh if he had everything.

"That's the fourth time you've asked him that," I said. I picked at the lacy edge of the paper placemat.

When Mrs. Emmons came over to refill coffee, my mother waved off the pot. There were half-moons under Mrs. Emmons' eyes. Her faded print dress looked as tired as she did.

"I'm jittery as it is," my mother said, rubbing the butt of a cigarette into the overflowing ashtray. "Charlotte, you're working too hard."

Mrs. Emmons smiled and said, "Rosie has a cough, kept us up all night." She picked up Josh's mopped-clean plates. "You were hungry."

"The Marines don't feed their recruits," I said to her. "It's a training technique."

Josh let out an exasperated sigh and checked the new watch on his wrist, a parting gift from Sally Fratti.

"It's all the excitement, makes you burn calories," Mrs. Emmons said. She looked at my mother's plate. "Alice, you should eat."

"Mommy's too sad," Annie said, shoving the last forkful of pancake into her mouth.

"Wipe your face, Annie," my mother said. She pulled a fresh napkin from the metal holder in the center of the table.

"Isn't she the sweetest thing?" Mrs. Emmons said, looking at Annie, then turning to my mother. "I'd be the same way as you, mind you. Thank God Jimmy's got Ingrid. She'll keep him around after you kids graduate." She winked at me. "One more year of school. I hope you don't leave us too, Sheila."

"I'm going to open a bar and restaurant," I said. "Maybe in Salinas."

"She's kidding," my mother said tiredly. "Aren't you?"

"I might." I shrugged. Who knew? I might fly to the moon too.

"I'd be devastated to lose my Jimmy," Mrs. Emmons said, biting her lip. She steadied the stack of plates on her arm. "You stay in touch, you hear, Joshua? People leave Tristes and forget all about us. At least, don't forget your mama." She hurried away to deposit the heavy dishes in the kitchen.

My mother wiped a tear with the napkin from her lap. She wore no makeup this morning and had pulled her hair into a loose ponytail. The dull sadness in her brown eyes conveyed lack of sleep and Josh's imminent departure.

"I refuse to cry," she said.

"See how mean you are, leaving," I said to Josh.

"He is not." Annie stared at me. "He is thinking of his future."

Josh's mouth trembled. He was trying not to laugh at Annie pretending to be so grown-up.

"Straight from the horse's mouth," I said, rolling my eyes at my mother. "It's amazing how well she mimics George."

"That will be enough, Sheila," my mother said. She poked

a fork at the yolk of one of the untouched eggs and frowned at me.

"Sorry," I said.

Annie pouted. I ignored her.

A few minutes later, the bus groaned into the station. Josh stood up, and my mother asked Mrs. Emmons for the check. Annie stuck her tongue out at me, and I returned the gesture. All was well again between us. I needed Annie on my side right now.

The sharp odor of exhaust filled the café. The bus rumbled at the curb where two other passengers who hadn't come into the café were waiting. The engine snorted, then died.

The driver, a pasty-looking man with a potbelly, came in and asked Mrs. Emmons for a medium-size coffee, extra cream, two sugars. The buttons strained against his uniform shirt.

"Burt," Mrs. Emmons said. "I think I know your order by now."

"You keep track of all the drivers?" he kidded.

"Only the ones who come inside for coffee," she said, winking at the driver and handing him change.

The four of us watched the driver make his selection at the cigarette machine near our table. It was as if this stranger about to deliver Josh to his new military life had an answer to a question none of us had yet. Josh picked up his suitcase.

"Guess it's time," he said.

"Hold on a minute," my mother said.

She went over to the cigarette machine and tapped on the

driver's shoulder. He straightened, keeping his finger on the Lucky Strike button he had just pressed.

"You take good care of my son," she said. "Get him to Imperial Beach in one piece."

"Ma'am?" he asked.

"That boy, my son," she said, pointing at Josh.

The driver retrieved the pack from the machine's tray and tapped it against his thigh.

"You enlist?" he asked.

Josh nodded and set down the suitcase impatiently. He looked at Annie fiddling with the pink ribbon she'd tied on the handle. She untied the ribbon and then retied it, double bows this time. Josh patted her head.

"You've obviously raised your boy right," the driver said to my mother. "My daddy was in World War Two. He was darn lucky." An easy smile gave his face a bit of needed color. "Rest easy, ma'am. I take boys from all along my route down to Imperial Beach all the time, 'specially during the war. Nine times out of ten, they're bawling before I've pulled out of the station."

"Mom, it's time." Josh nibbled on his thumbnail.

"I'll look out for your boy, ma'am," the driver said. He grabbed his coffee from the register counter and went out to the bus. The four of us followed.

Outside, the warm sugar scent from the Mexican bakery across the street mingled with the diesel exhaust. Sunlight poured between the bakery and the post office. Part of this familiar world was about to get on the bus along with my brother.

Jumping in place on the curb, Annie recited "The Cow Jumped Over the Moon," her first nursery rhyme. I remembered Josh teaching it to her when she was learning to walk. Annie would bounce up and down to the beat, her pudgy thighs like layers of dough. My mother and I had found this little dance adorable. Now, the red ribbon tied to the tail of Annie's braid danced back and forth as the rubber soles of her blue Keds kicked the curb. Her white bobby socks slumped.

I reached a hand to her, but she refused to let me take her hand. Josh knelt down to hug her, and she threw her arms around him. I felt a twinge of jealousy. Goodbyes seemed easier for Annie.

"Promise to send postcards," she said. "Or else I'll never talk to you again." She hiccupped, then giggled.

"If you promise to take care of King." Josh kissed the tip of her nose. He stood and grabbed me. "Take care of Mom," he whispered.

He smelled different, a new smell that seemed both faraway and close. Like the coast or a freshly opened paperback book. Not his familiar, vaguely cinnamon smell.

"See you when you're bald," I said, my voice thick with uncried tears and my eyes darting to the bus.

Behind the smoky windows of the bus, passengers peered out or slept. Some of them had families, some did not. Wherever they were headed, they were lucky not to be me, stuck in Tristes without Josh. Without Daddy.

The driver tossed his coffee cup into an overflowing trash

can. The cup rolled off the heap into the gutter. The white of the Styrofoam looked too clean against the oil-stained asphalt. I swallowed.

"Go," I said. "The bus is leaving."

"Don't tell me," Josh teased. "You're going to cry after all."

"Oh, shut up," I said, taking a half-hearted swing at his arm.

"Be good." He gave me another squeeze. "And stay away from the southerner."

He wrapped his arms around my mother's narrow waist and swung her around. She pounded him with her fists, demanding to be put down. Her sandal flew off her left foot. It bounced off the rear tire of the bus, and the four of us burst out laughing.

Josh kissed my mother on each cheek. The driver took his suitcase and slid it into the luggage compartment. The door to the compartment slammed. Josh's face crinkled into a broad smile.

"Call when you get there," my mother said. Two tears rolled down her left cheek. "Now go."

Josh turned away and boarded the bus. When the bus pulled out, Annie ran out to wave at him from the sidewalk. The laces on one of her shoes had come untied. I couldn't bring myself to tell her to retie it. And my mother hadn't noticed.

"There he is," Annie shrieked, shielding her eyes from the sun. "Bye, Joshie. Bye, bye, bye." She kept saying "bye" until the bus turned onto Main.

I handed the sandal to my mother. She put it on and tightened the strap, balancing on one foot, holding onto my shoulder with her other hand. The bakery clerk flipped over the closed sign in the window. My mother's fingers dug into my skin.

"I hope he sleeps," she said, looking at the space where the bus had been parked. "Otherwise, he'll be tired when he gets there."

"Mom, please buy me a cinnamon twisty," Annie cried.

She ran over to us and tugged on the hem of my mother's wrinkled white blouse that had actually been one of Daddy's dress shirts. I hadn't seen it on her in months. Not since she'd thrown out half her wardrobe and replaced it with crisp, bright dresses, skirts, and blouses, soft sweaters with feminine necklines.

"Mom, please." Annie gave my mother's shirt another tug. "Can I?"

My mother looked at her blankly. A stray mutt skittered past the bus station, sniffing the sidewalk for food. My mother watched the dog turn the corner. She let out a deep sigh, her eyes dry now. She smiled at me as I bent down to tie Annie's shoe.

An empty quiet infused Tristes. Sunday mornings, people slept in or went to church or were up early mowing their lawns to beat the heat. But the quiet now was like an ache I couldn't quite locate. It was in the haggard slump of buildings. In the stark, lonely quality of the light.

⁓

Annie tucked the giraffe that had belonged to me under her arm and crawled under the quilt. The upper half of the giraffe was limp, the stuffing having settled in the lower half. I had always insisted on carrying it by the neck.

"I thought Giraffe was too ratty," I said, pulling the quilt up over her bare shoulders.

"I like her now," she said. She blinked her golden-brown lashes to keep from drifting off.

"You're fickle, Annie Bananie," I said.

"Fickle-pickle," she said, yawning.

Her round face relaxed. She rubbed her eyes. I nuzzled her hair, smelled strawberry syrup. When she wasn't acting like a know-it-all, she was a sweet kid. I pretended to gobble her up.

I loved being in her room. Before she was born, Daddy had used it as his library. After dinner, he'd drink his whiskey and read. When Annie came along, he had to give up the room and his habit of retreating. That's when he started going to the Hero.

He'd complained he couldn't read his books there, that everyone wanted to talk to him about things he didn't give a damn about. He wanted to talk politics, literature, the perils of religion and big business. Occasionally, he'd try to engage Will Fratti in a conversation about Camus or some other philosopher. But Will's reading had never graduated beyond Louis L'Amour, and his travels hadn't taken him farther than Fresno, and L.A. a time or two. Daddy had been to Paris, New York, and Barcelona by the time he was twenty.

"Let's play night noises," Annie said.

"You remember how?" I asked, letting her snuggle against me.

"Course I do." She yawned again.

Outside, the chimes tinkled. Annie sat up and cocked her head. In the night-noises game she would listen for a noise, and I would say where it had come from.

"Chimes," she said.

"Chimes under the pomegranate tree," I said.

It felt good to hold her close. It had been months since I'd tucked her in. Tonight, George had taken my mother to the movies to help keep her mind off Josh. So it was just us. Me missing Dad and Josh, and sweet Annie about to drift off after a long day.

"Marigolds," she murmured, settling under her quilt again.

"Silly, marigolds don't make sounds," I said.

"They do so—when they open," she said. Her eyes flew open. "Listen."

I listened to the night, heard nothing.

"If you say so," I said.

"Stars," she said, yawning.

"You can't hear stars," I said. "I've listened hard many times, and they don't make a peep."

The spruce tree under the bedroom window rustled.

"Sparrow," she said, sighing and closing her eyes.

"Sparrow in the hedge," I said.

We listened, but the bird had fallen silent.

"Is Joshie there yet?" she asked.

"Not yet," I said.

Then we heard it. The whistle blew, long and determined. The ground began to shake. The window trembled.

"Train," Annie murmured.

"Train in the night," I said.

I held my breath. When it had passed I let out a deep sigh, and the windows were still. Annie slept.

I used to sulk over the loss of pomegranates we'd never had, and Daddy would make a special trip to the grocery store in Salinas that carried exotic fruit. I had sucked on the teardrop seeds on two occasions I can remember. The juice was neither pink nor red but certain to stain my dress.

A crescent moon blinked in the gap in the curtain. The chimes tinkled. But no sound came from the pomegranate tree, or the train, now long gone, past Greenfield, soon to pass through King City, then leave the valley entirely.

Four

Moths flitted about the kerosene lanterns John Tash the care-
taker had lit for our July 4th meal out at Paraiso Springs. Over
the hot springs bathing pool, steam hovered like loose lace in the
twilight. But no one would be swimming this evening. It was too
damn hot.

Although I hadn't wanted to come out to the Springs,
I had nothing better to do. Ing and Jimmy and everyone else
in town would be inside Tristes High Stadium tonight, where
the fireworks were pretty abysmal. Every year it was the same
fifteen-minute show. The mayor always insisted on staging it to
make the fireworks more dramatic. The show culminated in a
premature ejaculation of predictable colors. Seeing the fireworks
from the Springs would be a nice change or, at least, a change.

Sage and manzanita perfumed the air. Tash had started cook-
ing. My mouth watered from the salty apple juices of George's
grandfather's homemade sausages on the grill. When George's
father George Sr. died, Pepito, as his grandchildren affection-

ately called him, rekindled the Old World tradition his son had rejected. Pepito now hand-tied the sausages in his garage, a shot glass of grappa nearby to steady his hand. Annie and I had gone over to Pepito's house to watch. He offered me a sip, which I declined. The stuff was fire water.

After the barbeque, six of us planned to walk up into the foothills for a glimpse of the fireworks. Steve, a sandy-haired bronco rider from Fresno and Sister Sally's new beau, had come out to the Valley to see Sally for the holiday and ride in the rodeo next week. A beer in hand, Steve, with those friendly eyes and an easy way about him, helped Tash man the grill. George, Sally, and my mother sat at the table talking about the wedding. Annie and I engaged in a game of seek with a family of quail. We'd seen them skittering out from under the picnic table when we first arrived. The quail weren't about to make a second appearance, but Annie didn't need to know this.

It had been years since we'd taken the winding five miles of dirt road off of River Road and up into the Santa Lucias. Daddy, who had loved the sulfur smell of the place, had brought Mom, Josh, and me to the Springs many times on weekends. When Annie came along, my mother didn't see much point in swimming in a pool too hot for infants. So we fell out of the habit.

Will Fratti's truck pulled up just after we had sat down to eat. Waylon Jennings still blaring from the eight-track, Will stumbled out of the passenger side, cursing the fading daylight. Brother Will had supposedly sworn off drinking again. But holidays were always the exception. I braced myself for George's reaction.

"Damn him," George muttered. He set his buttered French roll on his bread plate and pushed the plate away, as if he'd like to treat Will the same way. "I told him this was a quiet gathering."

"At least he's not driving," Sally said. "Who's that with him?"

I couldn't believe my luck. Buck in the flesh. The first time I'd seen him since that afternoon at the packing shed. He and Will cut through the shrubs around the pool. Their T-shirts looked incandescent.

"Sounds like they've been at the firehouse picnic," Sally said to no one in particular. She turned to Steve. "Just remember he's a lamb when sober."

"You don't need to apologize," Steve said, giving her a peck on the cheek.

"You sure we're not intruding?" I heard Buck say.

"Hell, no," Will said, tripping over a poolside crack. "I'm family, aren't I? Sure smells good. What the hell does Tash do up here, anyway? The poor bastard's going to get sued one day."

"He shouldn't swear," Annie said, wiping her greasy mouth with her sleeve. She looked at George. "It's bad manners."

"That's right, sweetheart," George said. He took the red-and-white checked napkin from his lap and threw it on the table. He looked at my mother. "I'll handle this."

"Let him stay," my mother said, setting her fork on the edge of her plate. "You can't reason with him in that condition."

A barn owl hushed overhead. George stood there for a moment as if trying to decide how to proceed. Annie speared a sausage on the platter and dropped it onto her plate. It occurred to me that she'd never seen anyone drunk. Daddy had done his drinking late at night when she was fast asleep in her crib.

"Hey, brother," Will called. "Any of Pepito's sausages left?"

"You're drunk, Will," George said.

"Maybe we should leave, man," Buck said, putting his hand on Will's arm.

"Are you kidding? I'm famished," Will said. He shrugged Buck's hand away and pushed past George. "Hey, Sal, how about some grub?" He laughed and slid in between Sally and me. "Now isn't this cozy?"

Shaking her head, Sally handed Will a plate. When Will attempted to fill an empty glass, Sally took the wine bottle and glass away from him and poured Will a quarter of a glass. He grumbled when she handed it to him.

Buck held back until my mother insisted he sit down. Warmth poured into the space between his forearm and mine. My mother hadn't noticed the only place left at the table was next to me.

"Hey, kid," he said.

"Hey," I said. "Happy Independence Day."

"Same to you," he said.

I watched him split and butter one of the aluminum-wrapped potatoes Tash had roasted in the grill coals. He mashed the potato with the back of his fork. Tenderly, as though he appreciated the food.

Glassy-eyed, Will looked around the table. His lips were moist and pale. Steve gave him a careful nod. His high forehead, sunburned from days of bull-riding practice, glistened.

"Good to see you, Will," he said.

Will said nothing. Sally introduced Buck and Steve to one another. Will noticed the diamond glittering on my mother's ring finger. He let out a low whistle.

"Must be love," he said. "George Jr. doesn't let go of cash easily." He lifted his glass. "To the lovebirds."

"Don't start, man," George said. In the lamplight, squint lines gullied from the corners of his eyes. "You promised."

Will gulped the wine with his eyes closed. Will was bitter because the woman he loved had rejected him last year. She raised rabbits in King City. Will had always claimed she was too enamored of the bunnies to care about a man. But everyone, including Will, knew his drinking had driven her away.

"Don't start what, brother?" Will said, setting down the glass.

He turned to me. His eyes tried to focus. I'd seen him in this condition before, when he and Daddy had been drinking at the Hero. My mother usually locked the door on the two of them and let them sleep it off on the porch.

"It's Sheila." I fluttered my fingers at him.

"I know who it is, damn it," Will barked. He looked at Annie. "Roy's girls. I bet he's rolling in his grave, George, you being up here with them and their mother."

George's jaw tightened. His eyes got smaller and darker behind his glasses. My mother set down her wine and spoke to Buck. It was time to change the subject.

"Was it crowded at the park today?" she asked.

"Seemed like it was," Buck said. "But then again I've never been to the Fireman's Picnic. I can tell you that Will's a hell of a horseshoe player."

"I got lucky is all," Will grumbled.

"Horseshoes are supposed to be lucky," Annie said, popping a cherry tomato into her mouth. Her cheek bulged.

Will looked at her and mumbled something incomprehensible. I tried to catch Annie's eye. She looked worried. I didn't blame her. Will's mind got twisted sometimes. I didn't want him going off on her. Buck's arm grazed mine, and I wondered if he'd meant to touch me.

"I'm terrible at shoes," Steve said. "'Course, that's always after I've had a few beers."

"You ride bulls, hon," Sally said. She attempted to wrap an arm around Steve's broad shoulders, saw her arm was too short, and smiled shyly. "That's enough for me."

"Yeah, a real macho man," Will muttered.

"Will," Sally warned.

"What can I say?" Steve said, giving Sally an affectionate wink. "I love what I do."

John Tash came out of the lodge to see about clearing plates. He didn't make eye contact. Tash was painfully shy, and the Springs rarely got visitors. George offered him some wine.

"No thanks, Mr. Fratti." Flecks of purple light glinted in Tash's scraggly black beard. "Should I bring out the plum tart?"

"Fine, Tash," George said.

Buck looked up at the sky. The night was warm. I could

almost taste the salt on his glistening neck. I imagined brushing my lips over his skin.

"Venus is out," he said.

"That's Mars," Annie said. She looked relieved when Buck smiled at her.

"How do you know about the planets, little girl?" he asked.

She laughed. I wanted to kiss him right then and there for teasing her so nicely. For knowing Will had scared her.

"You talk funny," Annie said, scrunching up her nose.

"Annabelle," my mother said. "That's not polite."

"She meant no harm." Buck grinned at Annie.

He looked across the road at the mission. I followed his gaze. Indigo light outlined the small bell tower.

"Beautiful chapel," he said.

I had recently fallen in love with the Our Lady of Solitude chapel. This past February, on the anniversary of Daddy's death, Ing and I had driven out to the mission. She showed me the Our Lady statue and prayer room where I could light a candle for Daddy. It just seemed right, honoring Daddy there.

"You used to be able to just walk in until the cholos trashed it," Will said, his mouth full. "Carved their initials and slogans in the pews."

"The cholos respect the mission," I said. "It was drunk aggies making it look like cholos."

"Whatever. I need to take a piss," he said. He tripped over Tash's cat Sulfur when it darted across his path. "Damn vermin."

There was silence around the table. Far off, a hawk screeched. Steve looked at Buck.

"I've rode a few in Georgia," Steve said. "Nearly keeled over from the humidity. Nice, friendly people down there."

"No wind to cut the humidity," Buck said. "Not like here."

Buck loved the wind. He'd noticed how it made a difference with everything. How every day it washed the world clean. I felt ridiculously happy.

"Why don't you run and get the flashlight," my mother said to me. "Then we can take the path up."

"Will's got one in the truck," Buck said. "I'll get it."

"We don't need more than one flashlight." My mother frowned. "Do we, George?"

"One's plenty," George said. "If I know Will, the batteries in his flashlight are dead."

"I put fresh ones in yesterday," Will said, returning from the bathroom. "Surprised, brother?"

"Well." My mother put her hand over George's. "Maybe we could use a second flashlight."

Buck followed me to the truck. I didn't know how much longer I could play it cool. Thankfully, dog tags clinked against the bed, giving me something to do. I made George's mastiff Rusty sit, and I grabbed the flashlight from behind the seat while Buck checked Will's glove box.

"No flashlight here," he said.

I handed him mine, and he pointed it at the ground. Light

coned around us. Like a halo for two shining from below. I let out a little sigh.

"You don't much care for George," he said. His breath smelled faintly of garlic.

"He's all right," I lied. My heart pounded so hard I could hear it outside my body.

"He doesn't like me hanging around you," he said. "I can tell."

Footsteps crunched in the gravel. Buck smiled, his eyes always a different color of green. Tonight, they were pale, nearly gray.

"Time to get up the hill," George called.

"Told you so," Buck said, his laugh a flutter of sound. "Is Will joining us?" he asked, shining the flashlight at George.

"He's passed out on Tash's sofa. Where he belongs," George said. "Hey, Tash, are you coming up to the ridge with us?"

Tash waved him off and continued clearing the table. We joined the others. George set Annie on his shoulders, the flashlight in one hand. When we started up the trail, my mother motioned for me to go ahead of her. She fell in behind me, then Buck, then came Sally and Steve after they had stopped to steal a kiss.

As we went up the trail, the pungent scent of wild thyme filled my nostrils. I felt Buck behind me. How had he slipped past my mother? Our footsteps found their own rhythm. As if we were the only two people on the trail and the entire valley below.

Down the trail, I could hear Sally laughing against Steve's

mouth. She was definitely in serious lust, if not love. She and Steve had met on the highway a few months ago when he pulled over to help her change a flat. The next day he had called and told her she was the woman he'd been waiting for. An incurable romantic. He and Sally had been an item ever since.

George jiggled the flashlight over the hard, peeled-back bark of the manzanita on the path's edge. He held aside the branches, and we stepped onto the grassy ridge. Below, Salinas, Tristes, and King City were pearls on a darkened window, Soledad prison an industrial grid. Annie was hunched on George's shoulders, nearly asleep.

"Steve's knee's acting up," Sally called from the trail. "You go on."

"Go on up, Sal," Steve said, his voice strained. "I can manage."

"Steve, I've watched fireworks before," Sally said, then called up the trail, "We'll see you all back at the lodge."

"Okay," George called. He turned off the flashlight.

"Your little one," Buck spoke to my mother, "can sleep anywhere."

"She's always been that way," my mother said.

I listened to them, holding onto Buck's voice like a dream I didn't want to end. He stood next to me, purposely it seemed. Sparks of heat passed between us.

"Is your family in Georgia?" she asked. The wine and the night air had relaxed her.

"What family I have. My mother, a few cousins." Buck sounded wistful.

The grass was cool on my ankles. Down in the valley, the night swallowed starbursts yellow, green, then blue, then red. Buck's hand brushed my thigh. Had he meant to? A tremor of desire went through me.

Five

It was lunchtime, July 7th. I wasn't one bit hungry. I'd eaten very little since Paraiso Springs. I'd been cruising around town for half an hour, hoping to see Buck on his lunch hour. I finally spotted him eating a sandwich and sitting on the curb in front of Kim's, not two feet from where we'd first met.

I parked in front of the Hero, checked my hair in the rearview mirror. Before I left the house, I'd changed into a yellow halter dress and cracked open the Jean Naté Splash Ing had given me for Christmas. I felt very womanly, a new feeling for me.

Down the street, Mrs. Emmons untied her apron as she hurried home from her shift at the Depot. When I got out of the VW, I pretended I didn't see her. I had one mission, to see Buck. Shit. She saw me and slowed.

"Hello, Sheila," she called. "Heard from Josh lately?"

"He phoned last night," I said, wishing she'd get on her way.

"You tell your mother to call me anytime," she said. "I'm all ears."

"I will," I said. "Bye."

I could feel Buck watching me. I waved at him. Mrs. Emmons started to walk past Kim's, but when Buck gave me a nod she stopped. She looked from him to me. I wondered if my mother had asked her to keep an eye on us.

"Miss Sheila O'Connor," Buck said. Sinewy shadows danced across his tan face. "You're as pretty as a sunrise in that dress."

I turned to Mrs. Emmons and introduced her to Buck.

"Pleasure, ma'am," Buck said.

He stood and stretched his legs. He reached his hand to her. She didn't take it.

"You're the new guy at the packing shed," she said.

"News travels." Buck grinned and threw the sandwich in the trash can. "Strangest damn combination for a sandwich—ham, cheese, and kimchee. Spicy cabbage is new to me. Next time I'll stick to ham and cheese."

"Come down to the depot café for lunch sometime," Mrs. Emmons said, softening. "We've got a good patty melt."

"I might do that," he said.

He shaded his eyes and smiled. She looked away as if she'd remembered Buck was an outsider and regretted extending the invitation. Buck seemed to have that effect on certain people. He made them nervous. People in Tristes didn't trust wanderers. Anyone from anywhere else was automatically suspicious.

"I'd better be on my way." Mrs. Emmons patted my arm. "Rose and the boys are waiting for me. Be a nice girl for your mother."

She tucked the apron under her arm and hurried off. The hem of her navy blue dress flapped against the back of her knees. Her calves were strong from years of waitressing. Like my mother's legs.

"She doesn't trust me," Buck said. His tone was blunt.

"Don't feel bad." I smiled. "They're afraid of all strangers."

"Hell, I'm practically a local," he said, his eyes twinkling. "A Terra Dura resident at least."

George housed his workers at Terra Dura. The migrant camp sat on the freeway's edge between the cemetery and Soledad Correctional Facility. Buck had to be the only gringo living there.

This morning my mother had mentioned George had a meeting in Salinas today. Across the street at the packing shed, George's truck was gone, just as I had hoped. Buck was free.

"When's your lunch over?" I asked. My stomach was doing somersaults. I had practiced the question a hundred times in the car. "You want to go for a drive?"

Three business men were approaching the Pit. I recognized a friend of George and Will's who had dated Sally. When he opened the restaurant door, he noticed Buck talking to me and raised his chin at his friends. They exchanged words and slunk into the Pit. Assholes, I thought, let them talk. Buck didn't seem to notice. Or if he did, he didn't care much either.

"No harm in a drive," he said.

In the car, he lit a cigarette and offered me one, which I declined. I'd made it through half a Salem once. Ing had smoked five or six, turned green, and threw up. Smoking wasn't for us.

On the east side of River Road, the Salinas River—known as the Underground River—trickled down miniature valleys in the dry riverbed. The road ran the length of the Santa Lucia Mountains, some twenty miles, from Tristes to Highway 68, east into Salinas or west to Monterey, Pacific Grove, Carmel, and Big Sur.

The sweet grassy smell of new hay bales tempered the afternoon heat. Further on, in the fields at the base of the Lucias, pinto beans uncurled from furrows of black earth. Buck rested his elbow on the open window. I couldn't believe we were together in the VW. Alone. I switched on the radio. KPSA was blasting a commercial for rodeo week, so I changed the station. The KHTS DJ bridged from the commercial break. Linda Ronstadt sang "When Will I Be Loved?" with typical hearty sass.

"Fratti own all of this?" Buck asked. He gazed out at the fields.

"Pretty much," I said.

Under an oak, a little girl about Annie's age climbed onto a tire swing. I beeped and she waved. Buck laughed, which made me laugh. He would kiss me today. Maybe more.

"Where you taking me, kid?" he asked.

"You said you wanted to see the mission," I said.

"Will said it was locked," he said. "You know a secret entrance or something?"

"Sort of," I said. "Sometimes the side door is open."

Some quail skittered across the road, and I swerved to avoid hitting them. The chick at the end of the line tumbled over its sibling. Rejoining the family, the two quail escaped into the brush.

"That was close," I said. I relaxed my hands on the wheel, and my heart slowed.

"Good thing the suckers are fast," Buck said.

"It's up ahead," I said.

He was staring at me. I tried to focus on driving. A kiss for sure. Definitely more.

Just before the crumbling adobe wall, I turned off and parked. Behind the chapel, the shack that served as the priest's quarters was quiet. That priest liked his red wine and had a habit of sleeping through the afternoon.

Buck put his hand over mine on the gearshift. My breathing felt shallow. He fingered the strap of my halter top, cupped my neck in his hand. He told me to breathe.

In a freshly plowed field, a crow let out a throaty caw and then alighted from an irrigation pipe. I closed my eyes. Everyone kisses with their eyes closed. Buck's mouth was on mine. Ing hadn't described the carousel of light behind the eyelids—pink, then orange, pink, then orange. And his touch. Hard, supple. Empty. Full. I had kissed a few boys. But their lips had been tentative. Tongues had darted about my mouth, clothed hard-ons had probed and prodded. Buck's kiss was salty and deep and musky and animal.

"Shall we visit Our Lady?" His breath was soft on my earlobe.

It was chilly in the chapel. I immediately started shivering, so Buck draped his plaid work shirt over my shoulders. Buttery light filtered in through the stained glass above the small, cobwebbed mezzanine.

Disfigured lilies languished in dry vases set on pedestals on the altar last Easter. A hand-painted banner that claimed "He Has Risen" slid down the wall and onto the altar. Startled, Buck and I both jumped. On the crucifix above the altar, dried crimson paint dripped from Jesus' crown of thorns.

"Poor son of a bitch," Buck murmured. He studied the crucifix. "Damned if I understand why anyone would want to worship the horror of that."

"My best friend has nightmares about that cross," I said. "Her mom's into Jesus. She goes on and on about our sins and his suffering."

"My mother raised me Methodist," he said, ambling down the aisle towards the back of the chapel. "It never stuck, much to her chagrin."

The right back pocket of his jeans was frayed over the pressure of his wallet. I wondered what the wallet contained. Whose pictures he kept with him, if he carried other memories, a fortune from a fortune cookie, a love note from an old girlfriend. He had had many, I was sure.

"Religion's like politics," he continued. "Empty promises."

He stood under the stained-glass window of Father Junipero

Serra surrounded by adoring Indians. Father Serra's robes shone deep purple. In the background, a lush slope of vineyards and olive trees.

"Stained glass is a European cathedral thing," I explained, feeling like a tour guide. "The historical society made a big stink about it. The Frattis had it commissioned anyway. Come on, I want to show you something."

The tiny prayer room smelled of old wax, adobe. Shadows flickered on the walls. Our Lady smiled demurely, her eyes vacant and the same quiet shade of blue as her robes. An unlit votive waited in a glass on a narrow altar.

"Give me your lighter," I said.

A warm, clean honey smell filled the small room. Buck took the lighter from me. His mouth searched for mine. My heart pounding, I let him lead me into the chapel. He lowered me onto the cold pew and unsnapped my halter dress with one hand. The mark of experience. My nipples were pebbles.

"You new at this?" he asked.

I nodded, then gasped as he caressed my breasts, my belly. Out of the corner of my eye, I saw a mouse scurry from one pew and under another. I felt smaller than the mouse, more terrified and ten times more excited.

"We'll go slow," he said.

Buck's Levi's and T-shirt now lay crumpled on the clay tile. When I looked down and saw he wasn't wearing underwear I let out a little gasp. His penis seemed, well, large.

"You're good for the ego, darlin'," he whispered.

The rest of him was as lean and muscular as I had pictured him. A constellation of freckles showed through his rust-colored chest hair. But I hadn't accurately imagined what it would feel like, the solidness of his body, the sureness of his arms around me. His lips followed the line from my mouth to my navel.

"Relax," he whispered. "It's okay."

He peeled off my underwear, touched me where only I had touched. His hand brushed my pubic hair. He lowered his mouth to kiss me there. When his tongue started to probe I tensed up and twisted away from him.

"Not this time," I said. "I can't."

"You got it, kid," he said.

He looked up at me, and although I wanted to hide, I brushed the hair from my eyes. I had to be brave. Outside, the wind howled. This was it.

He came to me and kissed my mouth. I traced my finger around the triangle scar on his shoulder. It was ropey and red. I pictured him in a damp, mosquito-ridden jungle. He had bled, been wracked by pain.

"My ticket home from Cambodia," he said and caressed my cheek. "Now breathe."

Terrified of the tearing pain I'd heard about, I watched him slip on the condom. He used some spit to make it easier. But it still hurt. I stifled the cry. And then I relaxed. This new feeling was slow and undulating, and, finally, electric and sudden.

"That's it," Buck groaned, his face pink with exertion. "That's the way."

His body shuddered. Now I could breathe. Without encouragement.

⌐⌐

Later, he spooned me against the pew and traced his index finger over my hip. Every cell of me was blissfully, exquisitely happy. Even a truck whooshing up River Road made me smile. I read the graffiti on the pew bench. *Puta Madre. SJ loves RW. Pinche Cabrone* and other scratches I couldn't make out.

"You're a lanky one," Buck said.

"I'm part giraffe," I said.

I felt him smiling too. I closed my eyes, and he murmured "Goodnight." Our Lady, clutching a bouquet of white carnations, drifted across my eyelids.

⌐⌐

I woke to Buck smoothing my hair. The sun must have been passing under a cloud because above the pews, Serra's indigo robe turned pale plum. It had never felt so delicious to yawn. My mind was fresh, my body relaxed.

"Let's live here," I said.

"Too many mice," he said, a honey-colored arm reaching for his Levi's.

"So we'll put Tash's cat to work," I said. "He's local."

"Speaking of work," he said, "time for me to get back. I don't want George giving me hell."

He handed me my underwear and dress. Now that it was over I felt self-conscious being naked, so I dressed quickly, finishing before he did. Buck pulled me onto his lap and hugged me. His bare toes rested against the pew in front of us. A blue embossed Bible peeked from the rack. The *cholos* or the aggies, I didn't care which, had carved "Love Is Not Real," into the wood. What did they know, anyway?

The adobe of the chapel seemed whiter, the Santa Lucia crest etched more sharply into the blue. Even the air smelled new. Across the road Tash was sweeping up peppercorns around the pool as fast as the trees shed new ones. The cat dozed on the table where we'd had our 4th of July meal. Things were different now. I was older, more sure of myself.

"We're safe," I said, giving Tash a casual wave. "He won't talk."

"I hope not," Buck said. He saluted Tash.

Tash returned the salute and kept sweeping. Steam hovered pearlescent over the pool. I took Buck's hand, and we walked to the car.

"Come to Terra Dura tonight," Buck said, his elbow on the open window.

Beyond the outline of his face, the cold glare of the packing shed. He kissed me and got out of the VW. I would go anywhere, do anything. All he had to do was ask.

"Okay," I said.

As soon he was inside the shed, George pulled up. I accidentally threw the car into third, jerking it forward. I jammed the stick shift into reverse, but George motioned for me to stop. I had to think fast.

"Mom wanted me to stop by to give you a message," I said.

"What's the message?" He peered through the thick lenses of his glasses. His left eye twitched.

"Just to call her." I shrugged.

"I see." He seemed to be waiting for me to say more. "You and I have things to work out," he said. "It doesn't look right, you coming down here." He frowned at the hood of the VW. "You ask me, your mother keeps you on too long a leash."

"I'm not a dog," I said.

"That's not what I meant," he said.

He lifted his glasses, then let them rest on the bridge of his nose. I stared out the windshield. Tumbleweed had lodged under the fence between the packing shed and the tracks. I had an urge to kick it free. Instead, I threw the car into first gear, did two doughnuts, and left George in the dust.

Six

Ten minutes after I had dropped Buck at the packing shed, I parked the VW on the side of the road with no idea what to do next. I lifted the lapel of Buck's shirt to my nose and inhaled the soft, worn cotton. It smelled of sweet tobacco, dry oak, a tinge of peppermint. As if the front pocket had carried a pack of gum. I let go of his shirt and started down Main Street. Towards Ing's house. I had to tell her about him and me.

Betty Rodriquez answered the door. She wore her housecoat and slippers. A helmet of orange-juice-can-size curlers covered her head each wrapped with her jet-black hair. The vacuous floral scent of her perfume accosted me. I was pretty used to the aroma. If for some reason Betty hadn't applied perfume generously that day, I would have been hard-pressed to believe it was her.

She kissed my cheek gingerly so her lipstick would not smear. Like her husband, the Chief, Betty was fond of me. I suspect it was because, next to Ing, I seemed saintly. She gave my arm an affectionate pat.

"Hello, mija," she said. A gold cross wiggled between her large breasts pressing against her lilac housecoat. "Don't look too close. I'm only wearing half of my face."

She had painted her lips bright geranium-red and outlined them with a dark pencil. The effect was just shy of a prostitute's face on a work night. Blue shadow darkened her eyelids. She had not yet added mascara to her already thick, dark lashes. Betty always said Jesus liked a pretty face.

"Nice to see you, Mrs. Rodriquez," I said. As fevered as her love of God was, I had always been fond of her. Maybe because she drove Ing so crazy, and I felt sorry for Betty.

"You're such a good girl," she said. "Ingrita is in the kitchen."

As of an hour ago, I was far from a good girl. If Betty knew what I had just done with Buck in her blessed mission chapel, she would probably toss me out on the street, scoop up Ing, and run for the hills. And this would be after she called the Chief at the station so he could run Buck out of town.

I decided not to tell Ingrid that Buck and I had been in the chapel this afternoon. One day she might decide to spill the beans. If she asked me, I'd tell her we'd done it in the car.

"Thank you, Mrs. Rodriquez," I said.

Betty started down the hall towards her bedroom. She turned around. My stomach turned. What if she smelled Buck on me? What if she just knew?

"Mija, when are you coming to church with me again?" she asked.

"Oh, sometime," I said. I looked at the plastic-covered sofa. "I love your new throw pillows."

"You are very observant, Sheila. I bet someday you will be a scientist." She patted one of the loud orange pillows arranged in a fan in the center of the sofa. "Ingrid just noticed. I bought them nearly a week ago. JC Penney's annual sale."

Betty had thought converting me would be a good start to getting my mother to consider becoming a Catholic. This past Christmas, she had convinced me to attend St. Mary's Midnight Mass with the Rodriquez's. The glow of the candelabras on the altar and the massive, lit Christmas tree had almost taken my breath away. But the mass had dragged on and been dull and impossible to understand.

"Forget it, Ma," Ing yelled from the kitchen. "Alice isn't about to be baptized. She won't even go to church."

"Forgive me," Betty said. "But your mother should be married in the church."

This was not a newly expressed opinion, so I let it pass, and Betty shuffled off to the bedroom to finish putting on her face. The kitchen reeked of acetone. Ing was blowing on her nails.

She glanced at Buck's shirt in disgust.

"Who's shirt?" She loosened the cap from a bottle of clear polish. "You look like a wino."

"Thanks." I took a Coke from the fridge and giggled.

"Where were you?" she asked. "I must have called you fifteen times. Your mother said you were on your way over to my house."

I tossed the bottle cap into the garbage can under the sink and pointed to the backyard, our secret-telling spot since we were in kindergarten. Ing stuck the brush back into the bottle of clear polish and closed the cap. She followed me in her bare feet out the sliding door and onto the patio.

The sun accosted the black lid of the Weber grill. Two care-worn elms flanked the shrubs growing along the back fence, while dandelions and clover dominated the overgrown lawn. Betty hated the outdoors. In virtually every way, she and my mother existed on different planets.

"Were you with him?" Ing whispered. She glanced at the master-bedroom window. Fortunately, it was closed. "With Buck?"

Wind slapped at the swing's awning. We sat down, and Ing tucked her grass-stained feet under her. I jabbed the lawn with my foot. The swing creaked forward. A charm bracelet tinkled on Ing's wrist.

"Promise to keep this quiet," I said. "You can't even tell Jimmy."

"How far did you go?" she asked.

Her hands took on a life of their own when she was excited. Her blood-red nails flickered like blinking stoplights.

"Far enough," I said. I sipped the Coke and let her sweat it out. I was enjoying this.

"You did it. I can tell. Did he know it was your first time? Did it hurt?"

"Of course, dummy," I said. "It was obvious it hurt like hell."

I fingered the taupe button on the sleeve of Buck's shirt. "Well, not all of it hurt. Matter of fact, it was great."

"God, you're lucky. I adore his name. It sounds like a character in a movie or a novel or something."

A few weeks ago she had told me Buck was a dumb name and that he looked old enough to be my father. An exact quote. Suddenly she thought he was a movie star. Now she was being fickle about my love life.

"You're going to get your heart broken," Ing said. She examined the charm of the wrestler Jimmy had given her.

"I think my tailbone is bruised," I said.

I rubbed the spot, remembering the hardness of the pew, Buck's taut body pressing down on me, the thrust of his hips against mine. I shivered. An aftershock of pleasure.

"Was it that good?" Ing asked.

"It was pretty nice," I said, a small smile on my lips. "Not that I have anything to compare it to. But that's all the detail I'm going to give you. It's sort of . . . well, private."

I thought of the lit prayer room, the soft shadows on Our Lady and the walls, and Buck's breathing, warm and thick and wanting. These feelings and memories were mine and Buck's. I was obligated to tell no one.

"Private? Come on, Shee, I tell you everything."

"Shh," I said, nudging Ing's knee with mine.

Betty was standing on the patio dressed in a coral-colored pantsuit. She had teased and sprayed her hair. It looked like a spool of brown cotton candy. She shaded her eyes against the afternoon sun.

"Put the tuna casserole in at five," Betty said. "And remind your father when he comes home I'm at Bible Study. He forgets I go on Tuesdays now too."

"I'm going to Jimmy's," Ing said. She glanced at me. "Sheila and me are both going."

I had no intention of going to Jimmy's, and Ing knew this. One day I just might get enough of being in cahoots with her. Daddy had once told me that even best friendships go south sometimes.

"You're imposing, Ingrita. Charlotte Emmons has enough mouths to feed."

"But Jimmy ate here last night, Ma," Ing said. "It's my turn to go over there."

Betty didn't know, but I imagined that she suspected Jimmy and Ing had not spent last night playing Clue with Jimmy's siblings. They had been out at the river doing it in the back of Jimmy's Chevette. All Betty had to do was call the Emmonses to verify this. Yet she never did. My theory was she didn't want to know. Hence, the compulsive prayers for Ing. Prayers were a stand-in for confrontation.

"Just be here to feed your father," she said, frowning.

"He's a grown man," Ing called. "Can't he feed himself?"

Betty stopped in front of the patio door. She took a breath and spun around. A pebble on the patio shot out from under the heel of her white pump and landed on the grass.

"Ingrita!" she hissed at Ing. "Respeto!"

"Fine, Ma," Ing said, rolling her eyes. "Go to your group."

"Bye, Mrs. Rodriquez," I said. "Enjoy Bible Study."

"Kiss-ass," Ing said after Betty had gone into the house. "No wonder she thinks you're Goody Two-shoes."

She rotated Jimmy's class ring on her finger, a silver wrestler embedded in a large blue sapphire. It had taken twenty coats of clear nail polish over wrapped purple embroidery thread to make the ring fit her finger. She looked up at me.

"Don't get me wrong. I'm happy for you," she said. "It's just that sometimes I think Jimmy loves me too much. Sheila, do you love Buck?"

"It's hard to say," I said.

As much as I loved the wind every day, I loved Buck Hanson today, tomorrow and the next. Would the women at the sprayers wonder where he had been? Who he had been with? The idea of them speculating about us was exciting. Was he thinking of me too? Ing gave me a knowing smile.

"You didn't tell me where you did it," she said, nudging the grass with her toes to keep the swing moving.

"You'll never guess," I said.

"Not behind the gym?" She wrinkled her nose.

"He's in his twenties," I said. "Not high school."

"Okay, Miss Mature, then the VW," she said irritably.

I nodded. A small fib. But not about anything important. Maybe Betty would say a prayer for me.

"That must have been awkward," she said with a reedy laugh. "I did it with Billy Rollins in his brother's Pacer."

"You're kidding? I thought it was just that once on the baseball field."

"I don't tell you everything." She shrugged and looked away.

I realized she was jealous. For years she'd been the experienced one, and I'd gained on her in one afternoon. Worse for her, I thought I was in love. Ing did not love this way, and deep down she suffered. As if she had read my mind, she jumped up. The swing jerked about with me in it.

"I promised I'd call Jimmy," she said. "You know how crazy he gets when I forget." She stubbed her toe on the edge of the patio. She bent and crossed the foot over her opposite knee to examine the toe. "I'm bleeding, damn it."

From inside the house Betty called out a reprimand for swearing. I asked Ing if she was all right. She hobbled over to open the sliding door. It had served her right, stubbing her toe. She held back, played games. She had made poor Jimmy prove he was nuts about her, and now she didn't respect him. It was unfair. Jimmy deserved better.

The Rodriquezes' phone rang. It was my mother calling and needing the car. I had forgotten her shift at the Pit started at 4:30. In the kitchen, where Ing was applying iodine to her toe, the stove clock said 4. I was definitely in trouble.

I didn't care. If I found someone to watch Annie, I could have the evening with Buck. Ing and Jimmy could baby-sit her, and I would ride my bike out to Terra Dura. One night without necking out at the river wouldn't kill Ing and Jimmy.

"Watch Annie for me tonight," I said to Ing.

"He's going to think you're easy, seeing him again so soon," she said. She blew on the stubbed toe, orange with iodine. "Now I have to redo the polish."

"Give me that." I took a Band-Aid from the table and tore off the wrapping. "I've done thousands of favors for you."

"Thanks," she said, squirming as I put on the Band-Aid. She could be a baby about pain. "Okay, I'll do it, if you promise to be careful. If you get caught, I get caught."

"I learned from you, didn't I?" I smiled and gave her a quick hug. I hated it when we fought.

~

My mother pulled the pan out of the oven. The roasted chicken glistened, sputtered. She threw the oven mitt on the counter.

"You're mad," I said.

"Cook the green beans your sister picked," she replied, her voice tight. "We'll talk about this tomorrow."

She checked her lipstick in the toaster, fluffed the end of her hair. My mother didn't lecture. She "educated" us about better choices, better ways of behaving.

"You should know that I spoke with George," she said.

Asshole. Of course he had called her. He had probably seen me dropping Buck off.

"Mom, please quit acting this way," I said. "Talk to me."

"I'm acting like I always do," she said, "when you're out of line."

"And when was the last time I was out of line?"

She had no reply.

"See," I said.

I ran water over the green beans in the colander. I wouldn't have time to cook them, but I would worry about that tomorrow. Annie came into the kitchen wearing an organdy flower-girl dress at least two sizes too big for her. She did a few twirls around the kitchen. The dress belled out, showing a nasty scrape on her knee from falling off her new two-wheeler.

"It itches," she said, stopping. She clawed at the sheer tulip sleeves.

"Sweetheart, the bow goes in the back," my mother said.

I watched my mother's swift fingers retie the bow. The wedding was just three months away. I dreaded the pantyhose and high heels, the people staring, the banquet for one hundred and fifty. My mother turned to me.

"We found a dress for the bridesmaids too."

"Tell me it's not orange," I said.

"It's a nice shade of peach and tea-length," she snapped. "Sally picked it out."

"Mom, we just went for a drive," I said.

"I get to wear a crown," Annie said, touching the retied bow before taking another turn around the kitchen. "Who went for a drive?"

"No one," I said.

"I'm off at eleven," my mother said, kissing the top of Annie's head as she twirled past her.

"Am I grounded?" I asked, handing her the keys and remembering Buck's shirt on the floor of the backseat. It had seemed like a good place to leave it.

"You're a little old for that," my mother said. "However, we do need to have a serious talk. No guests, Sheila."

A serious talk I could handle. Maybe my mother wouldn't see the shirt. Maybe that would be the end of it.

Annie watched her back the VW out of the carport and onto C Street. This was Annie's ritual and had started when Annie was two, exactly a year after Daddy died. As if Annie knew it was the anniversary of his death and was frightened my mother might also have a fatal car accident. Disaster prevention from a childís perspective.

I made Annie a peanut butter and jelly sandwich and stirred three heaping teaspoons of Nestlé's into a glass of milk. I nudged Annie to get her attention, then handed her the glass of thick chocolate milk.

"How come you're being so nice to me?" Annie asked.

"Ing and Jimmy are going to watch you tonight," I said.

She studied me for a moment. I waited for questions. Instead, she just shrugged.

"I'll play with Rosie," she said. Rosie was Jimmy's three-year-old sister. "Are you going out with Mr. Handsome?"

Had she overhead my mother and George talking on the phone? I opened the fridge to put away the milk so Annie couldn't see the surprised look on my face. Annie sometimes had a sixth sense. But her question could be innocent, merely coincidental. I closed the door to the fridge.

"You have a chocolate milk moustache," I said to her.

She wiped her mouth on the sleeve of the sample dress and announced her Mary Janes were too tight. I bent down to unfasten the gold buckles. She slipped her narrow, almost size-one feet from the patent-leather shoes.

"Don't tell Mom, okay?" I said.

"That the shoes are too tight?" She wiggled her toes and sighed. "You know, Sheelie, you shouldn't lie."

"Who's lying?" I handed her the sandwich on her favorite plate. The one with the pansies around the edge and a big pansy in the middle. "I'm going to take a bath. Go watch *The Munsters*."

⌒

I slid into the hot, soapy water. The bubbles crinkled and popped. I made shapes with them on my tummy. Mountain peaks, islands, bowls.

Bubble baths were another new thing in my mother's life. Bubble bath had been too pedestrian for Daddy. He'd given my mother gardening tools and poetry books, although she preferred mystery novels and the occasional biography. George gave her perfume, lingerie, sachets, jewelry, and bubble bath.

I pressed my hand to my crotch. It was sore as if I had been horseback riding. But it had a warm tingling sensation, too. "Sweet darlin'," Buck had whispered in a husky, caring voice. I couldn't wait to see him again. To make sure he was real. And yet there was the tender ache on my tailbone, like a small badge of courage.

"Sheelie," Annie yelled upstairs. "It's Thing."

"Turn it down," I yelled back.

The volume of the TV stayed where it was. I hummed Linda Ronstadt while I shaved my legs. When I got out of the bath, I smoothed on lotion. Buck had touched this place. And this place. And here. And here. Outside the chimes rang *Buck Hanson, Buck Hanson, Buck Hanson.*

⌒

Jimmy revved the engine of the washed-out gray Chevelle he had envisioned painting cherry red. He'd run out of money repairing the car, and it had been dull gray for a year now. Annie settled into the front seat between Jimmy and Ing. I air-dried my hair with my fingers. Ing scrutinized my makeup-less face.

"You look plain," she said. "At least put on mascara."

"She looks older," Jimmy said. "Prettier."

"I told you not to say anything." Ing gave his arm a smack.

He looked at his bicep and laughed at her. Wrestling had turned his upper arms into river boulders. Annie sat up taller. Jimmy handed her a stick of gum. He was a sweetheart with kids.

"I just said she looks different," he said, pushing a Tower of Power tape into the eight-track.

"Sheila's in love with Mr. Handsome," Annie said over the music.

"Lucky guy," Jimmy said.

He grinned at me and sped off, burning a path of rubber. I had Buck now. But Jimmy still made me feel pretty.

Seven

Three boys were shooting hoops in Terra Dura dirt yard. The basket, a metal ring without a net, hung at the top of a trunk of a limbless pepper tree. Sweat poured down their naked backs. I got off my bike, bracing it and me against the wind.

"Mírala," the tall boy said to his friends. He dribbled and passed the ball to a boy wearing a bandana on his head.

"Hola," I said, feeling like a trespasser.

I spoke to them in Spanish. It seemed like the right thing, given they lived there and I didn't. The slighter boy among them wore a large crucifix on a leather strap around his neck. He gave me a shy nod. I'd seen him in the hall at school. But like the other students at Tristes High, I had never paid much attention to migrant kids. They came for one harvest, maybe two, then they were gone.

"Por favor. Dónde vive Señor Hanson? Please. Where does Mr. Hanson live?"

"El gringo?" the tall one asked. He looked bemused, probably by my accent.

"Sí," I said.

He pointed behind me to a clapboard shack across the yard and next to the chicken coop. Buck was leaning against a post, barefoot, damp hair tousled. My heart leaped into my throat.

"I thought I heard you," he drawled. "How about I make you a burger?"

I walked my bike over, and Buck rested it against the side of the house. White paint peeled from the window frames. Under the eaves of the small A-frame roof wasps hovered.

One of the boys whistled through his teeth. I resisted the urge to turn around and give him the finger. A white girl defying a Mexican never went over well in Tristes. And I didn't want to give them the pleasure of thinking I had something to hide.

In his tiny kitchen, KJAZ played static and saxophone intermittently. When I wrapped my arms around his waist, he squeezed my clasped hands and pulled away to reach for the plate of patties on the counter. He was acting strange. Or maybe I was just nervous.

I watched him salt-and-pepper the burgers. He opened a can of beans and took two Budweisers out of the squat fridge. The bottle opener slipped, nicking his finger. Blood seeped through the small cut. I tried to examine the finger. He withdrew his hand.

"I'll live," he said, laying the burgers in the waiting pan.

The radio played static. I tried to think of something to say. The room began to smoke. Buck lowered the flame on the burner and opened a window. The curtain, brown with grease and age, billowed and then settled. Out in the yard, a rooster crowed.

"Change the station, would you?" Buck asked. He seemed lost in thought.

"Sure," I said, relieved to have something to do.

KHTS was playing a commercial for rodeo week, which had started today. Sally would take Annie and me to watch Steve ride this weekend. My mother and George had to do a walk-through of the hotel's wedding facilities and taste-test the menu.

I set out two forks and two napkins while Buck laid the burgers and buns on paper plates. Today he'd held me close, and tonight I was invisible. Maybe Ing was right. I'd been too easy, coming to see him so soon.

Over dinner we talked about the people at the packing shed. I asked him if he missed Atlanta. I wanted to scream. What has happened, Buck? What has happened to us in four hours?

"Home didn't feel like home after 'Nam," he said, chasing down a bite of burger and beans with beer.

"You don't like talking about it," I said, relaxing.

"Home or 'Nam?" he asked.

"Either one," I said.

We were talking, thank God. I felt lighter inside. And dinner tasted delicious. The burger was cooked medium rare the way I liked it, the beer ice cold.

"Not especially," he said. He started to take my hand but jumped up to get another beer. "I had thought Tristes might be home for a while."

"What do you mean?" I heard my voice quaver.

"Fratti gave me a talkin' to today." His eyes narrowed. "Or more to the point, my walkin' papers."

Dinner turned to cement in my stomach. My legs and arms weighed three thousand pounds. In my mind, I pointed Daddy's .22 at George's temple. But there wasn't enough power in that gun to shoot more than a row of tin cans.

"Why?" I could hardly get the word out.

"Statutory rape, darlin'," he said. He sighed and pushed two beans around his plate, stabbed one and ate it.

"But that wasn't how it was with us," I choked out. "Is, I mean."

"'Course not," Buck said. "It's how they see it, though."

"Tash must have called George," I said.

Sitting still felt like dying, so I got up and went over to the window. On the freeway, drivers turned on their headlights. I wished I was one of them, just going down the road, not caring where I ended up. I had not considered how long I would be with Buck, just that I would be. And now George was sending him away.

"George Fratti has no proof," I said, the grief flowing into my voice like sand out of a sieve.

"All Tash told Fratti was he saw us out at the mission," Buck said.

He pushed his chair back and looked at his bare feet. Twin beauty marks decorated the top each foot. So many things I hadn't noticed yet.

"George can't do this," I said. "It's not his town."

"No, but it's the Chief's. And he and Fratti are thick as thieves." He got up to light a cigarette. "George considers this a precautionary move."

"To what?" I snapped.

"Calm down, sweetie," he said, exhaling smoke.

"Don't call me 'sweetie.' I'm not a child." I was crying, damn it.

I forced myself to breathe. To be a grown-up. Buck put his arms around me and curled a strand of my hair behind my ear. His neck smelled of mint shaving cream. We kissed, deep and hard.

"Sheila," he whispered. "We don't have to, you know. I should have thought this through, called you before you rode all the way out here."

"I want to," I said, wiping my eyes.

We went into the front room that doubled as a bedroom. Buck straightened the tangle of sheets and sleeping bag on the cot while I went to pee. The duffel bag hung behind the bathroom door. The corner of stars on the American flag patch had come unstitched. Had it been only a month since we'd met?

Would Buck pack carelessly or with regret? Would he miss

me? Forget he knew a town called Tristes? I washed my hands and then I committed the contents of the medicine cabinet to memory. Deodorant. Crushed tube of Crest. Razor. Shaving crème. A wrinkled UFW sticker peeked out from behind the glass shelves. I closed the cabinet.

Later, after we had done it the second time, I lay awake listening to semis roar past Terra Dura. Buck jerked in his sleep. He sat up and reached for his cigarettes, shaking his head as if to clear a bad dream.

"Nightmare?" I asked.

"I never dream," he said. "Not anymore."

In the newspaper and magazines, I had read the opposite story about soldiers. How they returned and couldn't shake the horror from their minds and bodies, awake or asleep. How the damage could not be undone.

"Where will you go?" I asked.

All night I had been afraid of his answer. As if my knowing the place would cause him to disappear in a puff of smoke.

"I've got friends in the Yucatan," he said. He draped the sleeping bag over us. "Come here. Don't cry."

Daddy had once taught a semester on Mexico. The Yucatan with its aqua seas, white beaches, papaya trees, and Mayan ruins had fascinated him. I laid my head on Buck's chest. His cigarette burned golden in the dark like a late summer poppy.

"I could come with you," I said, knowing this was impossible. "My Spanish is pretty good."

He didn't reply. I counted his heartbeats. When I got to one hundred I started over. Buck had drifted off.

~

The camp rooster woke me just after dawn. I'd thought I'd leave Buck a note, but I couldn't find a pen. So I watched him sleep instead. His face was a natural phenomenon, like rock sculpted by wind. But more than his looks had attracted me. I was hooked by every part of him. The hum of his lips and breath on my earlobe, his relaxed gait, the way he paused between sentences sometimes. Not to gather his words. Because he knew he didn't have to hurry.

Buck Hanson had left places before, and today he would leave Tristes and me. I hoped when he got down the road, he'd give us both more than a passing thought. He might even be relieved to have me gone when he woke. He wouldn't have to comfort me or explain one more time why he had to go. He would smoke a cigarette, shower, pack, maybe eat something. Then he'd walk out to the entrance to Highway 101 and stick out his thumb.

I was ready to leave. I headed outside. Blue-gold light filled the gaps in the pepper trees, and the yard smelled of pinto beans frying in lard. Workers hurried out of their bungalows—tying scarves, zipping jackets—and towards a waiting bus. From an open window came the sound of a mother hushing a crying baby.

My tears seemed to freeze the same moment they fell. I pedaled out the gate, past the cemetery and the chattering black-birds. Before George had ruined everything, I had thought I would visit Daddy. I had wanted to tell him about Josh joining the Marines and my mother's engagement. About Buck and me. Daddy had never given a damn about convention. "Love is rare, sunshine," he'd say. "Take it if it comes."

Eight

The sun flitting among the rooftops and alleyways did little to warm me as I pedaled slowly towards home. The lawns on C Street were dew-jeweled. I felt cold terror in my bones. Yes, my mother would be angry, but I also knew that when the day heated up, the hurt of Buck leaving would thaw, then burn.

Butts overflowed in the ashtray on the lamp table in the living room, where my mother was sleeping. I clicked off the lamp. Her eyes flew open. She shoved aside the afghan my grandmother had crocheted, sat up, and stared at me. Bits of sleep and mascara flecked her lashes. Her hair was flat on one side of her head. King lay at her feet.

"Thank God." She was pale with deflated worry. She picked up an empty pack of cigarettes and tossed it back on the table. "I was afraid you'd run off with him."

I sat down next to her and tucked my legs under me to warm them. King rose up enough to attack his rash. No matter how hard or long he scratched, the rash would always be there. I buried my head in my mother's uniform. The thick polyester smelled of Roquefort dressing and stale smoke.

"I hate George," I said.

I pulled away to look at my mother. King licked my freezing shins. I patted his head, grateful for his affection.

"Honey, he did what's best." My mother stared past me, her brown eyes brimming like puddles in sunlight. She spoke in a panicked whisper. "Did he use protection? What am I asking? You're only seventeen."

"Almost eighteen," I said. "And yes, he used something."

"Well, that's a relief," she cried. "Damn George."

I thought she was taking my side against George. But she was cursing him for hiding her extra stash of cigarettes. She got up and searched behind the framed pictures on the mantle, found nothing.

"Mom?" I said.

"What?" she snapped.

"There's a pack in the kitchen junk drawer," I said.

"I smoked them last night." She sat down again and took my hand. "George is trying to be a father to you, Shee."

"He's not my father or my stepfather. Not for three more months. If you marry him." This was wishful thinking of course.

"I'm sorry you feel this way." She let go of my hand. "I'm going to tell you something now." She spotted a long butt in the ashtray, dusted the butt on her apron, and lit it. "You need to keep busy. You think you're in love, and that thought will make you crazy. You have your whole life, Sheila."

"Which George is ruining," I said, letting out a shudder of exhaustion. "Did Annie tell you?"

"I hope that you will leave Annie out of this," she said. "She didn't tell me you were with Buck Hanson. When I saw Ingrid and Jimmy here last night, I immediately knew."

King lay his head in my hand, a request to scratch behind his ears. His leg thumped the tan shag carpet my mother had put in last year. My mother sighed.

"I need sleep," I said.

My mother got up to make coffee. King followed me upstairs. Annie had crawled into my bed. When I snuggled against her, she didn't wake. Had things worked out differently, she would have kept her mouth shut about Buck and me. I was proud of her.

The sun poured in the window over the garden, giving my room a dingy quality. The photo-booth strip of Ing and me goofing off, the dried marigold Annie had picked for me on the bulletin board over my desk. My Brownie cap and pin tacked to the wall. I wanted none of these things anymore. I hated everything in the room.

Nine

The noontime air was dank with the smell of fresh alfalfa and livestock. I scanned the rodeo crowd, a persistent, sick feeling in the pit of my stomach. For a few seconds, the remote possibility that Buck might be there eased the loneliness.

I spotted a man with Buck's red hair four bleachers below Sally, Annie, and me. When he turned to pay the beer vendor, my heart sank. Bumpy, sunburned nose, thin lips. Ugly as Buck had been handsome.

It wasn't like I thought I'd see Buck at the rodeo. It had been four days since he had left. He was long gone. Across the border and well into Mexico by now.

Next to me, Sally pulled back her sun-bleached hair into a silky Barbie ponytail and put on her white Stetson. She looked at me and sighed. On the drive up to the rodeo this morning, she had acted as if she was afraid I'd crack. We talked about the weather and the wedding and listened to Annie chatter. I knew Sally would bring up Buck eventually.

"Don't," I said to her. "Don't feel sorry for me. I'll fall apart for sure."

"I'm concerned," she said. Her brow, bleached from the sun, furrowed. "I hope it was all right, your mother telling me. I love you, Shee."

She glanced at Annie. Annie stared at a kid about her age wearing Coke-bottle glasses, reading the rodeo program ads aloud in a deliberately nasal voice. "'Mary's Western Wear has Wrangler Boot Cuts on sale,' 'Valley Feed, ten-dollar coupons,' 'the Surf and Turf two-for-one steak and shrimp platters.'"

The kid's mother fanned her face with a paper plate and ignored her son, while the father, weighing a good 350 pounds, watched the calf roping down in the ring. He tucked his fist under his chin. A diamond ring twinkled on his left pinkie. Sally waited for me to respond.

"Why should I be mad?" I said. "My mother's your best friend. You're George's sister. Why shouldn't you know everything?"

I didn't want to be mad at Sally. She hadn't made Buck leave. And yet she was one more person who thought Buck and me shouldn't be together.

The cowboy in the ring secured the calf's front legs and gave the rope a hard yank. The calf looked up at his captor with a dazed expression. The animal hadn't expected to be taken down so quickly. I knew how he felt.

The rodeo workers dragged the poor calf out of the ring. A tractor putted in and misted down the dust. The wheels cut an apple pie pattern in the dirt. I downed my 7Up and looked around for the soda vendor. He kneeled five or six bleachers down from us, making change, sweat stains like Africa under his arms. The loudspeaker crackled, feedback ripping a hole in stagnant air. Annie covered her ears.

"Give it up for the lovely Miss Suzanna Baroni," the announcer bellowed. "Salinas Valley Rodeo Queen 1975."

Miss Suzanna Baroni looked virginal, seated in the shade of the announcer's booth. The innocent look was all for show. Suzanna considered a bottle of Cuervo Gold fair exchange for a blow job. Rumor had it she'd go all the way for lobster on the Wharf. Truth had it she would be one of my mother's bridesmaids.

The Baronis and the Frattis were second cousins. George hunted boar with Suzanna's father and considered him a good father. I pictured George and Bud crunching over dried oak leaves in pursuit of boar, and George taking mental notes about how to keep me in line.

"Marry me, baby," some guy yelled.

The cowboys in the stands were rowdy, buzzed from drinking beer in the heat. Applause rippled through the stands. I smiled.

"It's good to see you smiling," Sally said. "Even if it is at my cousin's expense."

The truth was, I adored Sally. When Ing and Jimmy had started dating, Sally had spared me the "only fish in the sea" bit. She told me that she'd been there and had felt the very same way.

"I know how you feel. You got a hole inside you like the

Grand Canyon." Sally tried to signal the soda vendor, but he had turned around to go down the bleachers instead of up. "You'll find someone else. Someone more appropriate."

"I don't want someone else," I muttered.

The hole Sally was talking about was boundless. And no one could close it up. Not even Jimmy. When he heard what had happened, he called to say how sorry he was.

Jimmy wasn't seeing much of Ing these days. She'd gotten a summer job selling ties and shirts at Dick Brown's Mens Wear in Salinas. The Chief had promised to match her paychecks. If she had enough savings by the time school started, he'd buy her a Camaro.

The kid with the glasses scooted down the bleacher next to Annie. She scrunched her nose at him. I nudged her to be polite.

"My name's Bobby," he said, pushing his glasses up his nose. George was exactly like this kid, only older, established.

"My new daddy's going to get me one just like that black horse," Annie replied. She pointed to a saddled mare tied up outside the ring.

"My next horse's going to be twice that size," Bobby said.

"Bobby, don't pester," the father said, shifting his massive ass. The entire bleacher creaked.

"He's no bother," Sally said to the father. "They can keep each other company." She turned to me and spoke quietly. "You know George's heart's in the right place."

"Yeah," I said. "In his ass."

"You remind me of your father." Sally laughed and shook her head. "He never liked George either. Funny how your mom's going to marry him."

"Funny, yeah," I said.

I watched Suzanna ride into the ring on the black mare. She had changed out of her dotted Swiss gown into riding pants and a red-checked cowgirl shirt. Behind the saddle, the mare's haunches shone purple in the intense sunshine.

"A long time ago," I said to Sally, "you said Daddy was the only sane person in Tristes."

"I don't remember saying that," she said, her eyes on the scene in the arena.

Little kids on ponies paraded behind Suzanna and around the ring. The boys looked stiff in their new hats and blue jeans, the girls fluid with ribbons in their hair to match the ponies' manes. Annie watched them with envy.

"I'm going to ride in the rodeo parade next year," Annie announced.

"I rode last year," the brainy kid said. "It's dumb."

"Oh, please," I snapped at both of them. I turned to Sally. "You did say it."

"Then I believe you," she said.

She knew better then to challenge me. And she had made the comment about Daddy. Probably in jest, but she had said it.

"Steve's up soon," she said. She patted my knee. "Then we can leave."

The parade circled another time and followed the rodeo queen out of the ring. Workers scurried in to scoop up the pony shit. The announcer rattled off bull-riding stats. I pressed the empty cup to my forehead.

In the chute, Jeff Rianda from Leadville, Colorado, brushed his riding glove across his craggy face. Windtwister, the 1400-pound caramel-colored bull under Rianda nudged the front of the chute. Rianda whispered in the bull's ear. Threat? Plea? Either way, the bull would win.

The bell rang, and Rianda and bull shot into the ring. The bull's back legs bucked as if they were one, beast dipping and arching like a single muscle. The cowboy bore down, his rope hand tightening, then slid off the bull onto the dirt.

"Five and a half seconds," the announcer yelled over the noise of the crowd.

Rianda scrambled to his feet. But Windtwister was too quick. The bull thrust a right horn, nipping Rianda's shoulder. Rianda flinched, and the beast lowered his head, preparing to charge. Sally's fingertips dug into my knee cap as Rianda scurried for the fence, clearing it. Two cowboys, one on horseback, lassoed Windtwister. Rianda waved a trampled hat from behind the fence. Safe.

"See, Hon?" Sally put her arm around me and let out a sigh of relief. "The rider's fine."

"Is Steve going to get hurt?" Annie's eyes widened.

"Steve's an excellent rider," Sally said. "And the bull he got today is a softie."

"What's that mean?" I asked, tired of the whole show.

"It means that he's not likely to charge my sweetheart," Sally said.

"How nice for you," I said.

~

The brainy kid's mother came back from the snack bar and handed the kid a box of Cracker Jack. He shared a small handful with Annie. She popped the last piece of corn into her mouth and turned to me.

"I have to pee," she said.

"You want me to take her?" Sally asked, trying to be helpful.

"I'll go," I said.

She didn't want to miss Steve. Besides, my mother had put me in charge of Annie.

"Keep an eye out for Steve in the ring," Sally said, looking at her watch. "I told him we'd cheer."

Annie put her sticky hand in mine. We walked down the bleachers and around the outside of the ring, our sandals kicking up dust. The odor of fermenting human urine and shit floated from the Porta Potties.

In the ring, a rider shot out on Bruiser. The black bull gave Windtwister a run for his money in sheer size. Annie crossed her legs as she walked, trying to not pee her pants. Five feet from the converging lines to the Porta Potties, Annie stopped. She bent over and started to cry.

"Not here." I took her arm and tried to pull her up.

"I can't help it, Sheelie," she said. Pee streamed down the inside of her legs.

"Get up," I said.

Annie's urine mingled with the smell of bits of alfalfa on the ground. I was hot and tired. I wanted Buck back. I wanted George to get hit by a produce truck.

In the ring, the black bull thrust his horns at the rider's back. The rider cried out. The medical team surrounded him. A wave of nausea washed over me. Then the medical team moved back. The rider opened his eyes, and the stunned crowd burst into applause.

With the excitement over, people in the stands were watching us now. I picked up Annie, stumbling under the unexpected weight. When she was a baby, she'd weighed nothing, and Josh and I would fight over who got to carry her from the house to the car, the highchair to the crib. I didn't care that she smelled.

"Fuck them," I said under my breath.

"That's a very bad word." Annie wrapped her arms around my neck.

"Come on," I said. "Let's get you cleaned up."

I pressed my lips to her forehead and headed for the snack bar to get paper towels and water.

Ten

In August, a month and a half before the wedding, a John Deere tractor salesman bought our house on C Street, and we moved into George's place out on Bear Road on the Gabilan side of the valley. I was a little relieved actually. In the last month, I had spent too much time in my bedroom missing Buck.

The morning we drove away from C Street for good, my mother went into the garden to say goodbye. I watched her from the window. She sat on the garden path, maybe listening for the chimes, her nose tilted to the scent of the sweet peas. She didn't cry. Later, when I asked her why, she said the past did not deserve a second glance. She was on to a new life, a new family.

The movers went ahead, with a moving van packed to the brim. Annie and my mother rode out to Bear Road in George's truck. I watched from the front porch with King. Annie bounced on the seat, waving goodbye to the neighbors like a festival princess. She couldn't wait to play in the barn and in the pasture, where her new pony would graze.

A panting King hopped into the backseat of the VW and immediately began scratching. I backed out of the carport and stopped the car to look at the house one last time. It looked forlorn, run-down. The movers had torn one of the blinds in the front room, and the blind hung cockeyed, like a half-shut eye. The blue paint, already weathered, seemed even paler. I sensed the house wanted an official goodbye. My mother had taken care of the garden. I guess I was responsible for the house.

"Oh, come on," I muttered. "You're a house, not a person."

King's ears perked up. I patted his head. "I won't be long."

The heels of my Dr. Scholl sandals clopped through the empty rooms. Years of scooter races, dress-up high heels, and King pacing had left fossils in the hardwood. In Josh's room I made a mental note to come back for the jar of pennies the movers had missed.

Josh had called last night. We had had one last conversation in our childhood home. I could hear him tearing up on the other end. He had tried to pass his stuffy nose off on the cold making its rounds on the base. But I knew better. He liked his bunk-mates, still hated getting up before dawn, overall a decent report. He was halfway through Basic, looking forward to coming home for the wedding. I couldn't wait to see him.

In my room, dust bunnies scurried for cover that wasn't there anymore. The bed had left a dark rectangle in the floor, the legs of my desk, perfect squares. I had torn away my childhood posters, leaving tacks in the hospital-pink walls, Daddy's description.

I had grown attached to these walls. Under any other circumstances, I despised pink.

Out of habit, my mother had drawn the blinds in her room to keep the sun from bleaching the bedspread. I opened the closet to make sure she hadn't forgotten anything. A single wire hanger hung in the center of the rack where my mother's clothes had hung.

Salvation Army had come for Daddy's small trunk of clothes. She had not been able to let the trunk go until now. It had contained a pair of coveralls, a few shirts, ties Grandma Bea had given Daddy over many Christmases, and two sports jackets with suede elbow patches.

I had managed to retrieve his surviving desert boot before it too was carted off. Josh and I had spent many nights trying to figure out how the boot had landed on the tracks one hundred yards from where the train had hit the pickup. The police had been equally mystified.

A made-up rhyme came to mind. All things must come to a close. Just like a rose. All things must die. Even the gleam in your mother's eye. The rhyme ran through my mind as I wandered the rest of the house. I locked the front door, an odd thing to do since there was nothing to steal, and recited the rhyme once more. The house now seemed willing to let me go.

King barked at me from the open driver's-side window. I turned to go back for the pennies and then changed my mind. Let the new owner figure out what to do with a thousand faceless pennies.

The light was different on the Gabilan side of the valley where George and Will lived. At sunset, the mountains melded from gold to furry gray, and the outline of the oak trees was haunting and lovely. Ironically, I felt close to Daddy out here. He had loved the Gabilans, regardless of who lived below them.

Our new house, a two-story farmhouse, was not new at all. Pepito had purchased the farmhouse from a dairy farmer in the 1930s when the farmer shuttered the dairy and moved to King City. George Sr. and his siblings were raised in the house, followed by George Jr., Will, and Sally.

George had had it repainted in honor of his bride-to-be. White with the brown trim my mother had pretended to like. She had requested brick-red for the shutters and window frames. But Mr. Emmons, who painted most of the houses in town, had taken advantage of the Kelly Moore special on the brown and convinced George it was every bit as good as brick-red.

A reasonably intact picket fence enclosed Dottie's old garden. The neglect had begun when Dottie—George, Will and Sally's mother—became ill with cancer. My mother vowed to care for the roses first. Then she would prepare the soil for fall. She'd let George's house-paint goof slide. She would put her mark on the garden instead.

The day we moved in, George and my mother had their first argument. I overheard them from Will's old room upstairs. Will had agreed to move into the in-law unit out back. But he had left the room a mess. George was livid about the Skoll tins and dirty socks on the floor of the closet, the *Playboy*s under the bed that King was using as a hiding place. George's one hundred twenty pound American Bandogge mastiff, Rusty, was not King's cup of tea. He wasn't used to other dogs, especially big stupid ones.

"Honey, this is Will's house too," my mother said, trying to smooth things over for Will. She knew how George could get about his brother. "Give him a little time. It's certainly not worth all this upset."

"Let him move into the Meadows apartments," George grumbled. "He can waste away there."

The apartment complex was two blocks from Tristes High on the east side of town. Drug addicts and other people down on their luck lived in the run-down apartments there. At least once a year, a Meadows resident would wander onto campus at lunch time, looking for a handout, and the school superintendent would call the police.

"You're too forgiving, Alice," George snapped. "I'm going up there to clean it up myself."

I continued unpacking books, waiting for George to appear. He knocked on the door frame of Will's room. Rusty, named for the rust spots on his short white coat, snuffled in after his master.

He poked his snout at the dust ruffle around the bed. King let out a low growl.

"Rusty," George said. He snapped his fingers. "Here, boy."

Rusty obeyed. He sat in the doorway, licking the slobber from his mouth. George surveyed the room. His eyes rested on a *Playboy* on the floor, and his face reddened. I'd looked at the centerfold earlier. Miss June had Barbie-doll lips, breasts like moons.

"Go help your mother." He held my gaze. "You shouldn't be in here yet. The room's not ready."

I set a stack of paperbacks on the bookshelf and opened another box. I could feel him waiting for me to obey. He cleared his throat. I liked watching George squirm.

"Did you hear me?" he asked.

"I heard you," I said. "Now, I have something to say to you."

"What is it, Sheila?" He pushed back his thinning hair and sighed. "Though I suspect I know."

He stood in the middle of the room, waiting. A flush of heat went up my neck. This was it. I put down the books I was holding.

"Buck and me didn't do anything wrong," I said. "You didn't have to run him out like that. You ruined my summer. I hate you, George."

His face went white. I was breathing hard now. I was just getting wound up. I felt invincible. Alive. So damn alive, I could have kept yelling.

"Just don't tell me you did it for my own good. I'll vomit if you tell me that. I'll puke right here in the middle of the floor for Rusty to lick up. He would, too. George Fratti Jr. who thinks he owns everything, including my heart."

George closed the door behind him. It was just him and me now. The wind knocked a pepper tree branch against the window. The peppercorns scraped the glass. As if they were desperate to get in. As desperate as I was to get out.

"You can hate me all you want, Sheila," George said. His voice was controlled. "I don't need to justify my actions. You're seventeen years old. And one day you'll see I did the right thing. I'm just glad I got Buck out in time. Had he stuck around, there would have been trouble. For everyone."

He knelt down, did a sweep under the bed. He gathered the *Playboys* and shoved them under his arm. His knees cracked when he stood. Rusty lifted the dust ruffle with his snout. King growled again.

I had assumed my mother told him about the night out at Terra Dura. But she did the right thing. The safe thing. She had protected George and me from each other. George because he wouldn't have been able to handle the thought of me fucking Buck. And me because I couldn't stand him knowing. I stared at George.

"What is it, now?" he asked sharply.

"Nothing," I mumbled.

"Fine, then. Rusty, come," he ordered. "We have boxes to unpack. We're making a home, boy."

Rusty waddled down the hall. King slunk out from under the

bed, tail between his legs. This was Rusty's turf. King had some adjusting to do. I gave Fratti and his dog the finger and slammed the door.

—⁓—

The next morning, Will came in the house to make coffee. He looked hungover. My mother and Annie had gone down to the Pit to pick up my mother's last paycheck. George was down at the packing shed, pushing paper and probably on the phone arguing with the UFW, which was still lobbying to bring back the long hoe. Will had a coughing spell and spit in the sink.

"That's gross," I said, resting my spoon on the edge of my bowl of Cheerios. "Can't you use the bathroom sink, Will?"

"Sorry, kid." Will wiped his mouth with a clean dishtowel and peered into my bowl. "I take it you don't think I'm uncle material?"

"I guess it's an acquired skill." I laughed. "Uncle Will."

"I like the sound of that," he said, smiling.

"Thanks for giving up your room." I handed him the box of Cheerios, and he poured some into his mouth.

"Yeah, sorry it wasn't ready." He took a jar of instant coffee out of the cupboard and spooned the granules into a smiley-face mug. "How's it so far, living under the same roof with Georgie?"

"Not great." I poured more Cheerios into my bowl. "But we've only been here a day."

"It's pretty ironic, you living out here." He glanced out the window. "Speaking of which, it's George Jr. himself."

George stomped the dirt from his boots on the Welcome mat. The coat closet in the foyer opened. "Don't go reaching around in there," he'd told Annie and me, a warning about the hunting rifle he kept behind the coats and umbrellas. Guns in the house, that was a new one for us. Daddy had ranked guns right up there with the A-bomb. Tools of destruction. He had kept that old .22 rifle in the basement, but never in the house.

"I'll take my exit now," I said to Will.

"Good idea," he said, munching on a spoonful of cereal.

I went upstairs to shower. After I had dressed, I tossed a load of laundry into the washer. Soiled Pit uniforms were piled on the floor. Last night had been my mother's final shift, and Princie and the waitresses had thrown her a surprise party. She'd woken up slightly hungover but happy.

Downstairs, a cupboard slammed. I heard yelling. The clatter of dishes.

"Let it go, George." Will was talking. "As long as Sheila's not pissing and moaning about it, why should you?"

"The room was awful," George growled. "And show some respect. Clean up your dishes."

I sprinkled Tide over the sheets in the washer. Will said something I couldn't hear. A loud thump followed, then the crash of a ceramic object. I closed the washer lid and edged downstairs. The smiley mug was in pieces in the hallway near the kitchen. My hands shook.

"What the hell did you do that for, Will?" George shouted, his voice cracking a little. "That was Dottie's favorite."

"Dottie didn't have favorites," Will said. "Except among sons."

People had always said Dottie preferred George over Will because George was easier. They attributed Will's drinking to lack of mother love. I was torn between listening to the fight and getting the hell out of the house.

"Don't start the self-pity," George snarled. "She loved us equally."

Scuffling of feet and snorting noises pulled me into the kitchen. George held Will to the front of the fridge with his body. He pulled back a large fist, his face tight with rage. He saw me and stopped.

"Go ahead, brother," Will taunted, his eyes slits. "You've never held back. Pound away."

Cold sweat coated my back. Violence and me had never mixed. When fights broke out at school and everyone gathered to cheer, I went the other way.

"Let him go," I whispered.

"Sheila." George let out a haggard sigh.

"Just stop," I said, my mouth trembling.

"Damn," George whispered. He stepped away from Will and his breathing slowed. "I didn't know you were here."

"Not much fun around here, is it?" Will asked, touching a cut on his upper check. He was out of breath too. "See, Sheila, when it comes to me, George can't control his temper. Everyone else, he keeps a lid on it."

George held his arms to his body as if he had an upset stomach. Will went into the hall and picked up the broken pieces of the smiley mug. He put them in the trash can under the sink and left. George stared at the Fratti Farms cap that lay upside down on the newly tiled countertop. Like the hat, he looked crumpled, spent. Seeing him weak like this should have made me happy. So why wasn't I?

"Sheila, I'm sorry," George said, straightening to his full six feet. "I'm sorry you had to see this. Will and I don't see things the same."

"I can see that." I shoved my shaking hands into the pockets of my jeans. I preferred his righteousness over apologies. "I'm going to Salinas."

"Does your mother know where you're going?" George asked, following me into the foyer.

"Did she give you permission to have a fist fight with Will?"

I took the keys from the hook on the wall and looked him in the eye. He was back to being an asshole. Challenging him was easy.

"You still need to watch your step, girl," he said, lowering his voice.

"I guess that's a no," I said.

Eleven

The plane trees cast large shadows over the sidewalk on John Street. Ing was on her break. We were standing and talking in front of the JC Penney's, next door to Dick's Men's Wear. Leaves gathered in the gutter.

"Who won?" Ing asked, her voice rising. She relished a good fight.

"No one, really," I said with a shrug. "But it was ugly. George was shocked that I saw the whole thing."

I hadn't stopped trembling until I was halfway up the highway. I was remembering the time Daddy and Mr. Beckman had gotten into a fight over the Doberman shitting in our yard. Daddy had scooped up the dog shit with a newspaper and deposited it on the Beckmans' welcome mat. Beckman reciprocated. A fist in Daddy's face. The nosebleed seemed to go on for hours, and I had become hysterical.

"Did George throw Will out?" Ing asked.

She glanced at her reflection in the JC Penney's window.

Frowning, she unclipped the tortoise shell barrette holding one side of her hair in place, then neatly reclipped it. The ends of her hair, unaccustomed to this style, curled out.

"He can't," I said. "The house belongs to all three of them. Sally just prefers living in town in her own apartment."

"Smart lady," she said. "I've always liked her."

"George was embarrassed," I said.

"Maybe he'll be nicer to you," she said.

"I doubt it." I changed the subject. "Sally found a dress for the bridesmaids."

"I heard Suzanna Baroni is in the wedding," Ing said, pretending to pout. "How come your mom didn't ask me to be a bridesmaid?"

"At least you get to wear what you want," I said. "What the hell's a tea-length gown, anyway?"

"Don't you know anything?" She jabbed her anklebone with the edge of her hand to show me the length.

"Sally talked my mom into hiring a makeup artist," I said. "Can you believe it? Two years ago my mother didn't even wear makeup." I sighed. "I wish they'd elope."

A rickety pickup clattered past us. Across the street, a business man was locking up Wells Fargo Bank. The enormous key chain clanged against the metal door frame.

"That's Mr. Harris." Ing elbowed me. "I sold him that suit, plus twelve pair of gray socks."

In her first month Ing had sold more than any other salesperson had in three. Her best customer was Ben, an ex-tennis pro who worked for the real estate company up the street. The license plates on his hornet-green Corvette said, "DUIT4LV."

"Benjamin buys all colors," she said in a dreamy voice. "And ties to match."

Cupping her hands around her face, she peered into the JC Penney's window. I looked in. Furniture and dishes. Things Ing normally wouldn't give a damn about.

"Benjamin? Please." Had he asked her to call him by his full name? What a buffoon.

"He bought two suits the day before yesterday." She turned and tossed her head. "You know how much commission that is?"

"You're crushing, Ing," I said. "And on more than his money."

"What if I am?" She bit her lip. "I'm tired of Jimmy waiting around to see if I'll marry him."

"You talked about getting married?"

"Jimmy wants to," she said. She pointed at the dining room display in the window. "I love that table."

Two barrels formed the base of the table. A harvest theme. Frilly orange placemats and dishware with fall-leaf borders. What did Ing care about dishes? Domesticity bored her.

"Jimmy definitely loves you," I said. "But you guys are seventeen. No one gets married that young."

In fact, I could name at least three couples from Josh's graduating class that had tied the knot. Two of the couples before graduation. But I still didn't understand Jimmy's rush. He had plenty of time. Ing, too. If she cared enough.

"The problem is," Ing said, swallowing, "I can't bear to think about him working for his dad, coming home with paint under his fingernails, always reeking of thinner."

She was holding something back. I was pretty sure Ben was involved. The way she had talked about him was different. Intimate.

"Come on, Ing. There's something else." I stared at her. "What's wrong?"

"I think it's PMS," she said, shaking her head.

"I'm the one who gets sappy," I said. "You act goofy. Remember?"

She shrugged and looked at her watch. Her boss appeared in the window of Dick Brown's. He waved at her from between two mannequins.

"I should go," Ing said. "My break's over."

~

Jimmy met us at the Salinas drive-in that night. We sipped the Schlitz Jimmy had gotten Tall Larry to buy for us. Up on the screen, the shark in *Jaws* was turning a swimmer's leg into hamburger. The three of us sat in the front seat of Jimmy's Chevelle. The beer was warm.

"How often does he come into the store, anyway?" Jimmy asked Ing.

"I don't know," Ing said. "A few times a week." She didn't like Jimmy grilling her about Ben. "Shee, I got the munchies. Come with me to the snack bar. You want a soda, Jimmy?"

"I'm going to crack open the Old Crow." He was pouting over the Ben thing.

"I'll bring you a Coke," Ing said.

"I don't want a Coke," he snapped.

"Don't get all mad." She nudged me to get out of the car. "Coming?"

I climbed out. Outside of the Chevelle, the speakers hooked on each car window sounded tinny, comical. The shark cut an ominous line through the blue water.

"I'll stay." I wanted to talk to Jimmy. Let Ing cool down. "I don't want to miss this part."

"Fine," Ing said. "Be that way."

I climbed back into the Chevelle. The space Ing had occupied between Jimmy and me contained an eddy of unsaid words. He passed me the bottle of Old Crow. I tipped the bottle to my mouth. The whiskey burned going down.

"You think she'd go out on me?" he asked. "I saw how that guy looks at her. A real dick."

He had sensed the same thing. That Ing wasn't quite with us. Her being physically gone magnified this feeling. When I handed the bottle back to Jimmy, his hand accidentally wrapped around mine. We quickly wiggled our fingers apart. Warmth shot through my body. Not Buck temperature. But warm. Shit. I'd had feelings for Jimmy for years. But the Ben thing was stirring the pot for all of us.

"Do me a favor, Shee," Jimmy said, his face blue in the glow of the movie screen. "Go find her. Tell her I'm not mad."

"She doesn't deserve you," I said. "But I'll go."

Ing wasn't at the drive-in snack bar. I found her in the Ladies' Room. Her eyes were red from crying. I rinsed out my mouth to get rid of the whiskey and stale beer taste while Ing reapplied her makeup.

"Jimmy's all confused," she said. "Maybe he'll catch a bigger buzz and relax."

Last March on the full moon, Jimmy, Ing, and I had drank a lot of beer on Carmel Beach. The wave tips shone silver and Ing dared me to jump in. I surprised them both by stripping down to my underwear. I had waded around until I couldn't stand the cold anymore.

When I got out, Jimmy was starting a fire. He stared at the water pouring down my breasts. "Get dressed," Ing said when she saw Jimmy's eyes navigating my body. He couldn't help himself, and I liked the attention. It had been the first time a boy had appreciated my body this way. Now, I wanted to smack Ing for not appreciating Jimmy.

"How many times have you gone out with him?" I asked her.

"Who?" She gave me a coy glance.

"You know who. Ben."

"A few," she said, smiling secretively. "The first time we did it on the hood of his Corvette. Another time, in a motel. It was so fun. It's so different being with a man. You didn't tell me what I was missing."

"He's not married, is he?" I asked, knowing the answer before she said it.

"You must have ESP," she said. "I don't care that he's married." Her voice was shrill, a sure sign of guilt. "His wife had a miscarriage, and she's so depressed she won't talk to him. Ben confides in me."

The Ladies' Room door swung open. A woman wearing a flimsy red dress entered. She did a beeline for the closest stall. A couple of minutes later she came out and splashed water on her face.

"Jesus, Ing," I whispered. "Listen to me. Jimmy's good, you know he's good. Ben is a womanizer and an asshole."

Ing turned white. As if I'd spoken a truth she couldn't bear hearing. She looked daggers at me in the mirror.

"It's true," I said. "And you know it."

"You girls got a mint?" Red Dress asked, giving the polyester a tug to straighten it.

The Ladies' Room door opened again. A tall, stunning Mexican woman came in dressed in ivory slacks and a blouse. Her perfume smelled expensive. She floated down the row of stalls and went into the last one. Ing handed Red Dress a stick of Doublemint from her purse.

"Thanks, doll," Red Dress said, folding the gum into her large mouth.

She gestured at the Mexican woman going in the stall and waved her hand across her nose. As if she, Ing, and me were sharing a secret joke. I gave Red Dress a phony smile. I had an idea. An unusually catty one. Maybe spite would get through to Ing. Teach her to treat Jimmy like he meant something to her. To dump Ben like a hot coal.

"Ing, maybe this lady has some advice for you," I said. "Tell her about Ben."

"Sheila, I won't let you do this." Ing stared into the sink and bit her lip.

"What's wrong, sugar?" Red Dress asked, looking at Ing. She licked her lips, as if to prepare for a juicy discussion. "Love trouble?"

She touched Ing's arm. She wore the same shade of red nail polish as Ing. Creepy.

Jimmy had been good to me. Now it was my turn. And I was afraid for him. If Ing kept seeing Ben, Jimmy would find out, and who knew what he would do?

"Ing here has a boyfriend named Jimmy," I said. "But she's been messing around with Ben, who's married. A mess."

"Fate sent me into this Ladies' Room," Red Dress gushed. "Guaranteed the wife will find out and he'll dump you like the kitchen trash. I've been there. Stick with the boyfriend. I'd better get back to my honey. Bye, girls."

She yanked a brush through her overdyed hair and flounced out of the Ladies' Room. The smell of popcorn wafted in. The door swung closed.

"That was really low, Shee," Ing said, glancing at her reflection in the mirror. Since we were kids her own tears had fascinated her.

"I was trying to prove a point," I said.

"By humiliating me," she said, wiping away a tear.

The elegant Mexican woman flushed, came out of the stall,

and turned on the faucet. Ing and I watched the water run over the woman's slender fingers. She dried her hands slowly, as if they deserved utmost care, and left the restroom without a word. I pictured a clean-cut man dressed in a suit waiting for her outside.

"I'm going back to the car." Ing turned to me and yanked her purse strap onto her shoulder. "You do what you want."

"Ing, wait." I followed her out of the Ladies' Room. I had pushed her too far.

Under the neon "Snack Shack," Ing stopped and whirled around, ramming into me and jostling the popcorn the man behind us carried. I muttered a half-hearted apology. He glared at me.

"What do you want, Shee?" Ing spat. She tossed her dark curls. The screen framed her face, angelic in the glow of the movie. "I thought you were my friend."

"Look, I'm sorry," I said. "I'm really sorry. You're right. I was harsh."

We were two rows of cars over from Jimmy's Chevelle. I could see Jimmy. He put the half pint to his lips. Up on the screen, the shark devoured another tourist. On either side of the screen, car headlights pearled around the freeway overpass.

"My period's two weeks late," she said.

Ing stared at the screen, maybe past it.

Twelve

On Highway 1 North, five miles outside of Castroville, fog from the socked-in coast fingered up the sand dunes and over the artichoke fields. Ing was perched over the gutter on the side of the road. She'd had the dry heaves since we left Tristes. Saltines had failed to settle her tummy. We had stopped at Kim's for a ginger ale before we left town, but the cooler had gone down.

When she got back in the car, Ing still looked miserable. Her face was moist with fog. Her eyes watered from the cold and trying to barf. She licked her dry lips.

"Poor Ing," I said. As if being pregnant with a baby she didn't want wasn't enough. "You look awful."

"Gee, thanks," she said. Her head flopped against the back of the seat. "Take me to a store. I need a cold soda."

The "procedure" would take less than two hours. Asshole Ben had explained his wife was feeling better and they were trying to get pregnant again. He then handed Ing $300 cash and gave her a fatherly peck on the cheek.

Ing had had two counseling sessions on the phone with Planned Parenthood in San Francisco. We'd stay at her cousin Lorna's tonight. Ing would go to her appointment in the morning.

I turned the car into the 7-Eleven in Castroville and Ing and me got out. Day laborers loitered in front of the store, waiting for a farmer to drive up and offer them work. They tried to strike up a conversation in Spanish.

"Go jack off," Ing muttered in English.

Inside the store, she ordered a Cola Slushee, barely looking at the Chinese clerk. She had more than the abortion on her mind. The day after she had dumped Jimmy, who knew nothing about the pregnancy, he had showed up at the house and stood in the front yard screaming obscenities. Ing finally came out. He tried to hit her and hit the climbing rose bush instead. The Chief had informed Jimmy's parents if Jimmy set foot on the property again, he'd have him thrown in juvie.

"Machine broken," the clerk said, returning to his newspaper.

"How come?" Ing gestured at a laborer sucking on a large Slushee. "You gave the spics one."

"Machine broken," the clerk said. "End of story."

"Pinche cabrón! I'm pregnant." Ing's voice was high-pitched, bordering on hysterical.

The clerk barked Mandarin at her, and she shut up. I begged him to make the Slushee. He waved a small, delicate hand at Ing.

"She too young to be pregnant," he said. He turned on the Slushee machine. "So I make you one."

"I didn't know there was a drinking age for Slushees," Ing snapped.

She turned the rack of sunglasses near the counter. Frames in every color and style. Black, brown, tortoise shell, purple. Mirrored lenses, clear, polarized.

"I think he meant the other thing," I said, watching the brown ribbon of ice flow from the vibrating chute into a tall 7-Eleven cup.

"How do I look?" Ing slipped on a pair of the purple-framed sunglasses and flashed me a movie-star smile. My reflection in the glasses made me look oblong, with a pea-size head.

"Fabulous," I said.

The clerk snapped a lid on the Slushee. Ing slid the sunglasses down the front of her jeans. I tried to catch her eye before she stuffed a pair of tortoise shell knockoffs under her blouse. Too late. She winked at me and tossed a package of Fritos on the counter.

"One dollar and ninety-nine cent," the clerk said.

I pictured Ing and me at the police station, and George telling my mother that he'd told her so, seventeen-year-olds had no business driving to San Francisco alone. George had acquiesced after the Chief had given the trip to Lorna's his seal of approval. But he still worried we'd end up in dangerous places, doing dangerous things. My mother, bless her, had coolly informed him I was trustworthy.

The clerk handed me change, oblivious to Ing stealing. Outside, the laborers climbed into the back of a muddy white pickup truck. They waved. Ing gave them the finger, and one of the laborers let out a cat call.

"That was really stupid, Ing," I said when we got into the car.

"Don't be a narc. The chink didn't see me." She opened the bag of Fritos. "Remember the time Kim caught you with the Heath Bar?"

Another one of Ing's dares. I had begged Kim not to call my parents. In exchange for not telling them, he made me Windex the meat display case. Ing had stood by pointing out smudges and smears. We promised to never steal from Kim again. Then he loaded us up with bubble gum and sent us home.

"You were so scared," Ing said.

"This isn't funny," I said. "They handcuff people who steal from 7-Eleven."

"Nothing's funny anymore." She sighed and handed me the tortoise shells. "Here, they look better on blonds."

I put on the glasses to make her happy. Guilt makes people do strange things. Like steal.

I found the on-ramp to Highway 101 North, which would get us to San Francisco faster. It was good to be on the road again. I drove inland towards Gilroy and a sizzling blue sky. Eventually, Ing closed her eyes.

She'd told me the baby was moving last night and had kept her awake. I reminded her about Sex Ed. and fetal development. She said her baby was the exception, kicking at six weeks.

Fruit stands dotted the road. On a barnlike stand, an enormous garlic bulb advertised Gilroy, garlic capital of the world.

Tristes's Heart of the Salad Bowl was more poetic, but the reason behind the dubious claims was the same—small towns trying to seem bigger than they were.

Tomorrow the doctor would insert a skinny tube into Ing's uterus. They would give her a shot in the cervix, a Valium to relax her. She could expect bleeding and cramping. Yes, she would feel a tug or two during the procedure. But then it would be over. All over.

⁓

We passed the gleaming car dealerships of San Mateo and Burlingame. At the San Francisco airport, a TWA jet strained to gain altitude. The silver-bodied plane leveled off over the placid pewter bay. Candlestick Park hugged the water's edge. Ing opened her eyes and yawned. She looked out at Candlestick.

"Remember seventh grade?" she said. "Seems like a really long time ago."

I did remember. The Giants had lost, Jimmy bought Ing and me hot dogs. Ing had become jealous when Jimmy lent me his jacket. They had not yet dated. Still Ing had been possessive.

"We froze," I said.

"Yeah, it was cold," she said. "I love all the little houses."

Near the Army Street exit, boxy houses in every color covered an entire hillside. I glanced at Ing's curlicue handwriting on the note paper. Address but no directions. I thrust the piece of paper at Ing and gave her a blank stare.

"I think it's near Golden Gate Park," she said. "Lorna said a lot of hippies hang around the neighborhood."

The traffic thickened. Ing sucked on the dregs of her Slushee. Several miles later, I took the Broadway Street exit, just missing the lane to get on the Oakland Bridge. On Broadway Street, marquees advertised "Hot Love with Twins" and "Deep Throat Dreams." A woman wearing spike heels and a black miniskirt coaxed some guy into a red doorway. At a stoplight, a black hooker leaned into the open window of the silver Mercedes in front of us. They chatted for a moment, and the woman got into the car. The Mercedes sped off.

"Wow," Ing said. "Where do you think they're going? I bet she charges him a fortune."

"What do you care?" I said, flicking on the blinker to change lanes. "It's not some glamorous career."

"I'm just curious," she said. She pointed. "Hey, look at the Chinese people."

Unbelievable. Sometimes I couldn't fathom how Ing and me had ended up best friends. Down a side street, people dressed in Mao-style jackets and black, red rubber-soled slippers jammed the sidewalks, scrutinizing bins of shriveled roots and vegetables. We were obviously in Chinatown.

"I'm going to puke," Ing said.

The color drained from her cheeks. She opened her door at the next red light and let loose. The bus driver behind us leaned on his horn, and Ing yanked the VW door closed. She wiped a hand across her mouth. The car reeked of sour-smelling vomit.

I wondered if being pregnant makes puke smell worse than usual.

"Better?" I spoke through my nose.

"Much." She nodded. "Sorry about the smell."

I yelled out the window for directions to Golden Gate Park, and a Chinese man standing on a corner pointed up the street. We went through a yellow-tiled, exhaust-stained tunnel. On the other side of the tunnel, turreted doll houses in combinations of purple and lavender, red and gold, black and white lined the streets. On the west corner of the intersection, a church steeple pierced the sky. A hunched-over old man tossed bread to the pigeons on the church steps.

I spotted a pay phone and pulled into a parking place on the street, grateful my mother had insisted on teaching me to parallel park before this trip to Lorna's. She had me wedge the VW in between George's truck and her brand-new Firebird, an early wedding present from George. I had taken three tries to park. George was inside watching and sweating bullets. My mother said I was a natural.

Lorna's boyfriend Marco answered the telephone. He immediately asked how old I was. I told him forty-eight, wrote down the directions, and hung up. Another creepy guy. The world was full of them these days.

"I don't know about Marco," I said to Ing in the car. I drove up Van Ness Avenue to Pine Street, to Masonic Avenue and into the Haight Ashbury. "He sounds like the macho type."

"Lorna says he's a total fox," Ing said. "Of course, she always says they're good-looking until she breaks up with them." She glanced over at me. "Except for Josh," she said quickly.

"It's okay," I said. "Josh wasn't in love with her."

Ing and I both knew Lorna still had a soft spot for Josh. She'd never admit it. But when Ing had mentioned Josh had gone down to Imperial Beach, Lorna asked if Ing would get the address from me. Lorna wanted to send Josh "a little note."

Thirteen

At the corner of Haight and Ashbury, a record store advertised Bob Marley, Aerosmith, and Bob Seger's latest albums in bright orange window paint. A little boy scampered through the crosswalk, blowing on a pinwheel in his grimy hand. The bottoms of his bare feet were black, as though dipped in tar. A woman sitting Indian-style on the sidewalk called to the boy. He climbed into her lap and gave her braid a playful tug.

"Don't they bathe?" Ing looked at them in disgust.

"Apparently not," I said.

Down the block, a man with caramel skin and a mass of dreadlocks played a fiddle in front of a bakery. His eyes were closed. He gyrated to the music, his entire face twisted into a crazy grin that made me smile. He opened his eyes when a man dropped some coins into the beanie cap on the sidewalk at his feet.

"He's on acid," Ing said. "Look at him."

"Maybe he just loves music," I said, although the man did look pretty high.

The charcoal-gray Victorian where Lorna and Marco lived had sagging front steps. Newspaper and sheets of plastic were taped over the windows. "Impeach Nixon" bumper stickers plastered the front door. When Ing pressed the doorbell button, the doorbell sputtered like it had lost one of its parts.

"Some guy started throwing rocks one night," Ing explained, pointing to the windows. "The landlord's too cheap to replace them."

Lorna answered, dressed in underwear and a man's T-shirt, hair cropped at the shoulders. The soft mass of curls that had cascaded down her back, a trademark of the Rodriquez girls, was gone. We followed her down a beige hallway with a buckled wood floor. Jimi Hendrix and Led Zeppelin posters decorated the walls, and a scar of cracked paint ran down the middle of the ceiling.

Dishes overflowed the kitchen sink. Pots cluttered the grimy stove. On the fridge, a page torn from a magazine, Cheryl Tiegs, dressed in a yellow bikini. I asked Lorna how old the house was.

"Pre-1906." Lorna shooed away the black cat licking a puddle of leftover gravy on the counter. "This house made it through the big one." The cat jumped back on the counter. Lorna ignored it. "I hear your mom's marrying George Fratti."

"Yeah, in October," I said.

"You sound thrilled." Lorna peered into the fridge. "How's Josh? I still can't believe it. I thought he was against military stuff."

"Dad had a big influence on him," I said. "Now Josh's come around to his own way of thinking."

"We all have to grow up," Lorna said, taking out a loaf of Wonder bread. "Are you guys hungry?"

"I'm starved," Ing said. She pulled a chair away from the table and sat down. "I blew chunks in Chinatown."

"What were you doing there?" Lorna asked, dropping two slices of bread in the toaster slots.

A shower went on upstairs. The pipes thumped and screamed in the walls. Ing and I jumped. The rickety old house made us both skittish.

"We got a little lost," I said, laughing.

"I don't understand why you don't tell Jimmy," Lorna said to Ing.

Lorna had had an abortion last fall. I didn't know who the father was. Only that she'd dropped out of San Jose State because of it. Then she moved to San Francisco.

"Jimmy would want me to have it," Ing said. "Like I'm ready to be a mother."

"And you're sure it's his?" Lorna raised an eyebrow.

"Pretty sure."

Ing fed the cat some toast. Its coarse pink tongue licked at the butter. The purr sounded like the VW idling.

"Don't feel bad," Lorna said, her eyes softening. "I slept with my psychology prof while I was dating a perfectly nice guy." She stared at her open palm as if it were a cheat sheet. "When I told the prof I was pregnant, he said I should've been on the pill.

Didn't give me a penny." She looked at Ing. "Don't worry, cousin. After tomorrow it'll all be over. Come on, I'll show you Barry's room."

The Planned Parenthood counselor had told Ing the same thing. A relatively short, painless procedure. Afterwards there would be bleeding and some cramping. But nothing to worry about. Ing would be fine in no time.

⌁

Barry, Lorna and Marco's roommate, was in New York studying acting for the summer. His room had a swampy smell. Ing looked in disgust at the pilled brown blanket covering a mattress on the floor.

"I'll try to find some clean sheets." Lorna opened a window and headed to the bathroom shower.

I split the blinds and peered out. The pink house with white trim across the street reminded me of a birthday cake. A Bengal tiger covered the façade of the house next door. The tiger's tail curled around the side of the house. I half expected the tip to twitch. Ing came over to the window and stood next to me.

"Cool houses." She yawned. She stretched out on the mattress, tucking her sweater against her cheek to avoid the filthy pillow case. "I'm going to sleep. Just for a little while."

"Good idea." I thumbed through a paperback copy of *Death of a Salesman* I found on Barry's desk.

Under the desk, water from an overturned bong seeped into the hardwood. A streetcar screeched past the house. Voices drifted up from the street. One of the voices sounded calm, the other frantic. The fiddle player we had seen on Haight Street and another man stood talking outside the tiger house.

"It's all right, man," the fiddle player said to his friend. "There're other fish."

"She told me no more," the friend said, shaking his head. "I love her, man. 'No more' is not in my vocabulary."

"Come inside," the fiddle player urged. "Let me play for you. It'll calm your nerves."

The fiddle player's words came like smoke signals, lilted and delicate. The friend rolled up the sleeves of his soiled polka-dot shirt. He rocked on his heels as if trying to find his balance.

"No offense, man, but music won't cure this. I have to find her."

He unrolled the sleeves, then rolled them up again. He jerked his head about like a bird pecking the air for seed. The fiddle player looked up at the window and saw me staring down. Caught. I gave him a little wave and let the blinds close.

"I just got caught eavesdropping."

My heart hammered against my ribcage. What if the fiddle player was some creep, thinking I had the hots for him?

"On who?" Ing murmured. She flipped onto her back.

"The fiddle player we saw earlier."

"Maybe it's a sign," she said, closing her eyes.

"Don't be dumb," I said. When the fiddle player had looked

up, his eyes seemed kind. And anyone who lived in a tiger house had to be cool. "He lives across the street."

"How am I supposed to sleep?" Ing sat up. "I'm in San Francisco. Slide over my bag."

I gave her the bag, and she took out the diary she had started at the beginning of the summer. The cover had a nondescript floral pattern fastened by a flimsy gold lock. Ing wanted our last year before graduation well documented. She had code words to keep Betty in the dark. Sex was happiness, pregnant bad news, partying, going for it.

"I hope you're not still mad about the sunglasses." She wrote a few sentences and looked up. "So you're not mad."

"No, Ing."

Someday I'd tell her she was stupid and cruel for screwing up her life and Jimmy's. But today I'd go easy. She needed friendship, not truth. At times, these two things are mutually exclusive.

Santana pulsated under the floorboards. The sweet skunk odor of strong pot filtered upstairs and into Barry's room. Ing perched the pen against her bottom lip and smiled.

"I smell mota," she said. "Let's join the party."

I followed her downstairs. I wasn't up to partying, but I felt responsible for Ing on the day before such a big day. The cat sat on the bottom stair, licking its paws. Ing petted it as we passed.

Marco and Lorna were sitting in an overstuffed chair together. Marco, bare-shirted and wearing Levi's, sifting seeds. He had long lashes and full lips, a stocky, rippling physique. I immediately disliked him.

"What a hunk," Ing whispered after Lorna had introduced us.

"My cousin thinks you're cute." Lorna poked Marco.

"Tell me." Marco peeled two rolling papers from the orange ZigZag pack. He ran his tongue along the papers to attach them. "Are all the girls from Tristes as pretty as you three?"

I had to admit he had a nice smile. Decent lips, the chiseled jaw. But definitely full of himself.

"Flirt," Lorna said to him.

"Amo-o." Marco kissed the end of Lorna's nose.

I watched him sprinkle pot into rolling papers. With any luck, Ing would get high, pass out and be rested for the next day. When the joint came around, Ing and me had coughing fits. Marco laughed.

"My stuff is too strong?" he asked.

"Your stuff is good," Ing said and coughed.

Lorna sent Marco into the kitchen for drinks and something to munch on. Ing, Lorna, and me talked over one another, unable to zero in on one topic. The silver-painted radiator banged and hissed like a strange locomotive.

A little while later, the doorbell sputtered. Marco got up to answer it. He returned with Pete, a fat guy with expressionless eyes too small for his face, and Cindy, a wisp of a woman whose milky complexion probably didn't need cleansing. She wore a purple tunic, satin tuxedo pants, and scuffed Birkenstocks. Peace-sign rings decorated her bony middle toes.

Pete sunk into the sofa, crossing a black combat boot over his opposite leg. The hula dancer tattooed to his left bicep jiggled. Cindy waved both hands at us. Silver bracelets collided at her elbows.

"Hey, Marco man," Cindy said, sitting crisscross on the floor. She arranged the purple tunic over her knees. "Long time no see."

"Want to get high?" Marco smiled.

"I'm always good for a joint," Cindy said lazily. She turned to face Pete. "Pete?"

"I'll pass," Pete said. "I have to work tonight."

A bag of pretzels went around, beers were opened. Lorna and Cindy ignored one another. The tension between them was palpable. Cindy finally turned to me.

"I have an aunt living in San Luis Obispo," she said. "Is that close to Tristes?"

"That's about a hundred miles away," Lorna snapped.

"I grew up in Connecticut, what do I know?" Cindy replied, leaning blithely against Pete's legs.

It occurred to me that she and Pete might not be boyfriend and girlfriend. But he'd smiled at her several times. And there was the little sigh when her back touched his legs. I couldn't figure these people out. The plastic over one of the broken windows smacked the front of the house, startling all six of us. Marco laughed and lit up another joint.

"Smart girl," Pete said when I refused the second joint. "That shit fries your brain."

"Don't tell her that," Cindy said, patting her hand over a yawn. "I do my best thinking high."

"I've got the munchies." Ing reached for the pretzels and blinked her bloodshot eyes at me. "Good pot, huh?"

Cindy stretched out on the floor in front of the sofa. She crossed her hands over her chest and closed her eyes. Ing gasped. Ing's imagination did funny things on pot. But I knew what she was thinking. Cindy looked dead.

"Think about something else," I whispered.

"Cin's on cloud nine." Pete smiled, looked at Cindy and shook his head. "As usual."

"No kidding," Lorna said. She turned to Ing. "Cindy's Marco's ex. They broke up because she's always high."

"Not true," Cindy murmured. "Tell her, Marco."

"I'm staying out of this." Marco nuzzled Lorna. "Baby, let's dance."

When the song started to wind down, Lorna and Marco danced out of the room. There were giggling and shushing noises on the stairs. A few seconds later a door upstairs slammed, followed by more giggling.

"Some guys have all the luck." Pete squinted when he laughed. As if he was afraid of what was funny.

Everyone was longing for the love they didn't have. If Pete or the fiddle player's friend or Josh or Jimmy or Ing wanted love bad enough, that constituted love. For them, longing was love.

The record ended. The turntable needle lifted. The arm dropped into the slot. The room was excruciatingly quiet. There was a dull airy feeling in my head. A sensation of being physically in some other part of the house. I wished I hadn't smoked. I needed all of my senses.

"Is she asleep?" Ing nudged me and pointed at Cindy.

"She can conk out on a crowded bus," Pete said with a snort.

After a few more moments of buzzing silence, he asked us if we had fake IDs. "I'm working the door at the Watering Hole tonight."

"We'll dress up," Ing said to me. "I look twenty-one with makeup on." She looked at Pete. "Sheila, too."

"We didn't bring dressy stuff," I said, frowning at her. Her eyes blazed with excitement. She seemed hell-bent on partying. Maybe I should loosen up.

"Lorna has tons of clothes," she said.

"Make sure Marco's with you," Pete said. "My boss is a soccer freak, and he digs Marco because he's from Brazil, so he won't hassle you guys."

"I hate bars, Ing," I said. I stretched out my cramped legs. "But all right."

I had a hunch I would regret those three words. I imagined a cavernous dark bar with a grimy dance floor. Ing falling over drunk, Marco hitting on everyone. Not that partying would hurt the baby. Tomorrow, it would be history. I just wished Ing would get real about this.

Fourteen

Fog gusted in from the ocean and down Haight Street. It was the dead of summer, and Ing and me were freezing our asses off. The flimsy dresses we had borrowed from Lorna twisted like flags about our legs. The wind flapped against the ripped collar on the vinyl trench coat Ing had borrowed. I wore a thin fake fur coat, a cheetah pattern. Lorna had picked up the coat at the Goodwill. It smelled vaguely of B.O.

Our high heels clicked against the wet pavement. Marco whistled an inane tune as we walked. The rest of us were too busy shivering to say anything. We passed a café and the news kiosk where Marco worked. Marco said hello to his boss, an Italian-looking man unbundling newspapers.

Ing had done my makeup. Overdone it, I should say. I had not let her apply the blue eye shadow or the plum lipstick. Still, I felt like one of the whores we'd seen on Broadway Street this morning.

Ing looked twenty-five and "vampy," according to Lorna.

Lorna had dressed appropriately for the evening. Black wool dress, black tights, and boots. Yet she clutched Marco's arm like it was the last source of warmth on earth.

The fog swirled around newspaper stands and trash cans, bypassing the urine-soaked doorways that could have benefited by fresh air. I detested pantyhose, their icky grip, the ghastly flesh tone. I cared even less for walking up a strange street in a strange city at night. Bums loitered in front of the bakery. Marco exchanged hellos with a barefoot man dressed in a pair of tattered jeans, no shirt. Miraculously, the man did not look cold.

Unlike Ing, I had no misconceptions about the magic of bars. I could count on at least four hands the number of times Josh and me had crept into the Hero, past Felipe the owner, and into the poolroom to drag Daddy home. Nights my mother worked, we had to. Or risk Daddy spending the night there.

Ing hooked her arm in mine. She smiled at me, her porcelain cheeks dewy with fog. The long nap after the dope had refreshed her. I had spent the afternoon coming out of my own fog.

My pot brain haze finally cleared enough to read Roommate Barry's book of poetry while I watched at the window for the fiddle player. Sadly, he had never reappeared. He just seemed so damn happy. And loving. I didn't know anyone who possessed both qualities. Annie on occasion, but she was a child.

"Isn't this cool?" Ing whispered. Her breath was warm in my ear. "Thanks, Shee." She gave my arm a squeeze. "It'll keep my mind off stuff."

Lorna and Marco walked several feet in front of us. Lorna's

hair whipped around. She pulled the hood of her coat over her head. I slowed our pace.

"Just promise me you'll take it easy," I said to Ing. "A hangover's the last thing you need."

"Promise," she said, holding up her pinkie. The sacred Pinkie Swear meant the promise was air tight. "I'm sorry about today. You know, at the 7-Eleven."

Marco switched from whistling to singing in Portuguese, a baritone, and not half bad. Lorna tried to shut him up but he just sang louder.

"Never mind," I said, raising my voice so Ing could hear me. "You're going through a lot."

"You're a good friend, Shee." She lifted her chin at Marco. "Isn't he hysterical?"

"Yeah, he's hilarious," I said.

Marco was bad news. And no matter what Ing had said, it was going to be a long, unpredictable evening. There was no way around this.

⁓

The Hole was a basement bar located in a four-story building at the end of Haight Street. Pete pretended to check our IDs at the door. His boss was polishing glasses behind the bar and paid no attention to him or us.

A man onstage tested the sound system while a woman with hair that extended below her ass danced alone to music playing on the jukebox. A spinning disco ball scattered squares of green light on the parquet dance floor. Predictably, the Hole smelled of spilled booze, cherry syrup, and stale smoke.

"Cin's here," Pete said, pointing to a table in the far corner, beyond the dance floor. "She saved you guys a table. She's got some friends coming later, and I reserved a table for them." He turned to Marco. "She also has something else for you."

Marco gave Pete a knowing look and led us over to the table where Cindy sat. She had ditched the purple tunic for a sleeveless white chiffon pantsuit. Brass cuffs gripped her pencil-thin arms. She looked like the Greek Goddess Hera. A high Goddess Hera.

"You are so beautiful," Cindy murmured. She kissed Lorna, then Marco on both cheeks. A slow smile spread across her lips, as if her mouth and mind were out of sync. "Like Spanish gypsies."

The four of us sat down. Cindy didn't recognize Ing and me so dolled up, so Marco reintroduced us. Cindy studied us both and concluded we looked like models. She then slid a small folded square of paper across the table. Marco tucked the paper into his shirt pocket. Lorna's eyes shot daggers at him and then at Cindy.

A few minutes later, Cindy's friends arrived. Pete led them over to near the stage on the other side of the dance floor. Cindy picked up her gold drawstring purse.

"Goodbye, gypsies," she sang. She fluttered her fingers at the four of us and glided over the dance floor to the friends' table.

"Thank God." Lorna let out a sigh of relief. "What a pain in the ass."

A short white woman came to the table to take our drink order. Her small mouth sucked a peppermint and a pick-comb stuck out of her blond afro. She reminded me of a Kewpie doll.

"What can I bring you?" Her tongue thrust the peppermint to the other side of her mouth. "First round's on Pete."

Marco ordered a beer for himself, Cuba Libres for "the ladies." The waitress wrote down the order and scurried over to the next table.

"You told me you wouldn't," Lorna pleaded with Marco.

"One hit, amour," he said. "No more."

It had to be LSD. Ing's eyes fixed on the pocket. Not a good sign. I guess pinkie swears were no longer sacred. At school, only the real bad-ass *cholos* took the stuff. I had seen them camped in their low-riders along the perimeter of the park, Pendleton shirts loose at the neck, and cracking up hysterically at nothing apparent. The toughest *cholos* were usually too cool to laugh. Or unbutton their shirts.

"Let me try it," Ing cooed, snuggling up to Marco. "Come on."

"Forget it, Ing," Lorna said. She turned to Marco. "And don't you dare. My tio Pete would kill me."

"Come on," Ing whined. She fluttered her dark lashes at Lorna. "It'll be fun. The Chief will never know."

"He'd find out," Lorna snapped. "Knowing our history."

The Chief had once caught Lorna and Ing behind the post

office, smoking. Lorna twelve, Ing seven. Lorna's father, Ing's Tio Tony, had whipped Lorna with a willow branch. He then grounded her for a month. Ing got off without punishment. Too young to know better, the Chief had said.

Pete stepped inside to monitor the growing crowd. The band started their set with "Susie Q." The subject of Ing taking acid was dropped. For the moment, anyway. What did it matter if she managed to talk Marco out of a hit? I had run out of patience. Let Ing fry her mind. Let someone else hold her hand.

A group of bikers strutted in and sat at the bar. The chains looped to their belts clanked against the stools. They yelled their orders at the bartender. Smoke filled the bar.

"I'm ready to dance," Ing said, sucking down her drink. She looked around the table. "Marco?"

"You don't mind?" Marco asked, turning to Lorna for permission.

"Go on," Lorna said, smiling when Marco kissed her cheek. "Just remember what I said."

Marco nodded. He led Ing out to the dance floor. They fast-, slow-danced. Ing's butt wiggled under Lorna's slinky floral-patterned dress. Lorna shook her head and laughed.

"She's something, my cousin," she said. "I'm glad she's having fun. She needs this. Tomorrow won't be fun. And Marco loves a girl in crisis. He's also a terrible flirt."

"He knows about Ing?" I asked.

"Yeah," she said with a shrug. "He was cool when I told him about mine. We met a couple of days after my boyfriend and the professor dumped me, both in the same day. I was a mess. Marco consoled me. A week later, we moved in together."

A couple of the bikers asked the women at a table next to ours to dance. Each of the bikers draped a casual arm over their partners. Tie-dyed skirts swished next to black leather, chains, and tattooed biceps.

Marco's hand was low on Ing's waist. Lorna watched them and sipped her Cuba Libre. I'd taken one sip of my drink and found it too sweet. I drank the ice water the waitress had brought. Lorna reached for her purse. I watched her dig around in the inside pockets.

"So how is Josh, anyway?" she asked. Her long brown fingers produced a white tablet. "Quaalude," she said. "Want to split it?"

"I'll pass," I said. I had no interest in the unknown effects of this little pill. "Josh is fine, far as I know."

"He likes the Marines?" Lorna set the pill on her tongue and chased it down with ice water. "I still can't picture him with a buzz cut." She laughed quietly. "You know, I really liked him."

She sounded surprised by this. She shook her head as if to push Josh from her mind. When her eyes got to the bar, her face brightened. The source of delight was the fiddle player, talking to the bartender. His coffee-colored chest glowed in the dim light that shone over him. A medallion flashed between the lapels of his silky shirt. Ing was right. The guy showed up everywhere.

"Raj," Lorna shouted and waved at him.

"You know him?" I asked.

"He lives across the street from us," she said, a smile creeping over her lips. Her speech slowed. "Everyone knows Raj." The pill she'd taken appeared to be doing its trick.

The fiddle player seemed to float over to our table. He tried to hug Lorna in the chair. She stood up to give him a more substantial hug. He chortled and kissed her forehead.

"Lorna, dear, where's your sweetheart?" he asked. His teeth gleamed like a string of pearls.

"Dancing with my cousin." Lorna pointed a limp finger at the dance floor and turned to me slowly. Her words were slurred. "This is Sheila."

The fiddle player studied me. There was no way he would recognize me from this afternoon. Not with all the makeup. And he'd only caught a glimpse of me.

"Ah, it's the girl from the window," he said finally.

"I wasn't spying on you." I gave him a nervous smile. Now I was really caught.

"Don't worry, child."

I stared at the medallion. Brilliant gold, a face, it appeared. The fiddle player lifted the piece to show me. A crude face molded by inexperienced hands. It could have been a man or a woman.

"You like it?" he asked.

"Yes." I fingered the warm gold. I had never felt so relaxed around a stranger. "Is it Mayan?"

"Very good," he said, his eyes laughing.

"My father taught history," I said, setting the medallion

against the lapels of his bright green shirt. "He loved Latin America."

He removed the medallion from his neck and walked around the back of my chair. I turned around. He unfastened the gold clasp.

"You can't do that," I said. "It must have cost a fortune."

"The medallion was given to me," the fiddle player said. "Hold up your lovely hair so I can give you this treasure. It's yours now."

"Don't bother arguing," Lorna said. "He gives everything away."

"Everything but my fiddle," he said. "That I must keep."

He centered the medallion between my breasts and his smooth, dry fingers closed the clasp at the base of my neck. I was speechless.

"There."

Marco and Ing returned from the dance floor. Ing's jaw dropped. The fiddle player grinned.

"Why the surprise, young lady?" he asked.

"Everything is rushing," Ing murmured, sitting down. She stared at her hands. She traced her right index finger around the rest of her fingers.

"Goddamn you, Marco," Lorna said. Her hand knocked her glass. I caught it before the drink spilled.

"Like riding on a train with the windows open," Ing said, her eyes like small wedges of onyx.

"I have a gig across town," Raj said. "Until next time."

"Bye, Raj." Lorna blew him a kiss.

"Thank you," I whispered and held my hand out to him. He gave it a squeeze.

"You're welcome." He looked at Ing. "Maybe you should take her home. This bar can get strange. It could be . . ." He pressed his lips together. "Unsettling."

"Thanks," I said. He was right.

He smiled at Lorna and Marco French-kissing and walked out of the bar. I wanted to follow. He was the only sane person in the place. In the whole damn city, maybe.

"We'll meet you back at the house," I said. "Come on, Ing."

Marco groped Lorna's breast. She pushed away his hand, unpeeled her lips from his, and looked up at me. Both of them, Marco and Ing, wasted.

Fifteen

A dime-size moon bobbed behind the fog. I tucked Ing's hand under my arm to keep her from wandering off. If my memory served me, Marco and Lorna's place was pretty much a straight shot down Haight, turn right at the record store, then two blocks to Carl Street.

A lump slept under a dirty serape in the doorway of the closed health-food store. One person, possibly two. A chalkboard sign set atop a pyramid of loaves of bread in the shop window read, "Give us this day our daily bread."

"That is the most beautiful thing I've ever seen," Ing said breathlessly. Appreciation had never come this easily to her. "I wish the store would open."

She sighed and looked at me. Her eyes shone under the street lamp. She peered up at the light. A gauzy halo hovered there.

"So beautiful," she murmured.

A man approached us. He tugged nervously at the end of his

ratty beard and asked us if we had any pot. I steered Ing away from him.

"I'm hungry," Ing said. She was shivering.

"I saw a café up the street," I said.

"Is it very bright?" she asked.

"I don't know, Ing." I steered her down the block towards the café.

We were moving slowly but at least headed someplace warm where bums wouldn't bother us. A total of three winos lived in Tristes. Two of the bums lived in the old train station waiting room, the other behind Kim's Grocery. And as long as they had booze, they were no bother.

A scrawny kid loitered in front of the café door. He reached for the sleeve of his KISS T-shirt and wiped his nose. He looked eleven, maybe twelve. A smile unfurled over yellow teeth.

"You broads got any coke?"

"Jesus," I muttered. "Where are your parents?"

"They're dead," he said, tipping back his head and letting out a harsh, crazy laugh. His expression went deadpan. "Only kidding."

When I opened the café door, the kid pretended to lunge at us. Ing stared at him. Her eyes filled with tears.

"He's so old," she whispered. "So very old."

"Don't think about him, Ing," I said.

The inside of the café was cavernous and well lit. A handful of customers were scattered on benches at three long oak tables. The woman behind the counter looked up from a half-made tuna sandwich and wiped her hands on her apron. Ing had no clue what she wanted, so I ordered the chicken noodle soup, bread and butter, and two glasses of water.

We sat next to a couple playing checkers. I handed Ing a glass of water, which she ignored. She stared at the couple, the checkerboard. The LSD had pierced her ability to keep out the world. Now everything touched her. Her vulnerability scared me.

"Jimmy and me played once," she murmured. "He let me win." She stared at the floor, also checkered. "The tiles are rearranging too." She looked up at me. "Can you see them moving?"

"Yeah, it looks cool, doesn't it?" I set the bowl of soup in front of her. "Have some soup."

"I'm so glad you see it too." When she smiled at me, the sliver of iris around her pupils expanded.

Maybe eating would push the acid through her system faster. But food didn't interest her anymore. Outside, the kid with the yellow teeth jogged in place and hugged himself, rubbing his upper arms to stay warm. She gazed out the large window.

The soup and bread tasted good. I ate slowly. Glad to be inside, glad to be me.

⌒

The black cat wandered into Lorna and Marco's kitchen, meowing as though she'd lost a limb. Ing and I were sitting at the table. Ing stared at the wood grain. The cat looked down at the empty food bowl on the floor, then at me and let out a piercing cry. I didn't see any wounds, so I opened the fridge and fed the cat a piece of baloney. It devoured the meat in two pieces.

Ing nearly peed her pants watching the cat's jaws open and shut.

"I think it has ESP," Ing said. The cat licked her paws briefly and hopped into Ing's lap. "It happens, you know. I saw a show about it."

The cat's head followed the strokes of Ing's hand. At the base of the tail, the cat nipped Ing's thumb. She flung the cat onto the floor.

"It's evil." She stared at teeth marks on her hand. No broken skin. "Get it out of here, Shee."

I tried to shoo the cat through a cat door near the fridge. The cat glared at me and ran out of the room. Ing ran water over the bite. More dirty dishes filled the sink. Lorna had made spaghetti and salad. Food to suck up the booze, Ing had said only three hours ago. It felt more like months. I tore a paper towel from the roll on the counter and handed it to her.

"I'm a bad person," Ing said. The unused paper towel floated to the floor like a deflated parachute. She stared at the white square and shook her head. "I steal, I cheat on my boyfriend, and tomorrow I'm killing my baby."

"Don't, Ing," I said, looking around for something in the kitchen to distract her. Her purse sat on the table. "Let's see what's in here."

She watched me unzip her lime-green makeup bag. I removed

lipstick. Foundation. Blush. Mascara. A bottle of nail polish for touch-up. I lined the items up on the table and put on a plastic smile.

"Can I interest you in this shade?" I presented the nail polish to her like a salesperson at a beauty counter. "It's called 'The Devil Wears Red.' It's truly divine."

She burst out laughing, so I continued the game. After I finished "selling," she wrote Jimmy's name in lipstick on the table. Then she rubbed Jimmy's name out with the palm of her hand. Her mind shifted tracks again.

"I have to pee," she said, bending to retrieve the paper towel from the floor. She attempted to wipe the lipstick from her hand. "Will you come with me? Please? I'm scared."

I led her upstairs and waited outside the bathroom. I wanted sleep. Ing was in the bathroom for a good ten minutes when I finally knocked. She was on the toilet, pondering the wall paper. Hundreds of poodles on leashes held by no one, and a bright pink background.

"They're speaking French to me," she said and laughed. "I understand every word."

"Lucky you," I said. I helped her pull up her underwear and pantyhose.

She was still tripping when Lorna and Marco came home at 3 A.M. We listened to Lorna and Marco screw. Every half an hour or so, the streetcar on Carl Street screeched past the house. Ing tossed and turned. I closed my hand around the fiddle player's medallion and finally fell asleep.

Later that morning, I drove Ing to Planned Parenthood near downtown San Francisco. The receptionist was crankier than Ing. She told Ing to take a seat, but then the fiddle player's medallion caught her eye and she smiled at us. It had magical powers, this medallion.

We sat with our backs to the reception desk. There were three other women waiting. Two brunettes that looked like they could have been sisters and a blond girl not much older than Ing and me. The brunettes looked up from their magazines. If I had been them, I would be trying to decide which one of us had screwed up. But neither seemed interested in us or upset. They could have been waiting for a teeth cleaning.

Posters covered the clinic's mint-green walls. One poster pictured a man with a pregnant belly and the headline, "It takes two." A nurse dressed in a striped tunic, navy blue pants, and white Birkenstocks held a chart and looked at us.

"Rott-ree-gas," she called out.

I gave Ing's hand a squeeze and watched her follow the nurse behind a frosted glass door marked "Patients Only." The door swung shut on silent hinges.

I flipped through *McCall's* and found an article titled "Ten Tips for a Happy Marriage." As a joke, I tore out the article for my mother, then a recipe for Rice Krispies pie for Annie. The receptionist wrapped her fist on the desk.

"Those magazines are for everyone to read," she snapped. "Please be respectful."

I suddenly missed Annie. I went to call her from the pay phone in the lobby, but some jerk had unscrewed the receiver cap, yanked out the wires, and left a tangled mess of red, yellow, and blue wires. Probably a good thing. My mother would've answered. Or worse, George. I had forgotten to call them yesterday. He would want a full report. I hardly knew where we had been. The last twenty-four hours were a blur.

Last night I had dreamed Cindy and the fiddle player were dancing in a lettuce field. They moved along the rows in perfect sync, while migrant workers tossed heads of lettuce into Fratti Farms trucks. Then I had felt Buck's presence. I searched row by row, but the farther I went, the bigger the field became.

⌒

A different nurse appeared to take the blond girl back. More women who didn't want babies came into the waiting room. The brunettes struck up a conversation. It turned out they had a friend in common.

Lorna had told Ing about the machine. Like a mini-Hoover. Valium and a shot to numb the pain. The doctor inserting a tube into the uterus to suck out the baby. How was this possible? One minute pregnant, the next not?

An hour later, the nurse handed me some pills in a brown

bottle and a green sheet of instructions. Ing was resting, doing fine. She would be out momentarily.

"I can still feel the tugging," she said weakly. We took the elevator downstairs to the car. "It was horrible."

In the lobby, I stopped to fill a Dixie cup with water. When we got to the car, I gave her another pain pill and the water. She curled her body against the door of the VW and closed her eyes. I reached over to lock the door. Ing was already asleep.

Sixteen

In September the dry scent of tugged-at earth filled the valley. The bean and sugar beet harvests had ended. *Tristes Gazette* ran a front-page photo of Annie sitting next to a pockmarked thirty-pound sugar beet, a state record.

The same week, George presented Annie with a black pony. He had wanted Annie to name the pony something dignified, like Ebony. But Annie chose Beetle, a unique name for a horse.

The move had stressed King. Milky cataracts barely visible last spring now covered most of both eyes. My theory was he had simply decided to go blind so he wouldn't have to look at Rusty. Rusty, the alpha dog, ignored King for the most part.

In a last-ditch effort to cure the eczema, Dr. Wong had prescribed another round of Chinese herbs, which King vomited. Dr. Wong finally declared him a hopeless case. George and my mother had hinted at putting King out of his misery. I refused to listen. King still had me. He would go in his own time.

A few weeks before the wedding, I was washing dishes, with

my mother seasoning steaks at the same kitchen counter, when George came home from work for dinner. I watched him perform his nightly routine from the kitchen window. Porch steps two at a time. Unlace boots. Leave on socks. Set boots next to cap on the porch. Sit on top step to survey property. The ritual never varied.

He looked content this evening. The harvest was over, and the wedding was only weeks away. My eyes followed his. The natural fence of sycamores that George Sr. had planted as saplings nearly thirty years ago, now one hundred feet tall. The quarter-mile recently poured asphalt driveway. The tawny pasture that butted against the north side of the house and rolled up to the eucalyptus grove on the hill.

Since the fight with Will, George had been nicer to me. This change of heart was likely due to self-interest. I had no intention of telling my mother about the fight, but George didn't need to know this. I would hold onto my advantage for as long as I could.

He was being so nice that he had his eye out for a used car for me. He feared the VW would break down one night and leave me stranded. When I told him I cherished the VW, he called me sentimental, then quickly apologized. Though he appeared to be making an effort, I knew that given the chance he would have thrown Buck out of town a second time.

Annie slid down the banister to greet George. She was dressed in a pair of yellow culottes and matching blouse. She threw her arms around George's neck, and they exchanged twenty kisses, ten for George and ten for Annie. Another nightly ritual. One that no longer turned my stomach. I could see Annie needed him. Josh had been right.

George tried to kiss the top of my head and missed when I reached for the Comet and scrubbing sponge. Laughing awkwardly, he kissed my mother on the cheek. I concentrated on rinsing the sink. I felt off balance, confused.

"Coming, Shee?" my mother said.

She balanced on her arm the platter of steak and bowl of fresh peas she had shelled and steamed. George and Annie followed her into the dining room. I sensed George and my mother had had a conversation about me and him. Very soon he would officially be my stepfather.

George sat at the head of the table. My mother sat to his left, Annie to his right, then me next to Annie. We had sat in these chairs since the first day we had moved in, as if they had been assigned to us.

The dining room faced the back pasture. Above the eucalyptus, a red hawk soared. Beetle grazed just outside the barn. The evening breeze lifted her mane, then let it go.

"How was your day?" my mother asked, passing George the steak platter.

"Looks like César Chávez is going to get his wish," George said. He stabbed the large steak with the serving fork and lay the meat on his plate. "His people are working around the clock to push through this bill."

The UFW had been lobbying hard to ban *el cortito*, the short hoe. The farmers weren't too keen on using the long hoe to weed. It cut into productivity. Too tempting for a tired field worker to lean on. George would honor the ban if the senate passed the bill. But he wasn't happy about the change. Instituting the long hoe would cost Fratti farms in new equipment, new policies.

"What does Chávez wish?" Annie asked.

She had heard of César Chávez. Seen him marching through town with hundreds of union members, the red flag with the jagged design of a black eagle blowing proudly. She had heard them chant, "Sí se peude. Yes, it can be done."

"Mr. Chávez," George said. "Wants the farm workers to use a different tool." He gazed out the window at the pasture. "We farmers oppose this." He glanced at me and cut a bite-size piece of steak. "For many reasons."

The workers were demanding more than more humane tools. They wanted humane wages, the right to representation. My mother's eyes pleaded with me. *Let's keep the peace, Shee. Just a nice meal together. No confrontations.* George winked at Annie. She scrunched up her nose and both eyes, her version of winking. My mother looked at me and mouthed the words, "Thank you."

The phone rang. My mother got up to answer it. She stood in the doorway between the dining room and kitchen. My mother held the receiver a few inches from her ear and rolled her eyes at me. Grandma Bea. Once Grandma Bea got rolling, she didn't stop. Her nasally voice meandered the topic extremes, from reports on the contents of her fridge to the price of gas, which she didn't give a hill of beans about because she didn't drive.

Tonight she was calling about wedding attire, a subject they had already discussed.

"I remember Grandma sent me a dollhouse once," Annie said to me, and licked her spoon.

"No," I said. "She sent you dollhouse furniture. Mom put it away so you wouldn't choke on it."

"It's the thought that counts," George said.

The last time Grandma had visited was the year Annie was born. She had taken the Greyhound bus from Burbank to Tristes. The bus stopped fourteen times before reaching the depot here.

"I'm looking forward to meeting her," George said. "She seems wonderful."

Bea thought George walked on water. When he answered the phone, he listened to her with interest. He was the dutiful son-in-law Bea had never experienced in Daddy. Bea was also tickled my mother was marrying a rich man. She had always said there was nothing noble about being poor.

"I warn you," I said. "She's a pain."

"Your mother seems to feel the same way about her," George said, smiling. "I think your grandmother did a fantastic job, raising your mother on her own." He glanced at Annie.

"Annie knows about Eddie," I said.

"Who's Eddie?" Annie asked.

"Our grandpa," I said.

"Have I ever met him?" Annie chased a pea around her plate with her fork.

"None of us have met him," I said.

My mother's father had left Bea when my mother, an only child, was three. No note, no phone call from the road. Grandma Bea had once told Josh and me that Grandpa Eddie liked pumpkin pie and bowling. She evaded questions about his character. Grandma Bea simplified the complex to suit herself.

My mother had very few memories of Grandpa Eddie. She had shared an ice cream sundae with him on her birthday. She recollected the long marble counters at Swenson's, the thick sundae glass, her father's steel-blue eyes.

"That's okay," Annie chirped. "We have Pepito."

"Ice cream and sprinkles, anyone?" George asked.

He stood to collect the empty plates. A first, cleaning up after dinner and serving dessert. He and my mother had definitely talked.

"Mom, I've been trying to tell you it's not a black-tie wedding," my mother said, lifting the phone cord to let George pass. "Yes, the green dress will be fine. Don't waste your money on some silly gown." She twisted the cord around her index finger. "It doesn't matter that you've worn the green dress before. No one up here will know."

She nodded at the receiver and closed her eyes while Bea talked. In the kitchen, George whistled the old Smokey Robinson tune "Shop Around" while he prepared dessert. Spoons clattered, bowls rattled. My mother smiled.

"Someone will pick you up at the train station," my mother said. This, too, they had discussed. "Probably Josh."

Airplanes terrified Bea. Her apartment was six blocks from

the Burbank airport. She took Valium to drown out the noise. And the landlord hadn't raised the rent in twelve years. So Bea stayed. She claimed her "seddies" were an economic necessity.

George ducked under the phone cord and set down three bowls of rocky road ice cream. My mother's dress had already been altered, so she had to watch her weight.

"You're nice, Daddy," Annie said. "And I love ice cream."

George dabbed rocky road ice cream on the end of her nose. She wiggled her curly head at him and stuck out her tongue. George's eyes smiled behind his glasses. Annie had softened him, made him easier to be around. My mother told Bea she'd see her in a few weeks and hung up.

"She wants to come up early," she said.

"And?" George raised an eyebrow.

"I told her no," my mother said. "I have too much left to do without my mother sticking her nose in."

"Don't you like Grandma Bea?" Annie asked.

"I love her." My mother sighed. "I just don't particularly like her."

"Oh." Annie shrugged. "Well, sometimes she sends me presents."

⁓

A few days into my senior year, Jimmy approached me outside of Chemistry Lab. He wore his letter jacket in spite of the heat of Indian summer. His face gaunt. Like someone had sucked the life out of him. After Ing and me had returned from San Francisco, Jimmy had stayed away. The Chief's threat to throw him in juvie had scared the shit out of Jimmy and his parents.

I had seen very little of Ing in August. She had worked extra at Dick Brown's. She had called a few times. Ben Wilson had stopped coming into the store. As though he had died and the body hadn't been found. Ing had pulled away, and so had I. These days, a secret tryst with an older man felt like the only thing Ing and me had in common.

Mike Wong, the vet's son and my lab partner, brushed past Jimmy and me, heading into lab. I was grateful to see a wad of gum in his cheek. Halitosis could be distracting.

"Your turn to set up," Mike said. "Hey, Jimmy."

"Can you set up?" I said sweetly. "I've got to talk to Jimmy."

"All right," Mike grumbled. "You owe me, though."

At the other end of the lockers, Mr. Hasbin burst into the hall. He wore his trademark plaid short-sleeved shirt, polka-dotted tie, and Levi's. He hurried toward the lab, his wiry hair twisting in three directions. The second bell rang.

"O'Connor, Emmons," Hasbin bellowed. "Care to join us for some Chemiluminescence?"

"I got a dentist appointment, Has." Jimmy rubbed his jaw for dramatic effect. For a moment he actually smiled.

Ing had to know Jimmy was on edge. No one was that blind. I had heard she was screwing the captain of the wrestling team. I wondered if Jimmy had heard this too.

"A likely story," Hasbin said, turning to me. "And your excuse?"

"I wouldn't miss lab for the world," I said, blinking my lashes at him.

"Miss O'Connor," Hasbin said, trying not to smile, "your charm is never wasted on me. Just be inside in thirty seconds, or I'll be forced to mark you absent." He opened the lab door. "And, Jimmy, I expect you to make up this lab."

"Fine." Jimmy shrugged.

Down the hall, Jesus Rios slammed his locker. He lifted his chin at Jimmy. Like Jimmy, Jesus was a top wrestler. They were equally skillful on the mat and had helped take the wrestling team to the state championships last year.

"Man, Jimmy, you look like a goddamn skeleton," Jesus said, tucking *World History and Geography* under his arm. "I keep telling you, forget the broad. Broads ruin everything. Except you, Sheila. You're cool."

"Thanks," I said. I looked at Jimmy. "I have to go to class."

"Jesus," Jimmy called. "Tell Vandro if he talks any more shit about me and Ingrid, I'll kick his ass all the way to King City."

I had my answer. Jimmy did know about Vandro. This explained, at least partly, the look of torment on his face.

"I'm not your messenger boy," Jesus said. "But you got to eat, man."

Jimmy waved him off. Jesus shook his head and walked into World History. The class Daddy had taught. The same room in fact.

"Ingrid used to hate Vandro's guts," Jimmy said to me. "Now she's screwing him." He shook his head. "My mother wants to send me to a shrink, but my pop says shrinks are for pussies."

"I really should go," I said. I could see Hasbin through the netted glass, going over the day's experiment at the board. "Could we talk later?"

"Can I call you, really?" He grabbed my arm.

"Relax, Jimmy." I let go of the door knob. "It's okay."

"Sorry," he mumbled, staring at the floor. He looked up at me like a wounded animal. "Why'd she dump me, Shee? Why?"

"I don't know, Jimmy," I whispered. "But other people care about you. Me, your family. Think about your sister Rosie. When things get rough, I think about how sweet Annie is."

"See," he said, his eyes brimming. "I'm nothing but a pussy."

I'd seen Jimmy cry once. In the fifth grade a group of boys had been bullying a migrant kid. When Jimmy tried to defend the kid, one of the bullies pushed Jimmy into the Boys' Room and pounded on his face. Jimmy came out of the bathroom, snot and blood pouring out of his nose.

Ing's dishonesty and selfishness had pushed him to the edge. How could she not see how much he hurt? How could she keep up the lie about Ben and the abortion?

⁓

Mike Wong pretended to growl at me when I sat down. He used humor to cover up his incurable horniness. He peered through his smudged, black-rimmed glasses and jabbed his finger in my arm. I opened my notebook.

The rumor was he had never been kissed. Mike was the

antithesis of his movie-star-handsome father. Dr. Wong's marriage to Mike's mother, a wisp of a woman with the thinnest hair I had ever seen on a human, had been arranged in China. Mrs. Wong kept Dr. Wong's appointments, administered vaccinations, and took temperatures. The family lived above the clinic, out past the old dairy. Dr. Wong wanted Mike to become a vet so he could take over the practice when Dr. Wong retired.

"Are you and Jimmy Emmons dating?" Mike whispered.

"Of course not," I said. "I'm not stupid."

"What's that supposed to mean?" He stared at me.

"Nothing," I muttered, taking out my notebook.

I watched Mike mix potassium ferricyanide and hydrogen peroxide. I read the instructions on the board: 25 ml of each solution. Hasbin turned off the lights for the magic moment. Mike dumped the solutions into a clean beaker. He handed me the beaker.

"Swirl," he ordered.

The clear solution transmuted into a white-blue glow. There were oohs and ahs throughout the lab. A cold light, Hasbin explained. It seemed impossible that light that should give warmth didn't. I dipped my finger in the beaker. Cold.

"Big deal," Mike snorted. "We did this experiment in freshman Chem."

He pushed his pencil into the spiral binding of his notebook and looked nervously around the lab. Blue lights filled the room, one at every lab table. Hasbin wandered around, checking people's lab notes for accuracy.

"Are you going to the Crazy Hearts Dance?" Mike whispered. His glasses reflected the blue light.

"No. You?" I said. God, someone dance with him if he goes.

I had not even considered going. It seemed pointless. Buck had spoiled my already limited interest in school dances.

"My dad's supposed to lend me the car." Mike's breathing quickened. Beads of sweat collected on his upper lip. "How about you and me going to the dance?"

"Sorry, Mike," I said. "My parents are going out. I have to babysit my sister."

"I figured you'd say that." Mike sighed.

Hasbin opened the drapes and announced a quiz on Friday, the day of Crazy Hearts. Groans rippled around the room. Mike wrote up some more notes while I rinsed and dried the beakers. The Balers football team straggled out to the practice field. Coach Williams threw on his yellow slicker and scrambled after them, yelling, his normal speaking tone. A braid of cloud gathered over the Gabilans.

I considered ditching P.E. With possible rain, we'd be condemned to the gym for crab soccer. The next day I always felt like someone had been beating my thighs with a shovel. Worse, Ing and Ruthie were in the same class.

Mike handed me his notebook, and I started copying his lab notes. I glanced at the Chinese characters on the opposite page. He sat quietly.

"Is this some kind of secret message?" I asked.

He took my pencil from me and wrote in large, block letters, "I want to suck between your legs."

"You're disgusting," I said.

The bell rang. Mike shoved his notebook in his book bag and tripped over his stool. His face turned scarlet. He hurried out of the lab. The rest of the students filed out. Hasbin flagged me down as I was leaving.

"Sheila, how was your summer?" His wiry head dipped under the desk to retrieve his reading glasses. He was constantly losing them. "I understand you moved. How are you adjusting?"

"It's not so bad," I said.

The question under his question was: Did I like George? George had recently joined the school board. Already he had a reputation for pushing his agenda, regardless of what the teachers wanted.

"You're strong," Hasbin mused, picking up an eraser. "Like your mother."

"I'm late for P.E.," I said, sensing he wanted to say more.

I looked at the equation and waited for him to erase it all. *Luminol*, *aminophthalate* and cryptic abbreviations such as H_2O_2. I liked the strange language of chemistry. The mysterious results of combined elements.

"Let me know if you need anything," he said. He set the eraser in the chalkboard tray. "It's a crazy world. And funny enough, people get lost in small towns." He dusted the chalk from his tie. "Now don't be late. God knows your education wouldn't be complete without P.E."

Hasbin had worried about Daddy too. They had been close colleagues. Over the years they taught at T.H., Hasbin had tried to get my father to ease up on his drinking.

"Your wife's a catch, Roy," he'd say. "Don't ruin it."

Hasbin had a soft spot for my mother.

Seventeen

The sky let loose a hard, tepid rain. I zipped up my lime-green windbreaker and hurried toward the locker room to change into my P.E. uniform. On the south side of the gym, Balers collided out on the practice field. Frankie Jones, the quarterback, dropped back to throw a sideline pass. The ball grazed the receiver's fingertips and bounced off Superintendent Walker's red Caddie. It wobbled to a stop under a bank of drinking fountains.

"Frankie," Coach Williams shouted into the downpour. "You'd better thank God in heaven you didn't bust a window."

The Caddie was Superintendent Walker's pride and joy. A few years ago, a senior had spilled a Coke on the passenger door. He claimed he'd been shoved and that's how the Coke had spilled on Walker's Caddie. Walker, hard-ass, had made the senior wax his car every week for a month. Frankie's teammates ribbed him about the near miss.

"You jack-offs aren't going home until you get this goddamn play." Coach, rugged, with watery blue eyes, pushed aside the blond mop of hair that was perpetually in his eyes and gave me a wave. "Sheila, how are you, hon? We sure miss your mom over at the Pit." He started hacking.

"I'm fine," I yelled. "Guess what? My mom quit smoking."

"Wish I could quit," Williams yelled, shaking his head. He turned back to the players and clapped his hands. "Let's do it again, boys."

Rain rushed in the gutters around the gym. A small waterfall slapped the asphalt, splattering my tennis shoe. I spotted Ingrid and Ruthie heading towards the girls' locker room. Ruthie nudged Ing and whispered something in her ear. Ing reached for the locker-room door. When our eyes met, she turned away.

I entered the locker room behind them. Ing wore the gold cross Betty had given her for Holy Communion around her fleshy neck. She had never been heavy before. She'd changed her hair too, feathered it back, a new style for her. Ruthie twisted a piece of mousy brown hair around her finger, as if trying to get it to look like Ing's. Vapid little Ruthie, barely five feet tall, worshipped anyone willing to give her the time of day. I suspected she was an easy friend for Ing.

Steam from the previous class showering coated the locker-room walls. I smelled mildew and industrial soap. Several showers dripped, violating the Conserve Water signs Ms. Bob, the P.E. teacher, had slapped on our lockers yesterday.

I spun through my locker combination, said hello to Maxine Banini, and took out my uniform. White cuffed shorts, white blouse, white socks. I gave the socks a sniff. They would do.

"I got an extra clean pair," Maxine Banini said, stepping into her shorts.

Maxine sprayed deodorant under her arms, her biceps like small nectarines from working her father's farm. She was one of the few authentic aggies at T.H. The rest of the supposed cowgirls were wannabes. Most of them had never milked a cow, let alone slaughtered one.

"These are fine." I waved my pair of socks at her. "But thanks."

On the other side of the changing bench, Yvette Jimenez, who played a mean game of crab soccer, stood at her locker braiding her coarse black hair. I had never seen Yvette use a mirror. She probably could've braided her hair with one hand.

"Hey, Daddy Long Legs," she said, wrapping a rubber band around the end of the braid. Her nails, polished pear green, flickered like tongues. "You ready to kick some ass?"

"You bet, Yvette."

I smiled at her out of respect as much as fear. If Yvette sniffed a snub, she'd jump you. Or she'd get someone else to jump you. When you least expected it. Yvette was equally passionate about crab soccer. Everyone wanted her on their team.

"I don't care what Ms. Bob says, you're on my team today," Yvette said. She looked over at Maxine. "You too, Max. We'll cream them."

Maxine laughed and slammed her locker. Aggies and *cholas* were unspoken sworn enemies. I think Yvette respected Maxine for being the real thing.

The three of us went into the gym together. Ruthie and Ing

followed, chattering about the Crazy Hearts Dance. I heard Ing say she didn't think she was going. Ruthie didn't have a date. She said she might just "stop by" the dance.

"You want to borrow my red dress?" Ing asked her. "The off-the-shoulder one?"

"I could always try it on," Ruthie said. "It might look cute."

I knew the dress. The neckline would cave in over Ruthie's flat chest. I was tempted to turn around. To tell them no one cared what either of them did. Ing's cheating on Jimmy. His suffering because of what he didn't know but suspected. The way Ing had pushed me away and now palled around with Ruthie. Hard to believe I had been best friends with Ing.

Rain pummeled the roof of the gym, drowning out the loud motor spinning in the giant heater fan on the wall next to the game scoreboard. Ms. Bob stood in the center of the gym next to a large scuffed-up ball of brick-colored vinyl. She applied cherry Chapstick. The signal roll call was about to begin. She capped the Chapstick and dropped the tube into the pocket of her navy blue sweatshirt. Twenty-nine girls scurried over to fill the two lower benches of the bleachers.

"Abrams." Ms. Bob belted out roll in her drill sergeant manner.

Her real name was Sylvia Roberts. Her deep voice and crew cut had inspired the nickname years ago. For years students had speculated about Ms. Bob's sex life. But most of us didn't want to think about her doing it with a man or a woman. If anything, she seemed asexual.

"Banini. Camancho. Fernandez. Hamilton."

Ms. Bob went through the alphabet, looking up from her clipboard only when she didn't hear "present." Several girls were absent. They had probably ditched. Crab soccer had a limited following.

While Ms. Bob finished roll, the wrestling team in their street clothes and carrying workout bags entered the gym through the front entrance. Vandro combed his poker-straight, pale blond hair as he strutted past the girls. He flashed Ing a smile. But Ing's eyes were on Jimmy. Jimmy put his hands in the pockets of his letter jacket. He kept his head down. Vandro shrugged and pocketed his comb.

"Nice ass, Vandro," Yvette yelled, laughing when Vandro wiggled his hips. "Muy facho."

"Let's be ladies," Ms. Bob said. She looked up from her clipboard. "Shall we, Yvette?"

"Sí, Señora Bob," Yvette said.

The wrestlers filed into the room. They worked out in the small gym off the big gym. I wondered how Jimmy would manage on the mat today, knowing Ing was next door.

The far left door of the gym opened and threw a triangle of light on the gym floor. Tall Larry entered, carrying a ladder under one arm, a cardboard box under the other. Crazy Heart Decorations. The dance was three days from today.

"Miss Roberts." Ruthie raised her hand. "I have cramps."

"A likely story." Ms. Bob sighed. "Go ahead, Ruthie."

Ruthie picked up her book bag. Her short legs climbed to the middle of the bleachers. She took out her Spanish II textbook and a pack of sunflower seeds.

"I hope you don't plan on eating those, Ruthie," Ms. Bob said. "Larry has enough to do without having to sweep up your sunflower shells."

"Oh, no, Miss Roberts." Ruthie smiled demurely.

She put the pack of seeds back in her book bag. When Ms. Bob looked away to pick teams, Ruthie took the seeds out again. She placed the pack right on the open pages of the textbook.

The players sat on the floor. We placed our hands behind us, palms down, feet in front, crab style. Ms. Bob rolled the ball between the two teams. Ing faced me in the front line. Neither of us said a word.

Ms. Bob blew the whistle. The crab soccer ball hit the floor with a *thwop*. Ing gave it a swift kick. Max, the goalie, lobbed the ball to Yvette. Yvette cupped the ball between her feet and pressed up on her hands to kick. The ball flew out of bounds. Ruthie ducked. Ms. Bob blew the whistle.

The other team had the ball now. Joyce Hamilton, not known for her athleticism, delivered a hard kick. The ball rolled halfway down the gym. Her teammates cheered. I lifted my ass and crab-walked around the other side of the ball. I smacked the top of my foot at the ball, sending the ball into the bleachers straight at Ruthie. Ruthie fell backwards. Her book bag tumbled under the bleachers. Ms. Bob bounded up the bleachers. Ruthie sat up. She rubbed the side of her head. A bruise maybe, but no blood. The ball was light and couldn't do much damage.

"Ruthie," Ms. Bob asked. "Can one of the girls get you some ice?"

Ruthie shook her head and burst into tears. A ploy for attention. It worked. Ing scrambled to her feet. Her ponytail swung frantically.

"You did that on purpose," she said. Her breath was warm on my chin. "You meant for the ball to hurt Ruthie."

"Don't be stupid," I said, glaring back at Ing. "You know my aim isn't that good."

The rain had slowed to a light patter. I could hear the players grunting on the wet field outside. Ing's breathing quickened. I stepped back. Ing's slap grazed my cheek.

I hit her in the jaw, thumb inside my fist like Josh had taught me when I was eight. Ing's head flew back. She stumbled. Reaching up, she grabbed me around the neck. She pulled my hair, hard.

I heard Ms. Bob's whistle blowing. Girls surrounded us, their faces big and round and excited. The chant echoed. "Get her, get her." We were fighting on the floor now. Ing's nails gouged my cheek. I climbed onto her and pinned her arms. Her head tossed from side to side. Spit dribbled from her mouth.

"Larry." Ms. Bob's voice was like a lion's roar.

"Hit her, Daddy Long Legs. Hit her hard." It was Yvette rooting for me, the white girl.

I heard the hollow slap of rubber-soled shoes. Tall Larry bounded across the gym. In fifteen years as a high school janitor, he had broken up his share of fights. The urgency of his footsteps vibrated under Ing and me.

Larry's big black hands closed around my upper arms. He pulled me to my feet, held me still. His big black fingers curled around the sleeves of my blouse. Ing lay on the gym floor, holding her nose, her black eyes as wide as train wheels. Ms. Bob helped her up. Blood covered her nose and mouth. Ing hobbled toward the locker room.

"I'll see you two in Mr. Walker's office in fifteen minutes," Ms. Bob said sharply. She turned to Tall Larry. "I'm not sure what got into these two."

"Me neither," Tall Larry said. His eyes glistened like a fine, polished walnut. "It's a crying shame."

"It's over now." Ms. Bob let out a long sigh and turned to the spectators. "You can all go shower."

The girls straggled towards the locker room. I looked at the clump of my hair on the floor. Like a fallen bird's nest. Like unwoven sorrow.

"This ain't like you, Sheila." Tall Larry looked at me and shook his head.

It was just me and Tall Larry now. The only person I knew a foot taller than me. I touched my cheek gingerly. It stung.

"That's quite a scratch you got there," he said.

He walked over to the drinking fountain and stooped to drink. He drank long and deep. I watched him dry his mouth with the handkerchief he kept in the pocket of his brown work shirt.

"Miss Sheila," he said. "Are you in trouble?" He looked around the gym and lowered his voice. "Or maybe I should ask, were you in trouble?"

"What do you mean?" My mouth went dry. It was the tone of his voice when he had said the word "trouble."

"There was that young man this summer," he said. "A southerner. Worked for Mr. Fratti."

"What about him?" I asked.

Tall Larry was also a southerner. From Georgia, like Buck. I watched him open the box of decorations. He pulled out a huge construction paper heart attached to a long red ribbon.

"I knew your daddy pretty good." He set up the ladder. "So I've always felt the need to look out for you."

"Thanks, Larry," I said, letting out a sigh of relief. "But I'm fine." I smiled. "Mostly."

"Thank God." Tall Larry stuck in the end of the ribbon and started up the ladder. "What were you two fighting about?"

"Actually, Ing's the one who's been in trouble," I said. I watched him step a rung up the ladder. "She treated Jimmy real bad. Sometimes I can't stand her for that."

"Isn't that between them?" His long legs stopped midway up the ladder and he turned around. The red heart fluttered. "It's not worth you getting suspended over."

"I guess," I muttered.

It would have taken hours for me to explain about Jimmy. About the whole crazy summer. I didn't have one ounce of explaining in me. I didn't want to remember, didn't want to think.

Eighteen

Jimmy called late Friday afternoon to ask me to the Crazy Hearts Dance tonight. I nearly dropped the phone. My mother lay in bed upstairs with a sore back and a heating pad. Annie was in the den, watching TV. George had his monthly Chamber of Commerce dinner. King and me had been lazing around my bedroom, reading, listening to music.

"I can't," I said, still feeling the shock of Jimmy asking.

And yet I felt compelled to say yes. Me and Jimmy at the Crazy Hearts Dance. The idea had a sweet ring. Sweet and a little dangerous.

"And why not?" It sounded like the old Jimmy. Upbeat, ready to have fun. The Jimmy I knew a long time ago. Before he had dated Ing. "We'll party a little, dance a little."

In Chem Lab yesterday, Jimmy had been chatty. Too chatty. Hasbin had threatened detention if Jimmy didn't finish the lab. Jimmy was in some kind of strange mood. But a good mood. My mind riffled every item of clothing I owned. Nothing.

"Just as friends, Shee." Jimmy sighed. "Listen, I'm feeling good. Like maybe things aren't so bad after all. I don't want to just sit around the house. All I've done for the past two months is sit around."

"So what happened?" I asked. "How come you sound happy?"

"I can't explain it," Jimmy said. "Maybe I'm just tired of being miserable."

I wrapped the phone cord around my index finger. I wanted to go. To be with Jimmy. And if Ing showed up with Vandro, we would show her Jimmy could live without her.

Sally had given me that black knit dress last Christmas. The dress was still in the box, wrapped in tissue. Sally had made me promise to wear it for someone I liked. Jimmy qualified.

"Did you hear about the fight?" I asked Jimmy.

"Yeah, today." He was quiet. I heard Rosie and the boys playing in the background. "I'm surprised Walker didn't suspend you guys."

"Me, too," I said.

Walker had decided against suspension. He had assured Ing and me he would call our parents if it ever happened again. The Chief probably would have pulled Ing out of T. H. and sent her to Sacred Heart in Salinas. Walker hated losing students to the nuns. I suspected he had also wanted to spare George the public humiliation of me fighting in school.

"Listen, tell me about the fight later," Jimmy said. "When should I pick you up?"

"Give me half an hour." My stomach fluttered.

I would wear my hair up, leaving a few tendrils down around my ears. Maybe I'd put on a little perfume. I hadn't had a date since Buck. If I could call screwing in a church and a migrant camp dates. And I knew Jimmy. He wouldn't break my heart. Tonight we would dance, share a kiss if it felt right. Nothing serious.

"You're kidding," Jimmy said, laughing. "Ing always took two hours to get ready. Hey, Mom." Jimmy let out a whoop of delight and covered the phone, muffling his voice. "See you soon," he said when he came back on. He hung up before I had a chance to say goodbye.

King slapped his tail on the linoleum. He struggled to stand, then followed me slowly upstairs. His toenails clicked down the hall to my room. I got out the black dress, clean underwear, and a bra.

King wiggled under the dust ruffle and reemerged with George's slipper in his mouth. He sniffed the slipper and started gnawing. George had been looking for that slipper for several days. King had collected and stashed a number of such toys. Stray socks, work gloves, a troll doll Annie had given a haircut, the broken handle of a toilet scrub brush. I had not discouraged this new practice. Better that King chew on things than on himself.

I dabbed musk behind my ears. I had gone to Crazy Hearts in my sophomore year. I'd spent the night holding Ing's hair while she hugged the toilet. She'd overindulged on tequila. This year would be different. Let Ing see Jimmy and me together. Let her worry I might tell Jimmy about the abortion. So what if he knew? Ing had done all her damage.

I went into the master bedroom to tell my mother I would be going out. She looked up from the book in her lap. She had dug in the garden all afternoon, and her back had suffered. Lamplight muted her drawn complexion.

"Wow." She smiled. "That dress is gorgeous on you. Where are you going?"

"To the dance tonight with Jimmy," I said. I waited for her reaction.

"I didn't even know there was a dance." She turned to adjust the heating pad behind her. A stack of unopened wedding response cards on the bed fluttered to the rug. "Is Ingrid going?"

"They broke up, Mom," I said.

"Oh," she said. "I thought maybe they'd gotten back together."

"And that I was going to be the third wheel again?" I sat on the bed next to her and kicked off my black heels.

"That's not what I meant," my mother said.

King sniffed around to make sure the coast was clear. He came over to the side of the bed, tail wagging. The Holy Bible, *Time* magazine, and a book about how to have a wedding lay on George's nightstand. On my mother's side of the bed, the lamp, a jar of Ponds face cream, wedding to-do list, a chewed pen. I scratched behind King's ears. He groaned with pleasure.

"Poor thing whimpers all day until you come home," my mother said. She turned my face to see the scratched cheek. "Are you going to tell me what really happened?"

"I told you. Yvette scratched me during P.E."

"Ing and you haven't been speaking." She frowned. "Now, this?"

"Is George reading the Bible?" When in doubt, change the subject.

"Sheila Lorraine." She spoke sharply. "You and Ing have been friends for twelve years."

What did I have to lose by telling her the truth? She had already proven she could keep a secret. George was the problem.

"You won't tell George?"

"It stays between us," she said, holding up two fingers. "Scout's honor."

"Ing and me got into a fight," I said.

"A physical fight?" My mother sat up too quickly. Her face contorted. She reached behind her to rub her low back. "Why didn't the school call me?"

"Walker's protecting George."

"Everyone protects George." She let out a heavy sigh. "What was the fight about? God, how awful. Is Ing jealous? Of you and Jimmy?"

"It's a long story." The doorbell rang. "There's Jimmy."

I looked at my mother. Her expression vacillated between concern and confusion. Should she let me go out with Jimmy and risk another violent encounter with Ing? Should she chastise me for fighting at school? My mother had always been torn between disciplining us and letting us make our own choices.

"Honey, please," she said. "Be careful."

"I will, Mom." I leaned across the bed to kiss her. "Jimmy's not Ing's property."

"Is Bud Hasbin chaperoning tonight?" she asked. Her worried face brightened. "It would make me feel better."

"Hasbin chaperones every dance." I blew her a kiss from the doorway. "I'll say hello for you."

A crescent moon cradled the sky. The chill of fall was sharp. The starlight too, as if the stars braced for winter. The school parking lot was full, so Jimmy parked on the field near the gym. He nosed the Chevette up to the back of Hasbin's sedan and walked around the car to open my door.

Thursday's storm had soaked the field, which bordered the houses on the southern block of L Street. In a backyard lit by porch light, a tricycle lay upside down. A dog yipped. The trike's front wheel turned.

The field swallowed the tips of my heels. Jimmy scooped me up before I could stop him. I hugged his neck. His shirt collar was starched and cool. Ing had gotten him the sports jacket at Dick Brown's. A size too small then. But with the weight he'd lost, ten pounds minimum, the jacket fit perfectly. It felt good, Jimmy carrying me.

"I don't see Vandro's car," I said. "Maybe they really aren't coming."

"I don't much care," he said, setting me down on the pavement near the gym. "Let's just have fun."

I straightened the seams of my dress. The tennis courts across the parking lot were lit but empty. Some juniors passed a jug back and forth on a bench on the side of the gym. Probably vodka. One of the girls called out to Jimmy. He patted the flask in his jacket pocket and told her we had what we needed.

"I'm sorry about the other day, outside of Hasbin's class," Jimmy said, putting his arm around me. "I was feeling desperate.

"That's okay," I said. The gym doors opened, and a girl dressed in hot pants and platform sandals ran past us, crying. "I'm just glad you feel better."

"Yeah." Jimmy stared at the crying girl. "I'm glad too." He turned to me and smiled. But there was regret in his eyes. "When I picture Ing all beat up and blubbering like a baby, I'm glad. She deserves to hurt too."

Some freshmen girls hurried past us on their way inside. Their platform sandals clopped on the pavement. A short brunette I'd seen in the halls dropped her purse. A can of Coors rolled off the curb and into the gutter. She bent over to retrieve the beer.

"You look real nice tonight, Sheila," Jimmy said. He held the door for me. "After you."

On the stage, the band was belting out "Some Kind of Wonderful." People slow-danced under the sea of hearts Tall Larry had hung. The gym reeked of sweat and chewing tobacco and the Thai Stick smoke that had been absorbed by the *cholos'* dress Pendletons.

Jimmy and I sat near Jesus and his friends. Yvette was there with a guy named Ramon. They looked bored. Yvette saw me and gave me a thumbs up. The aggies, camped on the other side of the gym, spit rancid-smelling brown juice into Styrofoam cups.

"The cholos think I'm cool now," I said to Jimmy.

"I guess you're one of them now." He laughed.

Ruthie stood near the stage, talking to Mike Wong. She kept backing away from him. He lunged for her, and she shoved him and stomped off. Mike started after her, obviously drunk.

"I've never seen Mike at a dance," Jimmy said. "Or drunk."

"Me either," I said, feeling sorry for Mike.

The band launched into "American Band." Jimmy took my hand and we started down the bleachers. Maxine and her date, an aggie I didn't know, were doing the bump on the dance floor. Maxine said something to her date. He looked up and smiled at me. His braces gleamed in the stage light. I suddenly regretted coming to the dance. I felt exposed. Jimmy read my mind.

"No one cares," he said in my ear. "Hey, there's Hasbin."

Hasbin was ladling punch over at the refreshment table. He waved in our direction, pointed at his tie, and laughed. Years before, when my father and Hasbin had chaperoned dances, they had competed on ties. Hasbin, who regularly combed the racks at the Goodwill, usually had the loudest tie.

After the dance, they'd stop at the Hero for a nightcap, Daddy's four to Hasbin's one. Then they'd offer up their ties for the other customers to cast their votes for the worst of the two. The loser had to hang both men's ties on a wall in the poolroom.

It started a town trend. Pretty soon other men were putting up their ties in protest of tasteless convention.

The song finally ended. The lead singer announced it was time to slow down the music again. Jimmy's hand was firm on my forearm. But it was Joe Cocker. Jimmy had made love to Ing listening to Joe Cocker. As her best friend, I knew this.

"Shee, it's just a song." He pulled me close.

"But isn't this the song?" I whispered.

"No, Shee," he murmured. "You've got the wrong song."

He was lying. And yet his cheek was so warm against mine. No more Ing and Jimmy. No more Buck. Only Jimmy and me. One heart hung lower than the others dangling over my head. I reached up and grabbed it. I tore the heart from the ribbon, then tucked it into Jimmy's jacket pocket.

When we finished dancing, the band took a break and someone put "Let's Get It On" on the record player. The *cholos* descended the bleachers to slow-dance. Jimmy looked at his watch.

"Let's take a ride," he said.

Jimmy put his arm around me and guided me outside. There was a loud groan behind us. We turned around. Mike Wong stumbled around the corner of the gym. He wore new boots. Vomit-specked ones. He squinted at us, trying to focus.

"Mike, it's me, Sheila," I said. I held up three fingers. "How many fingers?"

"Peace and love, Sheila," Mike said. He started to wander off the curb.

"Who's your ride, man?" Jimmy grabbed him.

"Good catch," Mike said, letting out a snort of laughter. He turned to me. "You're sexy."

"Let's take you home," Jimmy said.

"I think he's driving his dad's car," I said.

"My cousin drove me." Mike hung his head. "He's screwing his girlfriend." He looked up at Jimmy. "I bet you get laid all the time."

"Not these days," Jimmy said. "Come on, we'll drive you home."

"My father wants me to be a vet. Dogs scare the shit out of me, and I hate cats. But he has his mind made up. It's the Chinese-son thing."

Jimmy took Mike by the arm. We helped him to the car, and Jimmy got Mike situated in the back seat. Mike took off his shoes and passed out. The ripe odor of sweaty socks filled the car.

"He lives out by the dairy," I said.

Jimmy clicked "Born to Run" into the eight-track. We sipped from the flask, although I didn't feel much like drinking. Out by the dairy, the feedlot was in full operation. Silos funneled grain into truck beds, filling the night with a cold dustiness.

We passed the dairy, shuttered decades ago. With each season, the dairy had slumped lower, becoming warped and brittle. Daddy had predicted that someday the wind would sweep up the dairy, leaving a quarter of an acre of dirt more fertile than any other between Salinas and King City.

For the next few miles, I saw empty darkness. Jimmy was holding steady at forty-five mph. I stared at the glow of the dash and Jimmy's profile, his nose, twice broken from wrestling. I felt as empty inside as the world outside. I slid over next to Jimmy and sighed. I'd been holding my breath and hadn't noticed.

Jimmy sang along with Springsteen. A jackrabbit bounded into the road. Jimmy braked in time. But Mike hit the front seat. He fell against the back seat, mumbling, and passed out again. The jackrabbit stared into the headlights, its ears twitching. Jimmy tapped the horn. The jackrabbit darted under a barbed wire fence and into the brush.

For some reason I thought of King and then Jimmy again. Jimmy's family didn't own pets. Mrs. Emmons had drawn the line of responsibility at children. She said four kids were enough wear and tear on her nerves and furniture.

"How much farther to the turn?" Jimmy asked.

"About half a mile," I said.

The Wongs' home and the vet clinic occupied a gray two-story house at the end of a dirt road. An upstairs light went on when we pulled up. The light went off, and a few seconds later another light flooded the porch. The doghouse on the porch stood empty. Next to it was a pile of blankets just sitting there.

"Hey, Mike," I said. "Wake up. Home sweet home."

"I feel like shit," Mike grumbled. He sat up and peered out the window. "I told you the son of a bitch would be up."

"Tell him some kid spiked the punch," I said. "And drink lots of water and take an aspirin before you go to sleep."

Mike felt around for his shoes. The springs creaked as he slid across the backseat to open the door. I thought about what he'd written in his notebook. A desperate case, Mike Wong.

"Hey, Mike," I said.

"Yeah?" He leaned forward, between Jimmy and me. I smelled regurgitated booze.

"You should tell him," I said.

"Tell who, what?"

"Tell your dad you don't want to be a vet. He probably already knows."

"Maybe I will," he said.

Dr. Wong opened the door. He eyed Jimmy's car, yelled something in Chinese at Mike, and they went inside.

"Poor Mike," Jimmy said, shifting the car into drive.

"He's got more balls then you think," I said.

"What do you mean?" Jimmy laughed.

"Never mind," I said.

We headed back to town, passing T. H. The dance was still in full swing. Across the street, the Meadowland apartment complex was dark. At the Main Street light, the mannequins in Mary's Western Wear stared out at us. The girl mannequin had on Wrangler's and a tuxedo-style blouse. The male one wore a shirt and cowboy hat, no pants. Jimmy finished the last of the whiskey in the flask he'd brought.

"Looks like Mary forgot to put her friend's jeans on," he said, laughing.

"You're coming back around, Jimmy."

"Being with you helps." His hand rested on my thigh. He let out a sigh. "Thanks for tonight, Shee."

"Sure, Jimmy."

Down at the Hero, the cars were two-deep outside. The Chief would be making his rounds soon to ticket. A man stumbled out of the Hero and dropped his keys. Daddy had done his fair share of the same.

"You want to see if Tall Larry will buy up for us?" Jimmy asked.

"I don't feel like drinking," I said. "Have you been out to the river lately?"

~

When we got to the river, Jimmy parked. The river gurgled below us. Daddy had always said it quenched the soul to hear the river flowing after a hard rain. In daylight, the trees that clung to the banks were thin and naked. But tonight I imagined their branches as a protective thicket.

"I'm thinking I should get out of Dodge," Jimmy said.

"Leave Tristes?" The rush of the river grew louder. "What about school?"

"I'll start new," he said. "My parents would be better off." He turned down the music and put his arm around me. "Maybe I'll join your brother." He laughed. "I never told you this, but that Buck guy, well, I was jealous of him."

"Don't talk about him," I said. "Not now."

"Never mind him." Jimmy spoke quickly. "Come with me. We'll move to, I don't know, Arizona or somewhere. It's crazy. But so what?" He turned to me. "Sheila, I want you to kiss me. Will you do that?"

I nodded. His leaving was just loose talk. He kissed me hard, and I pressed my body against his. I'd known Buck wouldn't stick around for long. But Jimmy, he'd be there.

Nineteen

The day of the wedding finally arrived. Not much had happened since Crazy Hearts. Jimmy and me saw each other a couple of times a week. Ing had transferred to Saint Anne's. The Balers went on a losing streak, and Coach Williams traded in his cigarettes for chewing tobacco.

Josh strolled across the wide lawn below me. He looked handsome, confident. Trousers just so. Shoes polished, reflecting the high clouds over Monterey Bay. The epaulets of his dress blues glinted in the muted sunlight. Annie skipped after him. Rose petals fluttered from the basket on her arm, scattering on the freshly mowed lawn.

Josh came up the terrace steps of the Highlands Inn bridal suite where me and three other bridesmaids waited for the wedding ceremony to begin. Behind Annie, the guests sat in white folding chairs, their backs to us. Suzanna Baroni, rodeo queen and bridesmaid, followed Josh's movements with her hungry eyes.

"Hi, gorgeous," he said to me.

"Have you met Suzanna?" I asked. "Our new cousin."

"Third cousin, step," Suzanna said. "I graduated Salinas High last year."

"Nice to meet you, Suzanna." Josh flashed her a smile and turned to me.

Nan, another of the extended Fratti clan and bridesmaid, rolled her eyes at Suzanna and adjusted her girdle. Nan had failed to drop the fifteen pounds she'd vowed to lose when Sally ordered the dresses back in July. But tight dresses were the least of Nan's problems. Her husband had recently left her to move in with a Mexican woman whom Nan had referred to that morning as "that spic bitch."

"Where's Mom?" Josh asked. Suzanna continued staring. "George sent me over to see if she changed her mind."

George was pacing the lawn over near the gazebo. Joe, his best man, was trying to distract him. George and Joe had been roommates at Cal Poly. Joe sold insurance in San Luis Obispo. Will hung back under the cypress on the cliff and smoked, while Alan, another groomsman, tried to engage Will in conversation. Will hadn't had a drink in several days, and he looked it.

"Her makeup's not done," I said. "Grandma Bea's inside helping. Sally's officiating. The makeup artist is ready to kill Bea."

Sally had managed to keep Bea out of my mother's hair all morning. When diplomacy failed, Sally had handed Bea a glass of champagne. My mother had been drinking champagne on an empty stomach. She burst out laughing when Sally told Bea to quit meddling. Offended, Bea had locked herself in the bathroom. This had been my chance to grab a Valium from Bea's purse. Just in case.

"Use plenty of blush," I heard Bea say from behind the French doors of the bridal suite. "My daughter loses color in social situations."

"Mother, please," my mother pleaded.

Today was a dream come true for Grandma Bea. She had finally gotten the wedding and the perfect son-in-law, and she hadn't shelled out a single dime for either.

I gazed out at the guests. Pepito dozed on the groom's side in front of the gazebo. A foghorn startled him, but he drifted off again. The Emmons family sat across the aisle from Pepito. Mrs. Emmons licked her fingertips and pressed a stubborn sprout of hair against Bobby's head. Mr. Emmons brushed a fleck of dandruff from his rented tux. He frowned at Rosie, squirming in Jimmy's lap. Jimmy turned around. When he saw me, his face lit up. I smiled. Seeing him there relaxed me.

I heard the soft rustle of silk satin and taffeta behind me. My mother stepped out of the suite and onto the terrace. Her eyes shone. Dottie's necklace of tiny emeralds glittered against her tan throat. Sally held her train. Josh stepped towards them. Annie ran over to my mother. Josh embraced the two of them. Bea held back, her smile thin.

"Where's my Sheelie?" My mother's eye caught mine. "Come here, sweetheart."

My legs resisted movement. This was it. Official end of Daddy. Official beginning of George.

"Go on." Sally nudged me. "She needs you."

I hesitated, then went over and slid my arm around my mother's narrow waist. The thick coolness of silk satin stilled my trembling hand. My mother's arms enclosed Josh, Annie and me. The four of us, close again. The last time this way.

"We're still a family," my mother said. She wiped a tear from her cheek. "We're just getting a little bit bigger."

"Don't cry, Mom," I said. "You'll smear your makeup."

"It's waterproof." She laughed through her tears.

"We're happy for you." Josh swallowed. "You deserve this."

"This is it, Alice," Sally whispered.

Annie bent to rub a spot from her Mary Janes. The lithe ache of Bach wafted toward the terrace. I helped Sally rearrange the dress train behind my mother, then lined up with the other bridesmaids. Annie picked up the basket of petals.

My mother looked across the lawn at George. She nodded and smiled. The minister opened his Bible.

~

At the reception, the wedding party sat at a long table. Josh described his first assignment to Suzanna. He'd landed a plum job caddying for a general at Camp Pendleton, plus some vague administrative tasks. Suzanna leaned closer and batted her lashes. Steve, George and Joe—boyfriend, groom, and best man—drank wine and reminisced about fishing up at Lake Nacimiento.

"The bass are prolific," George said to my mother. "Best camping in the state."

"We should go to the lake again," Joe said, chewing on rare prime rib. "For old time's sake. Bring the whole family. I'll barbeque. Is the old man still making sausage? Damn, I can taste them now."

Joe belched quietly. George turned to my mother and kissed her, as if to apologize for Joe's rudeness. Next to me, Cousin Nan watched with admiration as Suzanna attempted to seduce Josh. Will sat on the other side of me, drinking his coffee. He didn't look happy about this.

"Mark my words," Nan whispered in my ear. "Suzanna will have your brother in the sack by tonight." She motioned for the waiter to fill her wine glass.

"I doubt it," I said. "He's not that easy."

"Don't be so sure," she said. "Suzanna's a vixen."

"I promised the bride and groom," Will said, turning to me, "that I'd be good. But I got my own reasons, too."

"Do they have anything to do with the rabbit lady?" I said.

"You don't miss a beat, do you, kid?" Will cracked a smile. "Your dad would be proud. And yeah, matter of fact, the rabbit lady, AKA Linda, and I made a deal. I quit the booze, she gives up the bunnies."

"Sounds fair." I smiled.

Will was getting the better end of the deal. He'd never managed to stay on the wagon for more than a week. Daddy had beat him at two weeks once.

"I might even marry her," Will said. He looked over at Joe and frowned. One of the waiters was handing Joe a mic. "Big mouth's up," Will said under his breath.

On the other side of George and my mother, Sally's beau Steve whispered in her ear. Joe made a crack about marriage and expanding waistlines. He got a pretty good laugh. Sally looked at Joe and made a cutting motion at her throat.

"Okay, Sal." Joe blushed. "I can take a hint." He turned to my mother and raised his glass. "George always knew you two were meant to be. He vowed to keep on you as long as it took. Until you'd have him. And here we are. Congratulations."

Glasses clinked throughout the banquet room. When the guests set down their glasses, it sounded like a collective sigh of relief. Rich farmer had fallen for the town widow. And unlike Daddy, George was as normal as they came. Hardworking. Principled. One of their own.

The waiters cleared plates. My mother and George got up for the first dance. I gulped down one of Bea's pills. Will asked me to dance.

"Never danced with a tall one before," Will teased. "I hear you're pretty tough, too."

"Who told you?" I asked.

"Larry," he said. "I saw him at the Hero that night. He said he broke it up."

"Yeah," I said. A wave of relaxation passed over me. "It was ugly."

"Hard to believe it when friends turn enemies." Will shrugged. "What happened?"

Every time someone asked me this question, the answer slipped further away. Like the tail of a kite or a balloon a child had accidentally let go of. Did it matter what had passed between Ing and me?

"I'm not sure, Will," I said. "Lots of things I guess."

"Life's complicated," Will said, nodding. "But now I've got Linda."

"I'm glad," I said. "You need a woman, Will."

"You're a good kid." Will shook his head and smiled. "Your dad would be so proud, seeing you now." He laughed. "Maybe a little surprised, given the occasion."

"Yeah," I said. "It's her life, I guess."

"Sure is." Will nodded.

The Chief and Bea danced past Will and me. Bea looked wobbly. When I looked over at them the next time, the Chief was walking her back to her seat. George and my mother drifted by, eyes closed. The Chief came over and spoke to Will.

"Who is this lovely lady?" the Chief asked. I caught a whiff of Old Spice. "Mind if I cut in?"

"Not at all." Will surrendered me to the Chief. "Good timing."

Will turned and headed towards the bar set up against the far wall of the banquet room. I dipped under the Chief's arm, trying to avoid stepping on his feet. His big face smiled down at me. He looked handsome in his tuxedo. Like a man in a magazine advertisement. As a little girl, I had asked if the flecks in his eyes were real gold. He told me the angels had sprinkled them in his eyes at birth.

"How are you, mi hija?" he asked.

"Muy bien. Y usted?"

"Muy bien." His hand was firm around my waist. "Your grandmother is an excellent conversationalist."

"She's had a little too much to drink," I said.

"She is only having fun," he said, smiling. "She was perfectly well behaved."

He glanced over at the DJ booth, where Jimmy was talking to the DJ. Rosie and Annie were picking out records.

"I know about the fight at school," he said. "And last week, my brother, Lorna's father, found out that my niece left San Jose State nearly a year ago and has been living in San Francisco. Fortunately, Lorna is a terrible liar. I wish Ingrita were a bad liar, too. She would not be in this trouble."

He shook his head. Ing had caused the Chief great pain. I wished I could wave my hand to make the pain disappear.

"It's wrong of me to discuss this," he continued, "at such a happy occasion. But my heart is breaking for my daughter. She has changed in a bad way. And for this, she is finishing high school at Saint Anne's."

"Does Betty know?" I asked. Jimmy was over at the DJ booth, staring at the Chief and me. I turned to the Chief. "About the..."

"She knows about the fight," the Chief said. He loosened his hold on my waist, as if holding me was too much. "Knowing about the abortion would kill her. My wife is unstable, Sheila. And the more she prays, the less stable she becomes."

He stopped dancing and sighed. I waited. He closed his eyes, as if to mitigate the looming issue.

"Sheila, I have to know. Was the baby Jimmy's?"

My heart raced. Knowing about Ben Wilson would break the Chief's heart. But what would it do to Jimmy if I didn't tell the Chief the truth? The Chief stared past me. The gold flecks in his eyes receded into quiet rage. The DJ faded "Wasted Days and Wasted Nights" into "Brick House." The speakers thumped. People spilled onto the dance floor.

I took the Chief by the arm and led him over to an empty table. I'd explain everything to Jimmy later. He'd understand.

"Chief, Jimmy doesn't know anything," I said, sitting down. "Ing lied to him, too."

"I understand, mi hija." A quiet smile crossed his lips. "Thank you."

The Chief stood. He walked stiffly towards the bar, shook Will's hand, and ordered a drink. When the bartender stopped pouring the amber liquid, the Chief motioned for him to continue.

I needed time to think. I left the banquet hall without a word. A bellman directed me to the Ladies' Lounge, down a long plush hall with chandeliers the size of a small car. A Mexican attendant dressed in a white uniform folded linen hand towels. Foiled chocolates lay on a silver tray atop the long black-marble vanity sink.

I sat on a velour banquette and kicked off my pumps. The attendant smiled at me. I touched my stinging heels, peeling the pantyhose from my heels to let the blisters breathe. I dug my stocking feet into the thick burgundy carpet. I closed my eyes. My temples throbbed.

Things had been okay, until now. Jimmy and I had been keeping our relationship low-key around school. Ing transferring to Saint Anne's would take the pressure off. She had dumped Vandro, although he claimed he'd dumped her. Ruthie had been wandering around school like a lost puppy. I wanted nothing to do with her.

I knew Jimmy still thought about Ing. A few nights a week, he'd pick me up, and we'd drive out to the river to talk and make out. One night, when I had come outside to get in his waiting car, Jimmy was staring out at the pasture. "My Ingrita," he had murmured. "My Ingrita." He had not heard the car door open.

Jimmy deserved to know the truth. And now, with the Chief about to accuse Jimmy of getting Ing pregnant, I had to tell him. And yet he'd been in such a good mood since Crazy Hearts. He even claimed he was falling in love with me.

Twenty

Josh came out of the banquet room, Grandma Bea on his arm and out-of-her-tree drunk. The toe of her patent leather pump caught on the carpet, and she stumbled. I reached for her. The top of her ratted and sprayed head, dyed a soft red for the wedding, reached my collarbone. She looked up, as if trying to place me.

"Too much gin." Bea hiccupped and laughed. "Makes a girl ginny."

"What's her room number?" Josh asked me. He spoke to me under his breath. "She was in there flirting with the Chief."

"I was not flirting, Joshua," Bea said. She winked at a bellman as he passed us in the hall. "I was making conversation." She gazed up at the ceiling. "Is that gold leaf?" She sighed. "I just love this hotel."

She wandered ahead of Josh and me, admiring the carpet. She swayed dangerously close to a pedestal supporting a three-foottall brass statue of a mermaid. Josh grabbed Bea just in time.

"Oopsie." She giggled.

"We're all on the fifth floor," I said to Josh. "Did Mom see her like this?"

"I think I got her out of there in time," he said. "Let's go, Bea. Nap time."

Josh obviously needed moral support. I accompanied them onto the elevator. Before I was old enough to know that you didn't have to love your pain-in-the-ass grandmother, I had loved Bea. She had taught me to swim one summer, and we had played hours of checkers, which occasionally she let me win. And I used to think she was a good cook until I found frozen food packaging in the garbage. With Bea, the truth was a relative thing.

"George reserved the entire fifth floor for today," I said to Josh. "But I don't know the room number."

"I want to dance," Bea whined. "But my nephew won't let me."

Bea mock-pouted. She stumbled onto the elevator and looked at herself in the golden-veined mirror. Her age-spotted hands went to her hair, then to straighten her gardenia corsage.

"Your police chief said I was charming," she said, dropping the corsage.

When I wasn't disgusted, I felt sorry for Bea. Sometimes she made me laugh. Today wasn't one of those times. She was making a fool of herself. I picked up the gardenia and re-pinned it to her dress. She glared at me.

"Let me tell you something, Sheila." She wagged her finger.

"Your mother doesn't understand how hard it was to raise two children alone."

"Yeah," I said. "It's been a real cakewalk for her, raising us since Daddy died."

"We should get something for you to eat," Josh said to Bea. He shot me a warning glance. "You didn't touch your food."

Bea ate like a bird. My mother claimed the "seddies" curbed Bea's appetite. Her frail physique only made her personality seem more overbearing. How my mother had coped as Bea's child, I would never know.

When we got off on the fifth floor, Josh kept a tight rein on her. She riffled through her purse, looking for the room key. The bottle of Valium rattled. When I tried to help, she scowled at me.

"Why can't you be normal," she sneered. "Like Joshua? You're just like your father. I tried to tell your mother he was a drunk. Room 55, Miss," Bea yelled at a maid pushing a cart of supplies. "Where is it?"

I gave the maid an apologetic shrug. She clicked her gum as if she was used to people being rude and pointed down the hall. Josh and I thanked her.

"What are you thanking her for?" Bea snapped. "It's her job." She swayed as she tried to insert the key in the doorknob. "Do you think they'll have children? I bet not. Your mother's too old."

Josh took the key from her. Bea had crossed the line between happy drunk and downright mean. A tapestry of a stone house in the woods hung over the four-poster bed. A couple dressed in fancy clothes strolled toward the house.

"I'd love another granddaughter," Bea said, stepping out of her pumps. She lay on her back on the ivy-print bedspread. "The ones I have don't like me much. Annie is spoiled rotten."

I looked at Josh and he shook his head. I knew the look. *It's the booze, Shee.* Arguing with Bea in this, or any, condition was trouble. Daddy had had a similar mean streak, and it had usually fired up when Bea was around.

"In case she wakes." Josh set an empty ice bucket next to the bed. "And has to barf."

A gull's cry pierced the quiet. Bea was out. In thirty seconds, she'd gone from spouting ugliness to sleeping peacefully.

"Let's get some air," Josh said, sliding open the glass door to the narrow balcony.

We stood five stories up and over the Pacific Ocean. Kelp beds heaved below, the bay a sedate blue in a half-bowl of jagged cliffs. Sea lions around the point barked. The monotonous noise calmed me.

"Just like old times, huh, Josh?" I inhaled the sea air.

"I've never seen Bea drunk, Shee," he retorted.

"I was referring to Dad," I said. A fishing boat with its motor on putted toward shore. Gulls circled the mast, demanding their share of the catch. "Taking care of him, I mean."

"How many times do you think we yanked him out of the Hero?" Josh said. He sighed. "Too many."

I thought of the tall, polished bottles on the orange-lit shelves in the Hero. The din of men's voices. The crack of the pool game. Felipe trying to roust Daddy from his stupor so we could take him home. Josh had learned to drive when he was eleven, primarily for this reason.

"I miss going in there sometimes," I said. It was Daddy I missed, not the Hero.

"I don't," Josh said. "It stunk. Literally."

If it was before midnight, Daddy would be holding court in his booth in the poolroom. Will would be there at the table, and Tall Larry, if it was payday. There had been a woman once. Rosalinda, I think. Raven hair. Dreamy eyes. I needed to change the subject.

"Suzanna's all over you," I said to Josh. I tossed my head and ran my fingers through my hair, mimicking Suzanna. "I just love a man in uniform." I brushed my hand across his crew cut.

"Go on, Shee," Josh said, a flicker of a smile on his lips. "So what about you and Jimmy Emmons?"

"We go out sometimes." There was so much to tell Josh. Or nothing at all. We had been close. But now it was hard to say. "No big deal, though."

Below us, a quiet tide rolled in. The waves rolled back, then in again, covering more of the beach this time. As the tide rose, the urge to talk to Jimmy grew. I had to set him straight about Ing before the Chief tried to.

"You ever hear from the hitchhiker?" Josh frowned. "God, I hope not."

"Then why'd you ask?" I snapped. "You know I had a thing for Buck. You saw my eyes the day we met him outside of Kim's."

"Yeah," he said. "I had hoped to protect you." He turned to me, his eyes soft. "You still hate George?"

His complexion was clear, his jaw firm. That thumbnail no longer wandered into his mouth. He knew where he fit in the world now.

"I don't know." I hugged the peach-colored silk satin dress to my body. "Forget it, Josh. Okay? I got other things on my mind."

"Like what?" he said. "Tell me, Shee."

A pelican dove into the white caps. Seconds later, the large bird darted back to the surface, swallowing its kill in one gulp. The Buck thing hurt less and less. Sometimes it seemed as though I'd dreamed him up.

"In Basic, I learned that mental attitude affects everything," Josh said. "I've faced my demons, Shee." He hit his chest with his fist. "I feel the difference, inside."

He'd written to us about the Crucible, a fifty-six-hour test of physical and psychological endurance he survived early in basic training. Five miles into an uphill, ten-mile run that was part of the Crucible, Josh was crying so hard he couldn't see. But by the end of the run, his head was clear, and the anxiety that had plagued him was gone. "For good," he'd written, using five exclamation marks.

"That's funny," I said. "I learned the world is messed up no matter what I think."

"It's been tough for you, huh?" His voice softened. "Mom told me about the fight between you and Ingrid. I hope you're not turning cholo on me." He smiled.

"Cholo wouldn't be so bad," I said. "I'd have lifetime protection from Yvette and her friends."

I had meant this to be funny. But neither of us laughed. I was tired. Tired of the past. Tired of the present. Just tired.

"Mom's happy." Josh looked out at the water, then turned to me. "George is good for her. And for you, in the long-run."

"You don't live with him," I said. "We should get back to the reception."

"Yeah." Josh slid open the door. "She'll be fine."

Bea had turned over on her stomach. Her dress had wrapped around her knees. She snored. Josh pulled the spread up over her shoulders.

"I need to find the drug store," I said. "I've got blisters on my heels."

Actually, I worried the Emmonses had left the reception. But then I remembered that Jimmy had driven his own car. Knowing Jimmy, he'd hang around all night waiting to see what the Chief wanted. When Jimmy's mind got a hold of something, it hung on.

"You look like a grown-up," Josh said when we stepped on to the elevator. He ribbed me. "Like a woman."

"And brother," I said, smiling. "You look like a man."

"Weird, huh?" he said.

"Yeah." I wiggled his left epaulet. "It is."

Twenty-One

I found Jimmy and baby sister Rosie in the lobby, staring into a display of hand-painted china. Rosie fluttered her lashes and leaned against Jimmy's legs. She asked if Jimmy and me were going to dance. Jimmy looked pale. As if he and the Chief had spoken already. *Damn you, Bea.*

"Depends on Jimmy," I said, kissing the top of Rosie's red head. "I like your party dress."

"Thank you." Rosie curtsied for me and giggled. "I like your dress, too."

Nan, the bridesmaid with the absent husband, crossed the lobby, carrying a fresh drink and her pumps. She got on the elevator, and the door closed noiselessly in front of her. Done for the evening. I turned to Jimmy.

"Josh and me had to take my grandmother up to her room," I said. "She was acting like a fool."

"That's too bad." Jimmy stared at the floor. He looked up at me. His jaw tightened. "We need to talk."

"Look at her," Rosie murmured, pointing to a woman checking in at the front desk. "She looks rich."

The woman wore a floor-length mink coat. A pair of beady dog eyes peered through the handles of the woman's Gucci handbag. The clerk tapped a service bell, and a bellman hurried over.

"The Chief's got his eye on me," Jimmy whispered. "When are you going to tell me why?"

The Chief and Jimmy hadn't talked. I should have been relieved. But instead, I almost wished they had.

"You're being paranoid, Jimmy."

"Shee, don't lie." His face tightened.

"We'll talk later," I said. "I need some Band-Aids."

Rosie spotted her mother. She ran over, and the two of them walked toward Jimmy and me. Mrs. Emmons' cheeks were flushed from dancing.

"It's a lovely wedding," Mrs. Emmons said. "Aren't you two going to dance?"

"We're talking, Mom," Jimmy said.

"Are you okay, dear?" Mrs. Emmons studied Jimmy. "You look tired."

"I'm fine, Ma."

"If you say so, son." She smiled at me. "You look very nice, Sheila. So grown-up."

"Thanks, Mrs. Emmons."

"She should go to more fancy parties," Jimmy said when his mother and Rosie walked away. "She's happy for a change."

We stood there, not saying anything. Jimmy fiddled with the buttons on his suit jacket. The woman in the fur coat waited at the desk while the bellman wheeled her luggage into the lobby. The dog poked out his head and yipped at the bellman. The woman reprimanded the dog in German.

"I need Band-Aids," I said to Jimmy. My heels were on fire. "You think the front desk has any?"

"How should I know?" He looked around the lobby. "There's a store." He pointed across the lobby to a small shop.

In the shop, Jimmy picked up a tester bottle of Babe and held it to his nostrils. I picked up a pack of adhesive tape and a travel-size bottle of hydrogen peroxide, pretending to study the labels. What would I say to Jimmy?

I felt him behind me. I smelled nervous sweat from his body and acrid fear on his breath. I grabbed a box of Band-Aids and headed for the counter. My hand shook as I signed the bill.

"What's the name, please?" The white-haired clerk peered through her reading glasses at the bill. "I can't read the signature."

"Fratti," I said.

"Miss, you signed 'O'Connor.'" She lowered the reading glasses and frowned. "What's the room number?"

"She *said* 'Fratti,' lady," Jimmy said from the back of the store.

"I will have to call the front desk," the woman said. "To verify the name Fratti.

Jimmy approached the counter. I had never seen him snarl at

anyone. The woman's hands fluttered about the counter. Her left hand found the phone.

"Such rudeness is unnecessary," the clerk said, her lips pursed.

"I'll see you in the lobby, Shee." Jimmy glared at the clerk and left.

When I caught up with him in the lobby, he was staring into the glass display case of hand-painted china. He held his arms rigid. His left hand clenched, then the right. He spoke to my reflection.

"What did the Chief say to you?" His neck muscles were taut. "I know you were talking about me."

"He asked me about the fight with Ing."

"What else?" He was shouting now. "I know there's more."

I stared at our reflection in the glass. *What do I do? Daddy, help.* I heard a hissing noise behind us. I turned around. The concierge wagged a finger at us. I took Jimmy by the arm and led him over to some velvet chairs near the hotel entrance. I sat down and pressed my feet on the carpet. My knees knocked together. I took a deep breath and let it out.

Jimmy's knuckles were white against the rosewood armrests. My heart hammered. Outside, in front of the revolving glass door, a taxi pulled into the hotel's circular drive. I watched the passengers get out. The tall, thin balding man, the woman dressed head to toe in winter white. The other man, a fat cigar glued between his fleshy lips. I wished I could be any one of them.

"Ingrid got pregnant this summer," I said. I couldn't look at Jimmy. "The Chief thinks the baby was yours."

Another bellman entered the lobby pushing a luggage cart. The revolving door made a hushing noise as it turned. Jimmy looked at me and swallowed.

"Maybe he should ask Vandro," he sneered. "Maybe he shouldn't goddamn assume."

"It wasn't yours, Jimmy." I closed my eyes. This wasn't happening. Not this way. "At first Ing said she wasn't sure, but then with the abortion—"

"Abortion?" Jimmy whispered. "What?"

"I'm sorry," I said miserably. "But what did you think had happened?"

"Damn it, Sheila. Tell me." Jimmy jumped up, screaming now. "It was that jerk from Dick Brown's, wasn't it?"

I nodded slowly. Jimmy's eyes jerked around my face, as if looking for a safe place to land. His breathing quickened.

"But it could've been my baby, right?" His legs jiggled like a sewing machine pedal. "It could've been. I would've married her. You know I would've."

I did know this. As well as I knew Jimmy didn't love me like he loved Ing. I stared at the lobby revolving door, turning though no one was in it. Daddy would have had the answer. He'd know the right thing to say to Jimmy.

"But you set the Chief straight, right?" Jimmy said, wiping spit from his lips. "You told him it wasn't my baby, right?"

"You should've seen his face." I forced myself to look at him. "He's already so torn up over Ing, I couldn't tell him about Ben."

I wiped my eyes. My voice was high-pitched, desperate. Inside, I was all hollow confusion.

"You didn't tell him?" Jimmy stared at me. "You didn't tell him."

"When my dad died," I said, "my mom was sick with grief, and the Chief came to see us. Every day, he came, Jimmy."

"I hate her guts," Jimmy shouted. "I hate yours too."

He slid into the passing compartment in the revolving door. When he got to the other side, he started to run. Why couldn't he understand my loyalty to the Chief?

I followed him outside. The fog was rushing in from the Bay. I was immediately drenched. In the street, a taxi horn blared. The driver jammed on his brakes, barely missing Jimmy. Then Jimmy bolted up Pacific Avenue. He zigzagged around shivering tourists, parked cars. I lost sight of him a block from the wharf and stopped to catch my breath.

Below the street, a set of stairs led to tide pools teeming with purple-black mussels and eroded periwinkle. Daddy had brought Josh and me to see them, long before Annie was born. In one pool, a pale orange starfish had kicked one of its lower legs. When I crouched down for a better look, the starfish's leg moved again to meet the opposite leg so that it appeared to be clicking its heels. When we got cold, Daddy took us to the wharf for clam chowder and told us about Doc Ricketts, Lee, and the men who lived in the Palace Flophouse, the whole Steinbeck-Cannery Row gang.

I went down the stairs. In one of the larger pools, a small crab tried to free itself from a cluster of mussels. One of its claws was caught, and the opposing claw fought harder to compensate. A wave pounded the rock a few yards away, drenching me. I was too damn cold to cry.

I hobbled back to the Highlands Inn. The new concierge on duty in the lobby asked if I was all right. I nodded and kept walking. Josh and Suzanna sat in the velvet chairs, talking, kissing. I snuck past them and got on the elevator. As the elevator closed, Josh called my name. I pressed the button for the fifth floor. I'd lost Jimmy for good. It didn't matter what I said now.

Twenty-Two

The following Sunday before dawn, Jimmy hung himself in the Emmons' backyard. George heard the bad news before my mother and me. He had gone into town to pick up the Sunday *San Francisco Chronicle*. He was climbing back into his truck when he noticed the Chief out of uniform, heading into the Hero. George had immediately sensed serious trouble.

It was the first time George had set foot in the Hero.

Felipe the bartender had just poured the Chief a triple shot of whiskey. George ordered a beer and then spent the next two hours trying to convince the Chief Jimmy's suicide wasn't the Chief's fault. The Chief kept saying he should've known better, threatening Jimmy like he had.

My mother and I were finishing a late breakfast when George returned from town to tell us. He stood in the kitchen and held his cap to his belly as if to keep his insides from falling out. He stared past my mother standing at the sink, out at the barren sycamore.

"The Emmons kid is dead," George said. "Happened this morning."

I didn't think he meant Jimmy. Instead my mind presented the possible causes of little Bobby's death. Bad fall, car accident, accidental drowning. I pictured Mrs. Emmons, Bobby limp in her arms, that stubborn sprout of hair stuck straight up, regardless.

"Good God," my mother gasped. She left the water running on the soapy dishes. I felt her behind me, her hands firm on my shoulders. "I'm here, my love," she whispered. Despite her grip, her fingers trembled.

"It was a terrible thing," George said, turning to my mother. His voice stuck in his throat. "His mother found him."

King's toenails clicked in the hall. Rusty barked. George yelled at him to be quiet. A scuffle broke out between the dogs in the foyer. I was vaguely aware of George separating them. Rusty outside, King up to my room, George returning. George just standing there.

Then it hit me. They were talking about Jimmy. I saw the Chevelle in the ditch. Jimmy's face black and blue against the bloodied steering wheel. Had he been drinking? Engrossed in thoughts of Ing?

"God, these kids." My mother let out a teary sigh. "Was it a car accident?"

"Suicide." George glanced at me. "At home. Backyard, in fact."

I sat listening to George.

"Mrs. Emmons had come out to hang the washing. The neighbor heard her scream, called the police."

I imagined their voices competing with the hum of the new refrigerator. And—

"Sheila." Someplace faraway, my mother was on the verge of hysteria. "Talk to me."

"Leave me alone." I pushed her aside and got up from the table. I heard the *clop, clop* of her clogs coming down the porch steps after me. "Leave me be," I screamed.

"Let her alone, Alice," George said. "Let the girl be for now."

When I got to the road, an empty feed truck clattered by. Blinking dust from my eyes, I broke into a run. I ran down the broken yellow line on Bear Row. I counted the yellow rectangles aloud. I found a rhythm. I counted and walked. *Fifteen, sixteen, seventeen, eighteen, nineteen, twenty.* George's declaration filled the gaps between rectangles. *The Emmons boy is dead. The Emmons boy is dead.*

~

The day before Jimmy's funeral, I went to Ing's. It was midmorning. I had tossed and turned most of the night. I couldn't block the vision of Jimmy hanging from the locust tree in my mind. "You and Ing need each other," my mother had said. "Just go." Ing answered the door, the rims of her eyes raw, and her nose red, swollen.

We sat on the plastic-covered sofa in front of the fireplace.

Betty didn't allow fires normally. They were messy. Betty said the smell of smoke lingered in the furniture cushions forever. The embers beamed like jack-o'-lantern grins.

On the mantel, candles cast a pinkish glow on prayer cards. Jesus on the cross, Mary cradling Baby Jesus, a circle of praying angels. And a Polaroid of Jimmy in his wrestling gear. The blue sapphire on his class ring winked in the candlelight. Ing went over to the mantel and picked up the photograph.

"They beat Hollister that day," she said dully. "He looks so happy."

The gym had been packed that day. Josh had accompanied me and Ing to the wrestling meet. We sat at the top of the home-side bleachers. Josh had hoped Violet might show and wanted to watch for her. I had resisted pointing out the obvious, that Violet and her family had simply left Hollister. But I had searched the rodeo crowd for Buck. Now I understood Josh.

"I remember," I said.

I took the photograph from her. Jimmy wore his wrestling helmet, a mouth guard shoved between his lips, his forehead wet with sweat. But he was smiling.

"Where's Betty?" I asked Ing, handing her back the photo.

"In the kitchen with a migraine." She pressed the photograph to her chest and started to cry. "Jimmy came to see me last Friday and my crazy, insane mother pulled a knife on him. You know the one she uses to cut cow brains for tacos?"

I knew the knife. And the tacos stuffed with disgusting pieces of the gray, rubbery meat many Mexicans considered a delicacy.

"I tried to tell her." Ing paced in front of the fireplace. "That Jimmy and I had made up. Instead she asked me if they used a knife to cut out the baby. A *knife*? She's so stupid." Ing stared at the fire. "Someone called the police, and Daddy raced home from the station. He sees the knife and Jimmy holding onto me, and he takes my mother by the hand. He tells her, 'Go pray. Read your Bible.' 'Yes, Papa,' she says, like a child. Then Daddy turns on Jimmy. He says he'll kill him if he ever comes to our house again."

I had thought his only threat had been the threat to send Jimmy to juvie. Had the Chief also lost his mind? Ing set the photograph back on the mantel. She stood with her back to me. She whispered the Our Father. A pounding noise interrupted her.

"You have to defrost the chicken, Ma," she yelled. The pounding continued. "Ma. It's frozen. Are you crazy?"

I followed Ing into the kitchen. The mangled raw chicken lay on the cutting board. Betty held a hammer midair. Her unwashed hair hung limp around her unmade face. She looked at me like she didn't know who I was.

"Whores," she muttered, reaching to turn on the oven. She looked at Ing, then me. A crazy rage flashed in her eyes, so much smaller without the makeup. "Both of you."

"Ma, go lie down," Ing said with a sigh. "You've got a headache."

"Jesus took away my headache." Betty clutched her breast. "But I have other pain now." She wagged her finger at me. "That boy died for your sins too. You drove her to San Francisco. Jesus will forgive Jimmy, but he'll never forgive you girls."

She left the kitchen without a word, as if she had forgotten we were there. Unmoved, Ing opened a cupboard and took out a dish. She set the whole chicken in the dish and put it in the fridge to defrost.

Inside the open cupboard, Betty's pots and pans were neatly stacked. Thousands of servings of rice had been steamed, endless ladles of soup simmered. Through all of this, Jesus had been by Betty's side. Where was he now? Betty had finally lost her mind and her savior.

"When Jimmy came over last Friday," Ing said in a singsong voice, "he said we would go away, maybe to LA."

I should have known Jimmy would visit Ing after the wedding. He had told me he hated her, but Jimmy didn't have it in him to stay away from her. As for me, I had been a stand-in for Ing. Someone to fill in the gaps. I should have felt used. Instead, I felt relief.

"You don't believe me," she said miserably. She walked over to the table and collapsed into a chair. "I swear he wanted to take me away from here, to start a life."

"I don't know what I believe," I muttered. "But I know Jimmy was crazy about you."

Outside the kitchen window, a powder-blue pickup roared around the cul-de-sac. The pit bull in the truck bed gulped the wind like it was water. The white climbing rosebush in the Rodriquez's front yard shuddered on the broken trellis. Rejected by Ing, Jimmy had ruined Betty's singular attempt to beautify her yard.

But he had not killed himself over Ing alone. His soul had been weak. Some of us were born with the weakness and knew it. Others, like Jimmy, only discovered their weakness when love went bad.

"I have to go," I said to Ing.

"Please stay." Her dark eyes pleaded with me. She reached for my hand. "Come on, Shee."

"I can't." I pulled my hand from her trembling fingers. "Not after everything."

I felt the tug of our long friendship and habit. I wanted to say something to make Ing feel better. But the words were as worn out as I was.

Ing rocked back and forth, clasping her hands in her lap. Her tears flowed, unhindered by her usual concern about her appearance. If I had handed her a mirror, I suspect this time she would not have felt compelled to look at her reflection. She had finally reached pain. No need to see the pain was real.

In the living room, the embers had faded into ashes. I slipped the photo of Jimmy into my back pocket. This much was mine.

⌒

The Emmonses held a small reception at the house after the funeral service. Neighbors brought condolences and food. This bounty included five fruit salads of varying mixtures, three macaroni salads, two loaves of banana bread, an apple pie and a rhubarb pie, more than a few dozen brownies, varieties of cookies, three trays of cold-cuts, and two baked hams. Betty's *mole*, the first item delivered, was now the unintentional centerpiece on the table. The smoked sweet aroma of *mole* sauce filled the Emmonses' shabby home.

I had been to Jimmy's house just once, when he turned seven. Mrs. Emmons had thrown a birthday party for him in the backyard. Ing had arrived dressed in a pink chiffon dress. Forget-me-nots or some other tiny flower bordered the hem and collar. Jimmy's jaw had dropped when he saw her. He rushed over and offered to take her sweater. I think he fell in love with Ing that very moment. Years later, Ing told me she had no memory of the party or dress.

Mr. Emmons stood in front of the fireplace in the small living room. He and the men who had come to pay their respects spoke in somber tones. Mr. Emmons' paint-stained fingers clutched a glass tumbler of scotch on ice.

My mother, Mrs. Emmons and me sat on the couch. My mother held Mrs. Emmons' hand. A tarnished watchband hung loosely from Mrs. Emmons' thin wrist and her hands were work-worn. The plate of food my mother had fixed her sat in the lap of the thick wool dress she wore. Although they didn't speak, I sensed my mother's presence comforted Mrs. Emmons. They had a common pain now. The loss of a loved one.

My mother sipped her scotch. George had paid his respects at the funeral and was at home with Annie. His decision not to come to the Emmonses' had been a relief to my mother. She could now tend to Charlotte and me without distraction.

Mrs. Emmons' sister Ida came out to the living room, carrying a tray with a pot of coffee, cream and sugar. She set the tray on the coffee table in front of us. I watched her pour coffee for Mr. Hasbin sitting in a chair next to me. He thanked Ida when she set the Styrofoam cup on the coffee table. Hasbin wore a dark tie and a white long-sleeved, button-down shirt. A suit jacket hung on the back of the chair. New tennis shoes clashed with the navy cuffs of his unpressed trousers.

"That was a nice eulogy." Mr. Hasbin smiled at Aunt Ida. A paper plate of food balanced on his knees. "Quite moving."

Aunt Ida had traveled to Tristes from Boston to provide Mrs. Emmons the moral support that Mr. Emmons was too devastated to supply. Ida had given the eulogy. Jimmy had been a loving son and brother, admired by his peers, a gifted athlete. I recalled nothing beyond Ida's generic description of the nephew she had not seen in nearly fourteen years.

Hasbin sat with the students and some other faculty. Superintendent Walker had also come to pay his respects. He sat next to Ruthie, Mike Wong, Jesus, and the rest of the wrestling team. There had been other faces from school but they were a blur now.

"Why, thank you." Ida blushed and glanced at Mrs. Emmons. "I never was much of a public speaker. But it was a real honor."

"Well, you did just fine." Hasbin turned to me and spoke in a low voice. "How are you holding up?"

I watched the steam trail from the Styrofoam cup on the coffee table. I remembered the first week of school. Hasbin had been worried about me and Jimmy. Had he sensed Jimmy was worse off than I had?

"I'm sorry I've missed lab," I said. "I'll make up the work."

"Don't you dare worry about your grade." Hasbin sighed and tugged on the knot of his tie. "Mike Wong can always help you."

In the back of the house, the TV blared. According to Mrs. Emmons, Bobby and Michael understood Jimmy had been in a fatal car accident. None of the children had seen the body. Mr. Emmons had driven the Chevelle out to the river and simply left it there.

Mrs. Emmons had hung drapes to hide the backyard, but little Rosie, smarter than her three years, had taken to staring out the patio door. Every hour on the hour it seemed Rosie would ask her mother when Jimmy was coming home and why her father had cut down the locust tree.

"You Californians eat some strange things," Ida said, laughing. "But what is this mo-lay?"

"It's called *mole*, Ida," Mrs. Emmons said, turning her neck to see the table. "It's a Mexican dish. Betty Rodriquez sent it."

"They cut down the tree," I whispered to Hasbin. "Locust trees are tenacious. They grow back. You've got to dig it up, roots, everything."

"Your father would've thought of something to say to Jimmy," he said. He rubbed his eyes, as if to change what his mind was seeing. "Roy O'Connor knew what to say to make it all right. But I blew it. I had a chance to help, and I didn't."

Hasbin set his plate on the coffee table, upsetting the cup. Coffee pooled on the table. He stared at the spill. My mother got up to get a towel.

"It's not your fault." I put my hand on the sleeve of Hasbin's white dress shirt and watched my mother blot the spilled coffee with a paper towel. "If it's anyone's fault, it's mine. I told him about Ing."

"Sheila, please." My mother swallowed.

She looked around the room and sighed. In a moment, she would tell me it was time to go. That we needed to let the Emmonses grieve in solitude. My feelings of guilt had no place here.

"Let her talk, Alice." Mrs. Emmons pressed her hands to her ashen face. "Ed and me never let Jimmy talk. Parents need to let their kids talk."

"Charlotte, please." Mr. Emmons cleared his throat. "This is not the place."

"Don't, Eddie," Mrs. Emmons' voice cracked. "Sheila has a right. We all have a right to speak what's in our hearts."

Mr. Emmons stared into his glass. The other men looked uneasy. Mr. Emmons looked up, his face white.

"Pete Rodriquez had no right to threaten my boy," he said. "And his daughter had no right to do what she did."

"It's not worth getting mad, Ed." One of the men put his hand on Mr. Emmons' shoulder. "It's all done now."

"Not worth it?" Mr. Emmons jerked away. "My family's destroyed, man."

Mrs. Emmons got up and went over to her husband. She grabbed his hand and held it. His other hand slammed the tumbler on the mantel. I heard the bottom of the glass crack.

"Ed, get a hold of yourself," Mrs. Emmons said. "You got a daughter and two sons. You got me." Her breathing tightened. "And Pete Rodriquez had nothing to do with what Jimmy did."

Mr. Emmons glared at her, and her arms dropped like a rag doll's to her sides. She let out a weak groan. Mr. Emmons' friends stood there, waiting.

"She's not herself, Eddie," my mother said, trying to smooth things over. "She's upset."

"You weren't yourself when your Roy was killed." Mrs. Emmons' voice was cold. "Were you, Alice?"

"No, I wasn't, Charlotte." My mother sighed and stared at the coffee table. "I most certainly wasn't."

This was my exit. I needed to feel Jimmy, to make sure he was really gone. I pushed aside the drapes and slid open the patio door. The backyard smelled of green wood. The grass reached a foot high around the swing set. A lone wooden swing hung lopsided. The rope that had secured the other side of the swing was gone.

My eyes went to the locust tree, now in a pile of logs. Mr. Emmons had purchased a chainsaw the day they had found Jimmy. He had cut until he ran out of fuel, went to Qwik Gas for more, came home, and finished the job.

A Baler's T-shirt flapped on the clothesline. Mrs. Emmons had found Jimmy at six in the morning. She was pinning up Jimmy's shirt when she saw him. The morning sun poured over the top of the fence. Between the glare and her exhaustion, Mrs. Emmons thought she had hallucinated Jimmy.

When Mrs. Ramirez, the next-door neighbor, heard Mrs. Emmons' piercing scream, she had called the police. Mr. Emmons ran out in his pajamas to find her standing under Jimmy's body, and clawing at his ankles. Miraculously, Rosie and the boys slept late that morning. The Chief had found the bent flashlight Jimmy had used to find his way to a branch strong enough to hold him. The ladder now lay on its side on the grass.

I lay back on the cold slide. The sky was cloudless and bleached blue. A child's voice startled me. I sat up. Rosie stood on the patio, shivering.

"Hi, Rosie," I said.

"Hi."

She looked down and frowned at her furry red slippers. She appeared to have outgrown the black-and-white polka-dot dress she wore. She blinked her doe eyes at me.

"Do you like 'Rose' instead?" I said.

"Rosie Posies," she said. This had been Jimmy's term of endearment. She picked up a twig. "Can I sit with you?"

Before I had a chance to say yes, she climbed into my lap. Goose bumps covered her arms.

"Those people think Jimmy's dead," she said. "But he's coming back."

I wrapped my arms around her. Her fine blond hair smelled of baby shampoo and fresh air. She was trembling.

"When my daddy cut down the tree," Rosie said. She wiggled her feet. The left slipper tumbled onto the ground. "I had to cover my ears."

"I can understand that, Rosie Posies," I said. "That noise would've hurt my ears, too."

I hugged Rosie tight. Her little heart beat a mile a minute against my wrist. The T-shirt on the clothesline whipped and flapped.

Twenty-Three

George did his pathetic best to cheer me up after Jimmy's suicide. "Life goes on," he had said on numerous occasions. He also reminded me I had my whole future ahead. My mother, who knew better, left me alone. I would eventually come around. If I didn't, she'd cross that bridge when she came to it.

George's attempts to raise my spirits had the opposite effect. I was clearly damaged beyond repair. I sensed George feared me. I refused to pretend life would go on. Because it wouldn't. Not in the way it had for all these years. George feared change like he feared the *el cortito* ban and the migrant workers with their new long hoes and demands for better wages. He did have Annie.

Two weeks after Jimmy's funeral, I was home alone in the afternoon. So I had to feed the dogs. My mother and Sally were having their Thursday drink at the Pit before my mother picked up Annie at afternoon kindergarten. I'd been to Chem Lab, then P.E., and had just gotten home. School had become an empty routine. I went from class to class, counting the days until graduation. I had no plans after Graduation Day, so I just marked time. All I had was time. Long, endless stretches of it.

I had just made myself a triple-decker peanut butter and jelly sandwich when the phone rang. Rusty finished munching the kibble I'd poured into two bowls. To keep the peace, Rusty always ate first. King waited in the doorway. His nose followed my movements around the kitchen.

I picked up the phone without saying hello and listened to the unsteady wheeze. Ing's ex-sidekick Ruthie, again. She had been calling two, three times a night. My mother had threatened to get our number changed. But this time Ruthie identified herself. A car horn blared in the background. I could hear Coach Wilson yelling. She was calling from the phone booth outside the gym.

"I know it's you, Ruthie," I said, staring hungrily at the uneaten sandwich on the plate in my hand. "What do you want?"

King plodded over to the bowls. He was nearly blind now, and his sense of smell wasn't great. What remained of his coat had become a scabby salt-and-pepper. Ironically, the eczema had disappeared. But King had kept on scratching, like an amputee with a phantom limb.

"My doctor thinks we could be allies." Ruthie's voice cracked. "You know, help each other out."

I had heard Ruthie was seeing a shrink because she blamed herself for Jimmy's death. As if Jimmy had thought two seconds about Ruthie in the last seventeen years. King sniffed at his own bowl and then stuck his nose in Rusty's. Behind him, Rusty growled. King kept eating. "Listen, Ruthie," I said. "I'm glad you have a doctor to help you. But you and me…"

King looked up at me for more food. I held the receiver between my shoulder and cheek and poured out more food for King. Rusty eyed him. King ate more kibble. He lapped from the water bowl. The dogs had had scuffles before. Separating them for a while seemed to cool the dogs down.

"Please help me," Ruthie cried. "It's my fault. Jimmy wouldn't have died if I'd been nicer to him."

Rusty's tail slumped. He sniffed at King's haunches. Rusty was the alpha. I watched for pulled-back ears. His body tensed. The fur on his back spiked forward.

"Don't be ridiculous, Ruthie," I snapped, still eyeing the dogs. "Jimmy hardly knew you."

King turned suddenly, baring what was left of his teeth. His back was a sharp comb of fur. I reached for Rusty's collar to keep the dogs apart. The receiver hit the floor. Rusty lunged for King, his jaw nearly taking my finger with King's collar.

"Shit," I screamed and let loose of the collar.

King's paws slipped. He tried to gain traction on the linoleum. Snorting and snarling, he twisted away from Rusty's mouth. The collar unbuckled and hit the floor. Dog tags clanked. Ruthie's high-pitched screaming poured from the phone receiver.

Rusty's teeth clamped down. King let out a long yelp. Blood poured from King's neck. He fell onto his side. His chest heaved. I looked closer. Miniature valleys of blood flowed down King's beautiful, scabby chest. In one infinite second I felt every hurt, every bit of damage, every horror of the past years since Daddy died.

Rusty limped over to the water bowl. He was not a dog. He was a pig, a nasty, stupid pig. And he had tried to destroy the only love I could depend on. Innocent King. King who had never looked sideways at another dog until Rusty came along.

"You son of a bitch," I screamed. "How dare you?"

I ran into the foyer and threw open the closet door. My shaking hands pushed aside the mass of coats. Reaching to the back of the closet, I grabbed a tennis racket, a broom, a fucking umbrella. Where the fuck was George's hunting rifle?

I knew something about shooting. The Chief had taken Ing and me shooting out at the river one fall Saturday when we were thirteen. He brought a pistol and a .22 rifle. He believed girls needed to learn to shoot because it built confidence. I shot the row of empty beer and soda cans he had lined up for target practice.

I felt the cold barrel of the rifle. I pulled the gun from the closet and tucked it under my arm. Energy like fire coursed through me. I ran to the kitchen. There would be no more reason for King to watch his back. No more Rusty to hurt my King.

I stood in the doorway between the kitchen and foyer. King lay on the kitchen floor next to his overturned bowl. His body heaved. Rusty licked a fleshy bite on his left haunch. I set the butt of the rifle on my shoulder and steadied the sight on the white diamond on Rusty's forehead. His jowls were gluey with pink saliva. King's blood. I lowered the rifle to wipe away tears.

Rusty was such a dumb name. Not King. My father had named him King because he was a garden-variety black Lab. Daddy has said that if King heard this name often enough, he'd act regal. But he'd always been just King. Nothing regal, just pure trust and affection.

"Damn it, Daddy," I yelled. I raised the gun to my shoulder. "Where are you now?"

Through the sight pinhole, I saw the blur of Rusty. I let the tears fall anyway. I heard the clock ticking in the family room. My right index finger closed around the trigger. I placed my finger just so, the way the Chief had shown me.

"Goddamn you, you stupid, vicious dog."

I fired.

The kickback threw me into the hall, onto my ass. The noise of the shot pin-balled through the house, then ricocheted back. I let go of the rifle. The barrel clattered on the hardwood. I had chosen this. I had killed Rusty. Dense silence filled the room. A dark puddle gathered around one hundred twenty life-less pounds. And yet he seemed to float, as if the body had not quite surrendered. The busy signal blared from the receiver. I wondered why I had not noticed the noise until now. I heard guttural breathing.

"King," I whispered.

I scrambled to my feet and kicked the phone out of the way. I would kick George Fratti if I had the chance, and much, much harder. George must have known Rusty would turn on King one day. But George had done nothing. He had chased Buck out of town, but he had not had the guts or desire to control his own dog.

King's chest heaved. I yanked the tablecloth off the table, upsetting a vase of flowers. I improvised a tourniquet and diapered the excess cloth around King's hind legs, knotting it over his belly. He weighed seventy, maybe seventy-five pounds. Lighter than the hundred pounds he had weighed when Josh and I used to cart him around the living room.

I half-carried, half-dragged King down the porch steps and pulled the car up. I shoved him across the front seats and slipped into the car seat, positioning King's head in my lap. As I drove, I stroked his muzzle, where the fur was sparsely whiskered and smooth, like velvet.

"Please, King," I murmured. "Please hang on."

⁓

Dr. Wong reached into the car and felt King's heartbeat. I had honked from the turn to the clinic. Dr. Wong had come out, spitting mad. He thought I was one of his patients who hadn't the courtesy to come into the clinic to see him. He stopped and changed expression when he saw me with King.

King lay motionless across the front seats. I stared at his scaly coat. All of that scratching, and he'd never gotten more than a second or two of relief. No more scratching. No more precious King.

"It was an artery." Dr. Wong ran his fingers through his

straight black hair. "A dog rarely survives a wound in the neck, especially an old dog."

"I should've driven faster," I said, looking at Dr. Wong. When I saw his sad eyes, I turned away and murmured, "Maybe he would've made it."

"From what I could see, you drove eighty as it was." Dr. Wong's voice quavered. King had been his patient for fourteen years. "The dust you stirred up coming here." He opened the driver's-side door. "Now get out so I can lift King out. I'll take care of the body."

The word "body" echoed in my mind. Bowing my head, I stroked between his ears. One of my tears dropped onto his fur, then disappeared.

"Wait," I said. "I want to bury him myself."

"I can't help you." Frowning, Dr. Wong looked at his wrist-watch. "I'll get my son."

King's body was already losing heat. I pushed down his eyelids and stared out the windshield of the VW. Out in the asparagus fields, a crow cawed. A sound both empty and plaintive, as if the crow also knew King had gone.

"This is your end, dear King," I whispered, patting behind his ears.

It was mine, too.

My turning point should've been Daddy dying or Buck leaving or my mother marrying George, and if not these things, then most definitely Jimmy's suicide. But it was King. Sweet King, who'd been my companion through all of these things.

When Josh came home for the wedding, he had been shocked that King slept in my room and not in the guest room with Josh. I told him that King had switched allegiances out of necessity, not preference. King had needed me as much as I needed him.

Dr. Wong returned with Mike. Mike's face wore a serious expression, but he didn't hurry. Dr. Wong spoke to Mike in Mandarin. Side by side I could see a resemblance. Mike had his father's smooth profile. But Mike's hands were small, like Mrs. Wong's.

"Sorry about your dog," Mike mumbled. "He wants to know where you intend to bury him."

"Out at the river," I said, wondering why Dr. Wong hadn't asked himself.

"Make the hole deep then," Dr. Wong said gruffly.

They transferred King to the back seat. Dr. Wong went away and came back carrying a shovel and a thick wool blanket. He spoke to Mike in Mandarin again.

"The blanket is for you," Mike translated. "When you go into shock."

"I'm not in shock," I said.

"Not yet." Dr. Wong glanced at the bloodstains on my sweatshirt. "Now go, before it gets dark."

~

Sweat poured down Mike's temples. He threw down the shovel, took off his glasses, and rubbed his eyes. Behind us, alfalfa crops gave way to the green slope of the Santa Lucias. To the east, on the other side of the copper-lit river, fields shimmered, then the populated square of Tristes, more fields, and finally the Gabilans.

"Make the hole bigger," I said. Without thinking, I bent down to scratch King's ears. "We're not burying a Pekingese."

"Fine." Mike thrust the shovel at me. "Then you dig."

I shoveled sandy soil onto the growing pile. It felt good to move my body. In a nearby field, a flash of red caught my eye. It was Tall Larry, a new red cap on his head. He stepped back from the easel to study his work. He appeared to be painting the Gabilans across the valley. I'd never seen him paint outdoors.

"There's Tall Larry," Mike said, sitting on an abandoned truck tire. "Painting his nigger pictures."

"If you ever say that word again," I said, jabbing the point of the shovel at Mike, "I'll kill you." I started digging again. "It's getting dark. Get Tall Larry."

"You get him," Mike mumbled. He looked at his feet. "He's your friend."

"I hate this town." I threw down the shovel. "Hey, Larry," I yelled.

He didn't hear me, so I kept yelling. I jumped up and down waving my arms like a maniac. Tall Larry finally looked up from the canvas toward me.

"Sheila?" He took off the red cap. "What are you doing out here?"

"We need help," I called. "Come. Quick."

Tall Larry set his brush on the easel. As usual, his long legs seemed to arrive before the rest of him. He stared at King on the ground.

"Sweet Jesus," he said. "When it rains it pours."

He took the shovel from me and sunk the blade into the earth. The river rippled silver. Blackbirds swooped down and across the river. When Tall Larry had finished digging, the hole was twice as big as it needed to be. Then he lifted King's head and told Mike to take the other end of his body.

"You want to say a prayer, Sheila?" Tall Larry asked.

"I don't know any," I said, stroking King's left paw.

King wouldn't feel compelled to scratch anymore. Maybe for King this was some consolation for dying. I thought of Rusty, a useless mound of flesh and fur. Still, I'd shot him. What had I done?

"Dear God," Tall Larry said and bowed his head. "Take this animal into your arms, and bless the young lady who loved him."

A cry rose up in me. It clawed at my throat, climbed down my tongue and out my lips. There would never be another King. But there would be another Rusty. Dogs like him came around every day. I collapsed onto the ground.

Tall Larry and Mike helped me up and to the car. I wrapped the wool blanket around me and waited for them to finish burying King. I heard each slice of the shovel, each thud of the falling earth.

Mike returned to the VW with Tall Larry. Tall Larry looked in at me and asked if I was all right. I was shivering, but my teeth weren't chattering.

"A little cold is all," I said.

I would go to Josh. I would remind him that life did not run the course you expected in spite of rules and regulations you pretended to follow. Though he might argue this point, he had an obligation to King and me to listen.

Mike threw the shovel in the trunk. He tried slamming it shut but the latch was being temperamental. Tall Larry stood at the driver's-side window, watching. He wiped the dirt from his hands on his blue jeans. Mike slammed the trunk again.

"Leave the trunk," Tall Larry yelled at him. "I'll fix it."

"She can't drive with it like this," Mike snapped.

The latch finally caught. Mike got in the car. Tall Larry smiled at him.

"You don't like me, do you, kid?" Tall Larry asked Mike.

"I like you all right," Mike mumbled.

"Well, I'm glad to hear it." Tall Larry looked at me and winked. "Because I got the master key to the lockers."

"What's that supposed to mean?" Mike looked up at him. "I got nothing to hide."

"What did you do with the other dog?" Tall Larry asked me.

"Left him," I said. "My mother is probably cleaning up the mess right now."

"No telling what waits for you, coming between Fratti and his dog." Tall Larry stared at me. "You are going home, aren't you?"

Across the valley, a planet winked above the Gabilan range. I hugged the blanket to me. I had never felt so exhausted. I looked at Tall Larry and shrugged.

"I don't know if I can," I said.

"A smart young lady would go home," Tall Larry said. "Face the music, as they say." He unpeeled some bills from the roll in his pocket. "Just in case, take this. And no arguing."

"You can't run away," Mike said. "It won't solve anything."

"Shut up, Mike," Tall Larry said.

I mumbled something about paying back the money and stuffed the bills in my pocket. I still wore the fiddle player's medallion. I took it off, pried Tall Larry's hand from the edge of the window, and lay the medallion in his open palm.

"Ah, now," he said. "You don't need to give me that."

"I know," I said, closing the hand around the medallion. "Just tell me why you decided to start painting outside."

Mike shifted his feet impatiently. Tall Larry put the medallion in the pocket of his jeans and thought for a minute.

"Because those mountains are real, and there's no beauty in painting what's in your mind." He patted me on the arm. "You take care now."

I dropped Mike at the dirt-road turnoff to his house. I stared out at the blue-pink twilight and thought of King. Cold, alone, and unaware of either. It seemed impossible that he was gone. Mike picked at the dirt under his fingernails.

"What do I tell everyone?" he asked.

"Make something up," I said. "Or tell them the truth. No one but you and Hasbin care anyway."

I wasn't feeling sorry for myself. This was a fact. No Jimmy, no Ing, no Daddy. And Ms. Bob wouldn't miss me after Ing and me had stirred up trouble. Nor would Supe Walker.

"Where will you go?" Mike turned to me. "Aren't you scared?"

"I'm going to see Josh," I said. "Then, I'm not sure."

Fumbling, he lunged for my mouth. I pushed him off of me, but he managed to steal a kiss. Miraculously, his breath smelled all right.

"Call me when you get back," he said. "I'll be around."

He sauntered down the road, toward the clinic and home. I tapped the horn. Mike waved without turning around. I smiled. I'd never seen Mike Wong so confident. And in this sad-ass life, that was worth something.

Twenty-Four

I turned on the headlights and edged the VW onto Highway 101. The Salinas Valley was domed in stars and a new moon. Tall Larry would probably do the responsible thing and call my mother. Dr. Wong would call her too, to express his condolences.

I passed Terra Dura Camp. The sparsely lit dirt yard flitted in and out of view. I pictured Buck in Chile or some other South American country, playing poker with the locals, tangoing with sultry women. I remembered the rush of shame and excitement I had felt when the migrant boys whispered as I walked toward Buck's bungalow that evening. Buck's red hair curly and damp from the shower. The grin that had made my knees weak. And now King was gone too.

My mother would call the Chief, and he would either come after me or alert the Highway Patrol. Except that I wasn't a runaway. Runaways come back. And as Buck had once said about leaving, knowing you're coming back is for chicken shits.

In the rearview mirror, the glitter of Soledad Correctional Facility faded. KHITS played "Born to Run." When the song ended, the DJ made an announcement.

"That was a little song by The Boss," he said. "To Sheila from Mike."

I smiled and switched the radio station. John Coltrane, loud and clear. I rolled down the window. The fresh air cleared my head, dried the tears, and siphoned the smell of King's blood from the car.

I heard the distant thunder of the approaching train. Gradual it seemed, and yet the train had always arrived suddenly. This time I was moving too. The engine headlight funneled light along George Fratti's fields and moved at medium speed. We were neck and neck. But a mile or so down the road, the engine and boxcars thudded past me. I watched the rickety caboose fishtail down the tracks.

⁓

Fifty miles south of King City, I stopped to fill my tank at the 76 Station in Templeton, a town a quarter the size of Tristes and surrounded by oil pumps and sagebrush. The station attendant peered out of the station window. I waited a few minutes, then went inside.

An acne-faced boy about my age dusted off merchandise behind the counter. He mumbled something about not being sure I had wanted gas and went outside to fill my tank.

I set two cans of 7Up, a bag of Fritos and a pack of fruit Lifesavers in honor of Annie on the counter. I picked a comb out of a plastic canister and found some deodorant. I'd go to the restroom and clean up. T-shirts and sweatshirts hung on a long rack behind the counter, presumably where they would be safe from sticky fingers. When the attendant came inside, I asked for the gray sweatshirt.

"Were you in a fight or something?" He looked at my T-shirt and shook his head.

"Something like that," I said. "Do I need a key for the bathroom?"

"Door's open," he said, turning to the rack of shirts. "What size?"

"Large." I wanted to be extra warm.

I paid him for the sweatshirt, food, and toiletries. In the restroom, I spread paper towels on the floor and plugged a wad of toilet paper in the drain. I stripped to my waist. This had been Buck's method of roadside hygiene. He'd explained how to fill the sink and wash your upper body, before repeating the process for the lower half. This way, if you forgot to lock the door, at least you're partially clothed if someone walks in. I washed and combed my hair, then rinsed my mouth with rusty faucet water.

Good job for a rookie.

I jumped.

"Asshole," I whispered.

Didn't mean to startle you, darlin'. Buck's voice, aged twenty or thirty years. *You remembered my method.*

"Leave me alone." Shaking, I stuck my head through the neck of the sweatshirt and tugged it over my body. "I'm doing this myself."

You're still hurt.

"You should've stood up to George," I said. "But you didn't want to."

Ah, but you wouldn't have made it here without me.

"And it's such a cozy place," I said, tugging the new comb through my hair. "I especially love the smell of urine."

You'll see.

"I'll see what?" I said. "What do you know, Buck?"

Kid, I'm sorry about your dog.

"Get lost." I picked up the paper bag of soda and snacks. "I don't want you anymore."

~

I made it as far as Pismo Beach, and without Buck's running commentary. Why was he haunting me now? Daddy speaking to me from his grave I could handle. But Buck playing philosopher?

I spotted the empty parking lot of a closed diner, crawled into the back seat, and cocooned myself inside the wool blanket.

I dreamed Jimmy and I had gotten separated at Crazy Hearts, and Yvette was helping me look for him. People on the dance floor were shoving us. Yvette was yelling "Honky motherfuckers" at them. Tall Larry had turned the heat up high, and the gym reeked of sweat. I told Yvette I couldn't breathe, and she led me outside. Ruthie and Mike were smoking a joint. Mike was drunk and laughing at a joke Ruthie had made. When I asked Ruthie where Jimmy was, she said he'd just left with Ing to go to her house to fuck in front of Betty.

I woke in the middle of the night, thinking about King alone in that hole. Mike had promised he'd visit King from time to time. If Mike didn't make it out to the river, I knew Tall Larry would look in on him. Fog closed in on the VW. I drifted off to the noise of fog horns.

I dreamed King was still a pup. He wore a patent leather collar with a gold buckle. Daddy was throwing a rubber ball for King on the front lawn of a big white house with green plantation shutters. He handed me the ball to throw. When King brought the ball to me, my mother and George walked past the house, holding hands. My mother was wearing her wedding dress.

⁓

Sunlight slivered through the slats of the wooden fence that separated the diner's parking lot and a gray industrial building. Morning fog hovered in patches, but it was burning off. I pushed open the backseat window. The air tasted salty. I'd go down to the beach, wade up to my ankles, watch the gulls and the waves, stare at the horizon. Get my thoughts in order.

I got out of the car to stretch. A fan whirred in back of the diner. Through the backdoor screen, pans clattered. A spatula scraped a grill. The smell of ham made my stomach growl.

I reached into the car for the comb and found a rubber band in the glove box. Across the street from the diner, a man in shorts and a Hawaiian shirt walked his aging golden retriever. A dachshund the color of sunburned maple leaves trotted behind them. A wood-paneled station wagon cruised down the street toward the beach, blocking the man and his dogs from my view.

It's a new world, Sheila.

"Shut up, Buck."

A beige VW Bug the same year as mine roared into the parking lot. The young woman driving parked next to me. I watched her yank a brush through her mop of curly red hair. She wiped the sides of her mouth with her index finger and got out, giving the surfboard strapped to the roof an affectionate pat. She reached into the back seat for an apron. Her skin was tanned and freckled. She noticed me standing there and let out a yelp of surprise.

"You scared me. How long have you been standing there?"

I mumbled an apology. She clipped a green barrette in her hair and smiled. She tied the apron around her waist and hurried off.

"I'm late," she said. "What else is new?"

"Is the food good?" I called.

"It's breakfast," she said with a shrug.

She disappeared behind the back door and into the diner. I heard the cook interrogating her. I went inside and sat at the counter. Two workmen ate in silence. I studied the menu. My tummy growled. One of the workmen looked up and smiled.

I watched the cook attack the bacon on the grill with his tongs. He peeled two slices of American cheese from their plastic and dropped them over a puddle of bubbling scrambled eggs. He folded the eggs and cheese into a square.

The waitress started a new pot of coffee and straightened the place settings on the counter. The tabletops were glass over a picnic-style wax cloth. A vase of plastic daisies decorated each table. At one, a boy of eleven or twelve sat with his parents, waiting for food. The boy flipped through a comic book.

The waitress came out from behind the counter to plug in a Coors sign. A waterfall and some snow-capped mountains lit up. The cook bitched at the girl. He was worse than Princie, my mother's old boss.

"I took five orders for you, Charlene," the cook barked. "It's not my fault your boyfriend keeps you out late."

"He's not my boyfriend, Billy. And I've told you a million times, my name's Charlie."

"Charlie's a fellow's name," Sam growled.

"My daddy wanted a boy." The girl shrugged. "What can I say?"

"The restroom?" I asked, waving my hand in the air.

"You'll need this." She handed me a key and pointed to the back of the restaurant. "Don't leave it on the sink. People always do. Then I'll have to find the spare key, which is missing. You see my dilemma?"

"Absolutely." I smiled. I liked Charlie. She seemed easy-going, a free spirit.

The little boy was watching me. I caught his eye without meaning to. His cheeks reddened. His mother took the pair of sunglasses she'd pushed up onto her head and set them on the table. She frowned at the boy.

"Don't stare," she whispered.

"Ease up on the boy." The man with them chuckled. "Harry likes pretty girls."

"Robert, please," the woman said, frowning. "It embarrasses Harry when you talk like that."

"No, it doesn't. Does it, Harry?"

Harry reminded me of a younger Mike Wong, dorky and not quite sure where he fit. But unlike Mike, Harry would be vindicated later in life. He'd probably show up at his twenty-year high school reunion a stud, a pretty girl on his arm.

When I came out of the restroom, the waitress was serving Harry's family their breakfast. She refilled the man's coffee and set the check on the table. The woman smacked her lips in irritation.

"Why do they have to bring the check before we're done?" she said to her husband. "What if Harry wants more pancakes?"

"Ma'am," Charlie said, turning around. "All you need to do is order more, and I'll add it to the bill."

"I'll do that," the woman said with an exasperated sigh.

Harry looked out the window. Charlie sashayed behind the counter and dumped a filter full of coffee grounds in the trash, plopped a new filter into the coffee maker and pushed the Brew button. I wanted to kidnap Harry and save him the heartache of twisted parents.

I ordered orange juice, scrambled eggs, a waffle, and two slices of ham. The cook poured batter from a pitcher into the waffle maker. He took a drag off a cigarette and set it in the ashtray. The batter oozed out of the sides of the waffle maker. I rubbed my stiff neck.

I patted the fold of bills in the front pocket of my jeans. I had plenty of money to get to Camp Pendleton. I'd call my mother, convince her not to come after me. I gulped down the OJ. Charlie poured another glass and set it in front of me.

"Sleeping in my VW kills my neck, too." She wrinkled her freckled nose. "The beach is more comfortable."

"How'd you know?" I asked, feeling as if I'd been spied on.

"I saw your car in the parking lot last night." She frowned as I poured ketchup over the eggs. "Are you from inland?"

"North," I said. "Near Salinas. Do you surf a lot?"

"What a question." The cook looked up from garnishing a plate and laughed. "Charlene's hooked. All that waiting and waiting for the next big wave. Heck, I can wait on dry land."

Charlie laughed and went over to pick up the family's plates. The cook came out and poured himself some coffee. He took a sip.

"Too damn strong, like machine oil." The cook's face twisted in disgust. "Charlene's father used to drink it the same way."

He ate an orange slice and spit the rind in the trash. The waffle was like cardboard. I drowned it in syrup and ate.

"Waffles okay?" the cook asked.

"Delicious."

A few new customers filtered in. I watched the people order and the cook work. Charlie called most of her customers by their first names. The family came up to the counter and paid. Charlie started to hand the woman the change.

"Keep it," the man said.

"Dear," his wife said, "that's a five-dollar tip."

"So what?" The man laughed. He waved Charlie's hand away. "We're on vacation."

Harry, who seemed used to their arguing, stared at his Converse sneakers. His mother hurried out of the diner and over to a camper parked across the street. Charlie stuck the money in her apron pocket. Harry's father slapped him on the back, and they went out the door.

"You'll be a lady killer yet, Harry, my boy," the father said.

"She's going to leave without them, you watch," Charlie said to me. "I've seen this happen before. Couples always fight on vacation."

The camper's muffler spit out wisps of exhaust. Harry and his father shouted and waved their arms. They ran towards the moving camper. Charlie smiled.

"Told you," she said.

I watched her bus several dirty tables. She lifted the bus tub easily, as if the weight were no trouble. She slid the tub of dishes under the counter and bobbed up, wearing Harry's mother's sunglasses. The white frames extended two inches beyond her face. I laughed. The cook growled at her.

"She's the kind of woman who'll come back," he said. "Better stick them in the lost and found."

Charlie tossed the sunglasses in a drawer and gave me a shrug. Smiling, she wiped grease from a menu. I thought of Ing, ripping off the Castroville 7-Eleven. Charlie seemed so easy-going. She had Ing's charm, without the whiny manipulation.

Two women came into the diner and sat at a table against the wall. Charlie put down the salt shaker she was filling. She grabbed two menus, her pen and pad.

"My regulars," she whispered. "The tall one has oatmeal with skimmed milk. Dumpy has a patty melt with two eggs scrambled."

Charlie slid by me. I heard the heavy-set woman ask Charlie if she'd been surfing. Smiling, Charlie put pen to order pad.

"Every day, Pru. You want the usual?"

"Honey, bring me French toast this morning. I'm sick to death of patty melts."

Charlie clipped the order to the rack over the grill. The cook was in the back bitching at the dishwasher. Charlie asked my name.

"Gina," I said.

"You need a friend, Gina." She straightened the barrette in her hair. "Come down to the beach later. Paddle around with us."

"I have to leave," I said.

"Running away or towards trouble?" She laughed. "Gina?"

"Neither," I said, unsure of her tone.

The cook tossed a hamburger patty on the grill without looking at the order. Charlie watched me peel a twenty-dollar bill from Tall Larry's wad.

"I'm off at two," she said. "Come to the beach with us."

I wanted to, but I felt shy. And lost, suddenly. Her invitation had reminded me I was alone in a town I didn't know.

"Suit yourself," she said.

~

Up the street from the diner, people were coming in and out of shops and the post office. The air smelled saltier than earlier. The sky was bluer, as if a lid had been removed to make more room for the blue. Pismo Beach was about the size of Tristes, but it had the ocean and only one set of mountains, which made it feel borderless. I found a phone booth next to a surf shop. A sign on the surf shop windows advertised *50% Off Except Surfboards*.

"Sheila, where are you?" My mother cut the collect call operator off in midsentence. "Where the hell are you?"

"You're smoking," I said. It was a stupid thing to say. But I couldn't think about the mess I'd left her to clean up. Or about George's reaction to it.

"Sheila, you're seventeen years old," my mother said, her voice cracking. "You have no clothes and no money, and you're all alone out there." She sounded desperate. "Dr. Wong said King could never have made it." She let out a deep sigh. "Shee, did you shoot Rusty?"

The man with the dogs was coming up the street. The dachshund trotted along on leash now, leaving a light trail of sand under his paws. The retriever lagged behind.

"He was suffering," I said.

George would never accept the truth. But Rusty had killed King. This had justified my shooting him.

"And King?" my mother choked.

"He wasn't nearly as bad as Rusty," I said. I ran my fingers through my brows. My head hurt. "Mom, Rusty was almost dead."

"You just left, Shee." She was sobbing. "How could you do that?"

"Is Annie okay?" I asked. "She didn't see, did she?"

"Fortunately, I'd dropped her at the mailbox." My mother blew her nose. "I managed to haul Rusty out back and mop up before she came inside with the mail."

"What did you tell her?" I asked. "About King?"

"It was strange, she didn't ask about him. I told her Rusty was with George and that he'd taken him out to live with Will and Linda for a while." I heard a match strike. My mother inhaled. "He buried Rusty above the pasture. I tried to get him to wait. It was pitch-dark. He turned his ankle. He got drunk that night. It was horrible."

I imagined George scrambling around under the eucalyptus, jabbing his shovel at the earth and cursing me. I'd finally done something he had good reason to hate me for. There was a loud clatter in my ear. My mother had dropped the phone. She came back on.

"I'm headed for Camp Pendleton," I said. I heard Annie in the background. "I have to see Josh."

"You can't just show up, Sheila," my mother said. "They have regulations."

"Put Annie on," I said. "I want to talk to her."

"Call your brother," my mother snapped. "Here, I'll give you the number." I heard her fumbling for her address book. "Do you have a pen?"

I wrote down the number. Down the street, a rectangle of ocean connected the last two buildings on the block.

"Annie's out with the pony," my mother said. "Call back tomorrow, and you can talk to her."

I opened the phone booth. The warm air was tempered by an ocean breeze. The blue sea beckoned. Maybe the sun and sand would erase Tristes from my mind.

Twenty-Five

Down at the beach, waves rolled in, long and silent. Oil rigs perched along the horizon. Their sharp forms reminded me of the structures Josh used to make with his erector set. On the rare occasion, he had swapped a piece he had positioned for one I had handed him. I had caused the collapse of at least one of Josh's buildings. And now, there was King to tell him about.

I'd been sitting on the beach for nearly two hours before Charlie showed up with her friend Sam. The two of them paddled out and then in circles beyond the first line of breakers. Charlie stood on the board and thrust it into the wave.

The conversation with my mother had not gone well. She probably assumed I would come home after I saw Josh, provided they allowed me onto the base. When I tried phoning Josh, the Camp Pendleton operator had refused my collect call. I would have to just show up and see what happened.

I watched Charlie ride a wave in. She stopped near the shore, where the water went flat and foamy. She waved at me, flipped her board around like it was part of her, and paddled out again. She'd been surprised to find me sitting on the beach. She introduced me to Sam, stripped down to her bikini and wiggled her compact, freckled body into a wetsuit. Sam, tall, lanky, and in his early twenties, had looked at Charlie adoringly.

Now, Sam angled his board inside the curl of white water. He howled at Charlie paddling out. I watched him ride in.

"Nice day," he called and hopped off the board. "You want to try? I've got a spare wetsuit in my truck."

"No, thanks." I was too tired to attempt a new sport. "You're very good."

"Charlie's better." Sam unzipped the top of his wetsuit and pulled out a plastic bag wrapped in duct tape. "She could easily go pro."

"Why doesn't she?" I asked.

"Her mom didn't want her to." He shrugged. "Daddy's a pro surfer." He unrolled the package and pulled out a lighter and a joint. "He skipped out on them when Charlie was eight, moved to the Big Island. Charlie's mom hates him."

I wondered if Charlie ever saw her father. Sam handed me the lit joint. He dabbed a finger on his lip to remove a stray leaf of pot. Charlie floated beyond the breakers now. A seal bobbed to the surface. They floated there together.

"Have you seen *Jaws*?" I asked Sam.

"Bullshit hysteria." Sam snorted. "I knew a surfer who got bit down in Southern Cal, though. Guy learned to surf on one leg."

Frowning, I tried to picture the one-legged surfer. Talk about passion and determination. Sam nudged me and smiled.

"Gina, I'm kidding." He shook his head. "Is that why you don't want to surf?"

"No." I handed him the joint. I wished I'd thought of a different name to give Charlie. Gina sounded like a dumb-blond name. "I'm pretty wiped out from driving last night."

Charlie slid to a stop in front of us. She hopped off her board and slipped her leg from the leash. Water poured from her thigh-length wet suit and down her taut calves. Sam watched her come up to the dry sand. I recognized the look in Sam's hazel eyes. *Love me the way I love you.* Jimmy and Ing all over again. Charlie flopped down on the sand next to me.

"Looks like you and the seal have a thing going," Sam said to her.

"I swear it's the same seal we saw yesterday." Charlie smiled and raked her toes through the sand. "We're buddies."

The seal ducked under a wave. He resurfaced closer to shore. He blinked his onyx eyes at us. I thought of King. All critters' eyes, save Rusty's, had the same innocence. I turned my head away from Sam and Charlie. I couldn't cry. Not in front of two strangers. And once I got going, there was no telling.

"I think I'll take Mr. Seal home with me." Charlie laughed. "Let me have a hit, Sam."

Sam relit the joint. The erector sets swayed on the seam of sky and sea. I asked Sam what kind of pot we were smoking.

"Da kind," he said, patting the plastic pouch next to him. "Two hits and you're good to go."

"No kidding," I said.

The seal swam south along the shoreline. It seemed to have forgotten about us. Charlie piled sand with her feet and turned to me.

"Sam's brother owns a great bar in SLO." Sand clung to the bridge of her nose. "It's called Wink's. You can stay over at my house, leave tomorrow."

San Luis Obispo was twenty miles north. The wrong direction. I had to keeping moving. And the last thing I wanted was to go to another bar with two more broken souls. Sam cupped his hand to the side of his mouth.

"Charlie feels a kinship between you," he said, glancing at Charlie. "And we're curious about why you're in Pismo. Lots of people land here. But not many young girls like you, alone."

He pushed sand with his feet onto Charlie's pile. Charlie frowned at him and struck the pile with her heel. Sam pretended to pout.

"What I had said to Sam before we got here is," Charlie explained to me, "you've got a story. And in the right atmosphere, you'll tell us."

"No story," I said, thinking it might help to talk to two people I would never seen again. "I'm just driving south."

"See, Gina, we're bored." Sam laughed. "Looking for new blood."

A speedboat ripped across the water. The ocean churned in its wake. The seal had disappeared. Suddenly I no longer felt capable of saying what I wanted or being where I wanted to be. Maybe it was Sam's pot. I had finally run out of steam.

"Then it's settled," Charlie said. "We'll hang around the beach, take a drive, and then go to Wink's."

~

Sam's brother's place was shut down for termite removal so we ended up at another bar. I fell asleep beforehand and woke up as Sam pulled his white Toyota pickup into the parking lot. I sat between Charlie and Sam. This arrangement had seemed fine all afternoon, but now I felt trapped.

Charlie sprinkled some cocaine onto her fist and put it under my nose. I shook my head. She cleared it from her hand in one snort.

I wanted to be home, in my bed. Not Bear Road. C Street. King curled up at the foot of my bed. I'd been all over Pismo with Sam and Charlie. We'd bounced down a long dirt road to buy the coke from a dealer Sam knew. Rusted-out cars littered the front yard. Three German shepherds snarled at us from a side yard ripe with the smell of dog shit.

The dealer took a bottle of peppermint schnapps out of a mini-fridge he kept next to the sofa. Charlie, Sam, and the dealer talked at once, competing with each other and the noise of the TV. We had toasted. "To friends, man," the dealer had said.

"The bar looks dead," Sam said.

"No prob." Charlie ran her finger over her gums. "You like to dance, Gina? I bet they have a jukebox." She laughed a nervous, coked-up laugh. "Looks like that kind of place."

Who were these people, and what the hell was I doing with them? Rain pecked at the streaked windshield. A couple got out of an Opel sedan. They walked arm in arm into the bar.

"My dog died." I wasn't sure if I'd said it out loud.

"So this is what happened?" Charlie asked. Her tongue raced around her lips. She leaned closer to me and spoke in a somber tone. "This is why you're in Pismo?"

"She just said what happened, dummy," Sam said, his voice low and a little mean.

At the dealer's house, Sam had tried to kiss Charlie, and she had pushed him away. She told him she wasn't "in the space." Sam had been acting pissed off ever since.

"He was an old black Lab," I said, anticipating the next question. Had it only been yesterday? I had lost track of time. "I buried him next to the river."

"That's too sad." Charlie sighed. "I'm going to be tripping on it all night."

"Fuck, Charlie," Sam yelled. "Gina's finally telling her story, and you don't want to hear it? That's fucking cold. But then you're cold. So I don't know why I'd be surprised." He turned to me. "This is how she is. Charms you, then shoves you aside."

Charlie stared straight ahead. I could hear her heart pounding. Her hand fumbled for the door handle. Sam opened his door and got out.

"Come on, Charlie," he yelled. "Cut the drama. We've been on this bridge before."

I slid across the seat and followed Charlie into the bar. The rain was cold. My tummy growled. I hadn't eaten since the dry waffle at the diner.

⁓

The air conditioner in the bar was blasting. Charlie and I sat shivering in a booth while Sam went to order our drinks. The couple in the Opel sat at the end of the bar. When the woman talked, her straight dark hair swung in one motion.

"I had a Dalmatian," Charlie said. "He got run over by my school bus. My mother couldn't stand the dog. He used to jump all over her pink furniture. Sam says my mother's 'iconic.'"

Sam had flunked out of Harvard. He was now working on his electrician's license. His ex-wife and six-year-old daughter needed the income. They lived in Santa Maria, below Santa Barbara. "My kid's sweeter than an angel," Sam had said on the beach that afternoon. He saw her a few times a month if her mother cooperated with the schedule she and Sam had arranged.

The bartender plugged in the jukebox. The lights flashed and dinged. Sam set down our drinks, his face aglow in the jukebox. I took a big gulp of orange juice.

"Vodka," I said, grimacing.

"Sorry," Sam said. "I thought you wanted a screwdriver."

I pushed the glass away. Too bad the bartender hadn't carded me and thrown us out of the bar. My car was still at the diner. I wished Tall Larry were here. He'd get me away from Charlie and Sam and tell me where to go.

The man sitting at the bar got up and dropped some quarters in the jukebox. He shimmied back to his woman, snapping his fingers. Frank Sinatra crooned.

"Dance with me, sweet lady." He held his hand out.

"You're so funny, Eddy." She laughed girlishly. "Do you know how much I love you?"

The man had his eyes closed. His hand caressed the woman's back. His wedding band gleamed in the pinkish light of the jukebox. His wife whispered in his ear. Sam watched them dance. Charlie shook her head and turned to me.

"Sam's romanticizing," she said. "He thinks they have this perfect relationship."

"Shut up, Charlene," Sam said.

He shoved the table, joggling the drinks. He stood up and threw down a ten-dollar bill. Charlie stared at the bill. Sam grabbed his jacket and his drink.

"And unless you girls want to walk home," he said, gulping down the last of his drink, "you're leaving too."

⁓

On the freeway back to Pismo, Sam sped the truck to sixty, seventy, eighty-five. The Toyota rattled like a jackhammer. The speedometer edged to ninety, ninety-five mph.

"Slow the fuck down," Charlie yelled.

Sam took the Pismo Beach exit. He turned down a narrow, dimly-lit residential street. The truck engine quieted. Charlie sighed and wiped her eyes. I got the feeling they'd spent more than a few nights fighting like this.

"Piece of shit," Sam muttered. "Fuck my ex-wife and her bills. I'm buying a new truck."

"Where are you going?" Charlie asked. "Sheila wants her car."

The diner was in the opposite direction. Apparently Charlie had gathered I wouldn't be spending the night at her house. Or maybe she planned to stay with Sam after all. I figured I'd drive to Camp Pendleton and beg the guard to let me in to see Josh. If I had to, I'd sneak in.

A tabby cat darted into the street. Sam slammed on the breaks. I hit the dash. My head bounced, and I fell back against the seat. Charlie was screaming. Blood trickled from her forehead. The rearview mirror lay in her lap.

"You're a fucking asshole, Sam." She touched her forehead and started to sob. "I'm fucking bleeding."

Sam turned off the engine and flicked on the cab light. He examined the cut on Charlie's head.

"I'll take you to the emergency room." He reached behind the seat for a towel. "I have to make a quick stop, first."

"What?" Charlie screamed. She winced and pressed the towel to her forehead. "Are you insane?"

How had I gotten myself in this position? Pismo Beach was

no better than Tristes. The only difference was the ocean and that I was alone. I was so alone, I could hardly feel myself anymore.

Sam drove half a block and pulled into a short driveway. The house was dark. A "For Sale" sign jutted from the lawn. Sam left the headlights on. The light shone on the Radio Flyer wagon in front of the white garage.

"Sam?" Charlie stared at the cracked windshield. She had stopped crying. "What are you doing? It's a wagon, Sam."

Without a word, Sam got out of the truck. He didn't look angry anymore, just tired. A soft rain had started to fall.

"The wagon's his daughter's," Charlie said to me. "Her mother forgot to pack it when they moved last week." She rubbed her head. "I think I have a concussion. I'm dizzy as hell."

I watched Sam tip the red wagon on its side. Water trickled onto the asphalt. He carried the wagon to the back of the truck. There was a loud clatter in the truck bed. Then he got back in the truck.

Twenty-Six

West of Highway 5, the brown-pink sunrise saturated the cracker-box houses and buildings of Anaheim. Sleeping Beauty's Castle, a dull jewel embedded in the smoggy landscape. Daddy had once called Anaheim the armpit of Southern California.

I'd been driving for several hours on no sleep, aside from a catnap at 3 A.M. in the back seat before I left Pismo. I'd managed to catch a few winks before that in the San Luis Obispo E.R., where Charlie had her forehead stitched up. Sam had drowned his cottonmouth and remorse in Coca-Cola from the waiting-room vending machine. He had talked about getting custody of his daughter. A long shot, he'd admitted.

I looked in the rearview mirror to see if anyone was sharing the road with me. Buck cackled. I swerved at a white Mercedes. The driver shook his fist at me.

Poetic, isn't it—you and me on the road together?

"*You and me* don't exist," I said. "Get lost."

I turned on the radio. Big-band jazz. I cranked up the volume to drown out Buck's voice. The fear I'd been feeling since leaving Pismo felt looming and nameless. I had been trying to ignore this feeling. But every time Buck spoke, the fear grabbed me again. He seemed to leave me alone when I stood up to him. As I drove, the fear subsided and memories flowed.

The trip to Disneyland with Daddy, my mother, Josh and Bea. Daddy had driven through the night to avoid the summer heat. He stopped in Burbank to pick up Bea. Bea had insisted on accompanying her grandchildren to meet Mickey Mouse. Josh and me sat with Bea in the back seat. I was about to lose my first tooth and kept my tongue busy poking at it. Bea tried to get me to leave the tooth alone, her theory being that a left-alone tooth falls out sooner than a forced tooth. This memory stood out in my mind more than any other aspect of Disneyland.

That night, the four of us were supposed to crash on Bea's living room floor and pullout couch. Somewhere south of San Luis Obispo, I woke up in the car. Bea was gone. My parents had dropped her off in Burbank. My mother was driving.

"I don't know what you want me to say, Roy." She spoke in her deliberately calm tone.

The headlights on a southbound car flickered on Josh's face. His eyelids twitched. In the front seat, my father yawned.

"For Christ's sake, Alice," he said. "I was dreaming. People say all kinds of things in their sleep."

The lighter clicked in the dash. A few seconds later, the lighter popped out. My mother took a drag on her cigarette.

"What would you do if I made a 'mistake,' as you call it?"

"I'd try to forgive you." My father turned to stare out the passenger-side window. "It's over, Alice. I keep telling you this."

"I'm not so sure you're done." My mother's fingertips drummed the top of the steering wheel. "You just said her name."

"Don't tell me men don't look at you," my father snapped. "And that you don't look back. What about George Fratti? Always eyeing you at the Steak Pit."

"Looking is one thing, Roy." My mother sighed. "And George isn't like that."

"George." My father snorted. "How affectionate."

"Shut up, Roy."

I worked my tongue over the loose tooth. It was holding on by a thread. I thrust my tongue sideways. The tooth fell out and into my open hand. I wanted to make an announcement. But my parents were preoccupied. I didn't understand their words, but their import was clear. They were fighting.

"Let's get a drink at the pink place," my father said.

"What about the kids?" my mother asked.

"Let them sleep," he said. "It's the Madonna Inn exit."

The car buoyed over some potholes and parked. I closed my eyes. My mother leaned over the seat to check on us. I smelled cigarette breath, lemony perfume. She pushed down the door locks.

"They'll be fine," I heard Daddy say.

Their voices faded into the night. I sat up. The Madonna Inn was lit up like a birthday cake. Josh was sound asleep. I poked his shoulder several times, but he didn't stir. I ran my finger around the tooth, so tiny in my hand.

~

I drove through El Toro, Mission Viejo, and San Juan Capistrano. The Spanish names of these towns comforted me, made me forget the other Spanish name. Rosalinda.

In San Clemente, leaf-blown driveways led to hidden mansions. Rolls Royces gleamed like trophies. Daddy had betrayed my mother. But had he loved this other woman? Wasn't my mother the love Daddy had waited for?

Farther south, San Onofre Beach sparkled from the pine-studded coast to the cloudless horizon. A sign said "Camp Pendleton, 10 miles." After Josh, I'd drive to Mexico, through Central and South America. I'd find a job. I'd save up and take a boat to Africa, then Australia. I'd learn the languages and break a few hearts. Daddy and Buck Hanson would have nothing on me.

~

The armed guard at Camp Pendleton's main entrance wore combat fatigues. He ran his right thumb down a clipboard. Stubs that had been fingers seemed to wiggle involuntarily. I pictured the grenade going off before he had a chance to throw it at the enemy. The dismembered digits blown to bits. Forever separated.

"Here you are," he said. "We had you arriving yesterday, Miss."

For a moment, I was surprised when he located my name on his clipboard. Of course. My mother had called the base to make sure Josh knew I was coming. I'd be more likely to come home if I got on the base.

"I had to make a stop," I said.

The guard came out of the station house. His combat boots shone. He taped an orange pass to the inside of my windshield.

"Private O'Connor is waiting at the First Marine Division headquarters." He handed me a map. "Take Vandergrift Boulevard, turn right on Fourteenth Street, go past the Red Cross. Headquarters on the left."

"How big is this place?" I asked.

"Two hundred square miles, seventeen of them pristine coastline." He saluted me. "Welcome to Camp Pendleton."

I'd expected barracks and concrete bunkers, not green land and wildlife. A decent-size river ran along Vandergrift. Starlings flitted along the banks. On the other side of Vandergrift, a golf course cut a velvet swath along the coastal hills. Josh, also dressed in fatigues, was waiting out in front of the Red Cross. He gave me a long hug.

"Your hair's growing out," I said, not quite ready to discuss King. "I'm famished."

"There's a dining room," he said, studying the gray sweatshirt I'd picked up at the 76 Station. "It's just a few minute's walk from here."

"I guess you talked to Mom," I said. "The guard with the blown-off fingers let me in, no problem."

Josh stopped walking. His hand was firm on my arm. I tried to pull away, but his hand closed around my wrist. The Marines had made him stronger.

"Watch what you say around here," he whispered. He let go of my wrist. "People have made sacrifices. They deserve respect."

"Yes, sir."

"Please." He sighed. "Don't mock me."

"I wasn't mocking you." His words stunned me. "I promise."

A golf cart whooshed past us. Josh saluted the driver. The cart squeaked to a stop. A spry elderly man with a full head of snowy hair hopped out. His golf cleats clattered on the street.

"That's Major Marino," Josh whispered. "Please be nice."

"This must be your lovely sister," the major bellowed. He put his arm around Josh. "Josh is popular around here. We're working on getting him assigned permanently."

"I'd like that, sir," Josh said.

"Damn straight, O'Connor." The major gave Josh a hearty slap on the back. "I don't want to lose my best caddy."

The major turned to me. I was acutely aware of my dirty jeans and messy hair. There was no doubt I looked like hell.

"Aren't you a little young to be gallivanting around the state?" The major's blue eyes twinkled.

"She's old enough, sir," Josh said. "Nearly eighteen."

"I'm sorry about the family dog." The major frowned and shook his snowy head. "I've seen men die, but a dog dying hurts like nothing else." His legs did a little skip. "I'd better go, now." He smiled at me. "The missus wants me home."

The major hopped back into the golf cart. The cart went around a towering elm. The clubs in the black golf bag in the back of the cart jiggled as the major made the turn. I turned to Josh.

"You didn't tell him about Rusty," I said.

"I left that part out," he said. "It's a little gruesome."

"I don't know why I came here," I said. "It's all black and white with you. You used to be able to see the in-between."

"Admit it." He caught himself chewing his thumbnail and shoved his hand in his pocket. "You were looking for revenge. Rusty might have lived."

"See it as you like," I snapped. "I don't know what Mom and George told you, but you weren't there."

"You still want to eat?" He kicked at the ground. "The food's decent."

"I guess so," I said.

We walked toward the cafeteria without speaking. Above the golf course, oaks dotted the hills. A trail wound among the trees and up to a ridge. A red-tailed hawk floated in the empty blue.

"It's pretty here," I said.

I wanted to reach for his hand. To let him know I was sad about King. Sad about a lot of things.

"I'm lucky," Josh said. "Supposedly, it's the prettiest base in the country."

I thought about how Mike Wong, Tall Larry, and me had

dug the grave and the river had been copper-lit in the falling sun. Josh should have been there, too. Then he'd see that King dying and me shooting Rusty had been unavoidable events. As fated as Jimmy dying and Daddy dying and Ing's and my friendship shattering. It seemed to me that according to the new Josh, you don't pull a gun on your stepfather's dog. Not even if he's killed your family dog of fourteen years.

~

The cafeteria was teeming with people. I smelled bacon, and my stomach growled. We got in line. Josh handed me a tray and nodded to a Marine with an acne-riddled face. The Marine turned around to ask the young woman behind the cafeteria counter for two ladles of gravy. The woman wore a net over her red wavy hair and a plain T-shirt under a base-issued apron. She poured the gravy and handed the plate to the Marine.

"O'Malley," Josh said. "This is my sister, Sheila."

"You drove all this way to see this clown?" O'Malley smiled at Josh and shook my hand. "My sister would tell me to jump in a lake."

O'Malley's hand was clammy, his laugh adolescent and high-pitched. Like Josh, he was young and had not yet experienced real combat. Probably the Marines had been a career choice because nothing else had sounded good.

The gravy girl gestured with her ladle. I asked her for extra gravy on my biscuits, and Josh and me continued through the line. The people in line with us looked like regular people. Civilians who worked on the base, military personnel in fatigues. Most of them seemed relaxed, happy to be there.

Josh and I sat at an empty table. I dug into the biscuits and gravy on my plate. The gravy tasted salty and warm, the biscuits doughy. Josh put down his fork and looked around the dining room.

"I'm sorry I lost my temper outside," he said.

"I could say the same thing," I said, wiping gravy from my mouth. I felt my stomach relax. "I guess I'd been hoping you'd listen to my side of the story. Being that I was there."

"Mom says you were in Pismo," he said.

"Yeah," I said, following his lead. He did not want to discuss King. Not here. "I met some people. Surfers."

"You can't just run away, Shee." He frowned. "You've got school."

At the next table, O'Malley got up to reload his tray. He chatted with the redhead wearing the hairnet. She smiled and wiped the strip of counter around the clean plates.

"School's overrated," I said. "Even Hasbin thinks so."

"When did he say that?" Josh asked.

"At Jimmy's funeral." Hasbin had said no such thing. But at the funeral reception at the Emmonses', he had acted like nothing mattered to him anymore. "Hasbin feels real bad about what happened with Jimmy."

"Me too," Josh said. He stared straight ahead. His jaw twitched. "I shouldn't have left." He turned to me. "I mean, do you ever think it works that way, Shee?" His eyes filled. "One change of plans changes everything that follows?"

"No, Josh," I said, leaning closer. "Leaving is good."

"Then do it the right away," he said, swallowing, his eyes now dry. "Finish school, Shee, then decide."

"The right way," I muttered, shoving another bite of biscuits and gravy in my mouth. "You mean your way?"

"Let's take a walk." He pushed his tray aside. "There's something I want to tell you."

~

The Marine Memorial Golf Course had just been watered. Our shoes made squishing noises in the grass. Moisture seeped through the seams of my sneakers and into my socks. A squirrel scampered across a raked sand trap and up a tree trunk. The bushy tail flickered sunlight. A bench sat under the tree.

"So where do they hide all the weapons?" I asked, sighing. Eating had made me feel my exhaustion. "Or is that a secret?"

"Fallbrook Weapons Station." Josh pointed northeast.

"This place reminds me of summer camp," I said.

"A lot of people say that," he said, smiling.

There was pride in his voice. He loved the place. And not only because the base wasn't Tristes. He had grown up, seemed to feel better in his own skin. It would be unfair of me to begrudge him this. I asked him if he remembered our trip to Disneyland. He smiled.

"Are you kidding? The Pirates of the Caribbean traumatized me for life."

"Yeah." I sat on the bench. "Anyway, in the car on the way home you and me were sleeping in the backseat. I woke to Mom and Dad fighting."

He raised an eyebrow. Fighting had not been unusual. I shifted on the bench.

"Daddy had an affair, Josh," I said, swallowing. "I just figured this out."

"More than one." He reached for my hand. "You need to hear this, Shee."

"Hear what?" I choked. "So he had affairs."

I sensed Daddy's infidelities were only part of the story. Josh looked up the fairway. A cart sped along the edge of the course. A small group of golfers moseyed towards us. The jagged leather things on their shoes flapped as the men walked. A caddy jogged behind them, weighed down by a golf bag on each shoulder.

"Shee." Josh turned to me. "Dad committed suicide. You know that, don't you?"

"Over a woman?" I said. "Don't be stupid. He was drunk. It was an accident."

"Goddamn it, Sheila. He meant for that train to hit him, and you know it." Anger flashed in his eyes. "Maybe it wasn't over a woman, but he did it. He was sick, Shee."

"What about Mom?" A sob erupted from way down deep inside me. I forced the tears back. "What does Mom say about this? Did she tell you to tell me this?"

"She knew that night," he whispered. "This is just you and me now, saying the truth aloud."

There was a whispering sound behind us. A great egret perched at the top of a large pine tree. The bird unfolded its glorious wings. As if on marionette strings, the egret sailed up the fairway. It landed on another pine tree, a few hundred yards away. I turned to my brother, desperate for an explanation. I could hardly get the words out.

"What about that?" I pointed at the egret. "Remember what Daddy always said? 'Find the beauty, no matter what.'"

"We can find it, Shee." Josh wiped his eyes. "You can. You always do. That's how you're different."

My body began to shake. The truth approached, jarring yet familiar. The feeling retreated for a moment, but then it came again, along with all the times I'd wondered how my father hadn't seen the train, loud as it had been and often as it had passed through.

"Now I know for sure," I whispered.

Josh pulled me close. Just like I had pulled Rosie close in the Emmonses' backyard the other day. I buried my head in Josh's fatigues.

In my mind and body, in every part of me, the wheels pounded the rails. The house shook uncontrollably, and the windows rattled. And then all was still.

The egret soared toward us. A wingspan of easily four feet. When the bird got close to us, it ascended in a *whoosh* of temperate air. The egret's flight leveled out above the tree line.

"Come on." Josh grabbed my hand. "Quick."

At the far end of the golf course, he led me up the trail through the oaks. I was out of breath, dripping with sweat. But I kept going.

"That bird's long gone," I called, inhaling the scent of oak. "Long gone."

"We're not after the egret," Josh yelled. He turned around and grinned at me. "Hurry up, before I get caught acting like a crazy man."

At the top of the hill, a dozen sheep grazed in a clearing. Their tails flicked, shooing away flies. I looked for a place to sit down to catch my breath. Leaves crunched under my sneakers.

"You dragged me up here to see sheep?" I asked.

Josh put his finger to his lips. He pointed at a small man napping on a boulder. The man's face was creviced, the color of molasses. He opened his eyes and stared up at the sky. Josh nudged me.

"He's the base's shepherd," Josh whispered. "Just wait."

The shepherd straightened his canvas hat and sat up. One of the smaller sheep baaed. A ewe nudged her lamb.

"Ah, tú quieres música," the shepherd said and chuckled.

He took a wooden flute from the inside pocket of his peacoat. Smiling, he waved the flute at the sheep. They came toward him, their white heads turned as if to better hear the music the shepherd would play. When I reached for Josh's hand, he was right there.

That night, I slept in one of the Camp Pendleton apartments reserved for family visitors. I lay on the lumpy mattress and closed my eyes. I felt Josh untie my sneakers, the weight of an extra blanket over me. His footsteps retreated down the hall, his step lighter now. He'd done what I'd come for him to do.

Twenty-Seven

Carlsbad, Leucadia, Moonlight, San Elijo, then Cardiff. The glittering beaches unfurled below Highway 1. Sailboats dotted the flat water. A toy-size aircraft carrier headed toward Imperial Beach Naval Air Station, where Josh had done his basic training. I felt as though I could drive forever.

I'd left Pendleton this morning without saying goodbye to Josh. He would have wanted to know my plans, and I had no clue where I was going. South and that was all I knew. He had probably called my mother to let her know I was safe and reasonably sound. Someday I would have my own conversation with her. By phone, letter, or telegram if I had to, but not in person. I was done with family, done with Tristes.

Just outside of Chula Vista, a gunshot, or so I thought, exploded behind me. I gripped the steering wheel to avoid swerving into a station wagon in the slow lane. I reached out the open window, adjusted my side mirror. Left rear tire, blown. The deflated rubber *whapped* the road.

I edged onto the shoulder, turned off the engine, and got out of the car to examine the flat. An embedded nail, twisted into a question mark. I walked up to the front of the car. Cars sped by, the motion whipping my hair around my face. An Arco gas truck barreled past, horn blaring. I stumbled against the front bumper of the VW.

I recovered my balance, then took Mike's shovel from the trunk and set it against the front bumper. Dr. Wong had probably read Mike the riot act for forgetting his shovel. River dirt drifted from the blade and turned to dust.

I lifted out the spare and wheeled it over to the flat. A sleek black car approached in the fast lane. The car switched lanes, slowed. White top and door, marked with a gold star. Fucking Highway Patrol. My heart dropped to my stomach. The patrol car crept onto the shoulder and parked behind the VW.

"Shit," I muttered. "Shit, shit, shit."

I capped the lug wrench around the first bolt. Was the cop looking for me, or simply helping a motorist in distress? Act busy and the cop might receive a critical dispatch and head on down the road.

Loosening another bolt, I looked sideways so as not to appear guilty. The cherry top-lights on the patrol car blinked to a stop. The cop at the wheel wore mirrored sunglasses. Small nose, feminine lips. A woman cop. The first I'd seen. She appeared to be looking at the VW license plate. She spoke into the radio mike.

Then two shiny black boots stepped out of the patrol car. Fitted khaki uniform over a stocky build, hand on the billy club.

Dark brown hair tightly braided and pinned to the top of her head Heidi-style, just a hint of lipstick.

She sauntered over. To my surprise, she smiled. Then she nodded at the spare leaning against the wheel well, as if changing a flat was a unique concept. I finished loosening the lug nuts. Praying she wouldn't throw me into the back seat of her patrol car and redeposit me in Tristes.

"Can I see your driver's license?" she asked.

I put down the lug wrench and jumped when the metal clattered on the asphalt. I took my wallet from the glove box, careful not to show the wad of cash. My back produced copious sweat. My armpits were drowning. This morning's shower on the base had been a waste of time. I handed the cop my driver's license, glancing at her name tag. Sergeant Wilson.

"Tristes?" she asked. "Is that far from here?"

"It's near Salinas," I said. She had to be playing dumb. I wedged the jack under the car, adopted a casual tone. "Steinbeck country. Pretty place."

I lifted the flat off the axle. A year ago, I'd spent the day with Jimmy and Ing at the King City Fair. We had been about to leave when Jimmy noticed the flat on the Chevelle. Left rear, just like the VW now. I helped Jimmy change the tire while Ing went to pee. Off in the distance, the Ferris wheel lit up, and the sensuous drone of electric guitar floated across the parking lot. A hot, damp night, not a shiver of a breeze. Jimmy's arms had glistened. His breath smelled of cotton candy and beer. I had been tempted to kiss him that night. Would have had Ing not returned so quickly.

"Not many girls know how to change a tire," the cop said, watching me crank up the jack. "I'm impressed."

"My brother's at Imperial Beach."

Lying was getting easier. I wiped my greasy hands on my filthy jeans. The cop had my name but not my destination. By the time I got to Mexico, I'd have a whole string of lies behind me.

"I'm on my way to visit him," I added.

"I see." She glanced at the shovel. "You planning on digging a hole first?"

"The shovel belongs to a friend," I said, setting the spare on the axle. "I forgot to return it before I left."

She folded a stick of Juicy Fruit into her mouth and looked out at the ocean. Her sunglasses reflected the first line of breakers. She turned to me.

"You tell your brother . . . what's his name?"

"Joshua," I said. "Joshua O'Connor."

Hell's Angels buzzed by, a kaleidoscope of chrome exhaust pipes and sissy bars and wild-haired, tattooed men. The cop eyed the caravan of motorcycles. She was either gathering her thoughts or assessing the risk of letting the Hell's Angels go on their merry way. When they'd passed, she turned to me again.

"It's good of your brother, serving his country," she said, working the gum in her mouth. She gestured at the view. "Too many kids think all of this comes without a cost. You strike me as a conscientious person too. Loving to your family, etcetera." She eyed me again. "Am I right?"

"Sure, I love my family." I said, going along with her story. "Everyone does."

"Not necessarily." She shook her head. "Least they don't always demonstrate the love. Last summer, a young woman, not quite eighteen, runs away from home. Family's devastated, authorities looking for her. The whole bit. The girl finally shows up in Tecate, Mexico. Her mother was just sick about the whole thing." She nodded as I tightened the last lug nut. "I'm darn thankful I'm not a mother myself."

I lifted the flat into the trunk, tossing in the jack, lug wrench, and Mike's shovel. The latch didn't catch as usual. The cop nudged me out of the way, lifted the hood, peered at the latch.

"Bent," she said, slamming the hood. "There's a Chevron in Chula Vista, about a mile and a half south. Take the second exit, then go east four blocks. They'll fix your tire and your trunk." She smiled. "I promise I'll keep an eye out for you, coming back this direction. Make sure you don't have any more car trouble."

I muttered my appreciation and got into the car, still sweating like a rodeo bull. I edged the VW into the flow of traffic. The cop sped past me, radio mike to her mouth.

Home was out of the question. But if I kept driving south, I'd have the cop and her buddies on my ass. What was the saying? Someone to watch over me. *Daddy, where the hell are you when I need you?*

~

The Chula Vista heat in November made Salinas Valley in the summer seem mild. The mechanic at the Chevron station was backed up with cars until later this afternoon, so I left the VW and walked over to the Woolworth's to kill some time. I'd heard the border police only checked ID if you were entering the U.S. They didn't give a shit who entered Mexico, only who was leaving.

A white woman with bags under her eyes stood at the cash register. I asked her if the store carried hats and cold sodas. She looked me up and down as if I might try to steal something.

"Hats in aisle four." She clicked her frosted pink nails together in a semiprayer gesture. "Soda fountain's closed."

I tried on a straw cowboy hat like those the wetbacks in Tristes wore. Perfect fit. I wandered over to the dime-store paperbacks. *Nemesis* by Agatha Christie, *Jonathan Livingston Seagull*. I returned both books to the rack. I had to save my money, plan for the future.

Maybe I'd try the Baja coast. Years ago, Daddy had taken a few weeks' vacation alone and driven to the tip. He had returned to Tristes weathered and tan and full of stories about wide-ocean fishing, hospitable natives, and eternal sunshine. My mother, who had been left at home to tend to us, didn't speak to him for days.

I perused the postcard rack. Tall Larry and Mike Wong deserved a report. While I paid for the hat and postcards, a large Mexican woman waddled into the store. Her toes extended beyond the toe of her beige sandals. A Chihuahua peered out from the armpit of the woman's purple polyester blouse.

"Perdóneme," she asked the clerk. "You have Boney Donie?"

"It's pronounced 'Bonnie Doone.'" The clerk's mouth twisted in contempt. "Woolworth's has a no-dogs policy, lady."

The Mexican woman looked at me with confused eyes. I glared at the clerk and let the Chihuahua sniff my hand. His master's silver front teeth gleamed when she smiled at me. She could've been a worker from the packing shed.

"My English no good," she said, shaking her salt-and-pepper head. She stroked the dog's tiny head. "He is called Corazón." She placed her open hand on her blouse, under her enormous left breast. "Like here."

"Es bonito," I said. I looked at the clerk, daring her to throw out the woman and her dog. "Isn't he adorable?"

The Chihuahua licked my palm and blinked his shiny brown-button eyes at me. The dog lifted two front paws onto my shoulder. His pink tongue licked my chin. Like King's love in a much smaller package. The Mexican woman chortled. The clerk tried not to smile.

"He kisses me only." The Mexican woman poked my arm gently. "Now you. Bravo."

Her crepe soles shuffled over to the makeup counter. I set the cowboy hat on my head and refused the clerk's offer of a bag for the two postcards. As I left the store, the Mexican woman approached the cash register. She set her purchases on the counter.

"Adios," she called. She lifted the dog's front paw to make him wave. "Muchas gracias."

"De nada," I said. "Señora."

In front of Woolworth's, a Chula Vista city bus spewed diesel exhaust at the curb. An old man and a boy holding a leather book bag got up from the bench. I sat down and watched the two get on the bus. The book bag swayed from the boy's shoulder. Behind him, the old man lifted his legs slowly up the steps. He dug into the pocket of his baggy suit jacket and pulled out some coins. The change *pinged* into the fare box. The bus doors clamped shut.

Watching the bus pull away, I thought of Josh leaving Tristes. My mother's inability to stop him. And now me. Seventeen and on the road.

I wrote out the postcards. Mike Wong's showed a crude map of California's missions, Tall Larry's, a frothy stretch of the San Diego coastline.

Hi Mike. Tell Hasbin I'll make up the chem final. I have your shovel. Sincerely, Sheila

Dear Larry. If you visit King, say a prayer for him and me. One day, maybe you can paint the ocean too. Yours, Sheila O'Connor

I addressed the postcards to Tristes Union High School, Tristes, California. 93926. I had never written to anyone in my hometown because I'd never left it. My writing looked foreign, and I questioned what I'd written. Maybe I should just call.

I dropped the postcards in a mailbox kitty-corner from

Woolworth's, on the sidewalk between a three-story office building and Sambo's Restaurant. Down the narrow alley, I heard the soft gurgle of a fountain. A wood bench sat under an olive tree. A respite for the workers, maybe. I was tempted. But I had a phone call to make.

I spotted a pay phone just inside Sambo's. I gambled on Annie answering. I burst into tears when she said, "Hello." After two attempts by the operator, and me talking over her, Annie accepted the collect call. Annie was a constant. Like the valley wind, I could always count on her to be there.

"Hi, Sheelie," she bubbled. "We got a puppy."

"How come you're not at school?" I turned my back on the dining room. "It's one o'clock."

"Because it's Saturday." She bit into something crunchy. "Want some apple?"

"Sure." I made crunching noises into the phone. "How's Beetle?"

"Boring. All he does is eat." Annie's breathing quickened. I pictured her prancing on her tiptoes. "The puppy's name is Wrinkles. George named her. We're training her to pee on the newspaper. Tell Joshie 'Hi.'"

I heard soft yipping. Annie giggled. The puppy had probably been my mother's idea. Let the dead dogs lie. And George naming the new dog was a good sign.

"I'll give Josh a kiss for you," I said, feeling a pang of guilt.

"Okay," she said. "Mom's out in the garden. You want me to get her?"

"Not now." I swallowed. "Annie?"

"What, Sheelie?"

"I love you."

⌒

The waitress in Sambo's brought coffee over to the booth where I sat. An infant slept in a bassinette on the table next to my booth. The mother read the newspaper and ate her lunch. I ordered a ham sandwich, drank the stale brew.

There was a man at the counter wearing a hat like the one I had just bought. He motioned for the waitress, and she hurried over, carrying a full pot. He tapped a fresh pack of Camels on his thigh. The waitress refilled his coffee and flirted with him.

"Is Buck really your name?" She plumped out her lips and laughed. "Sounds like a movie star."

"It can't be," I whispered and noticed the weather-beaten hands.

Not *the* Buck, *my* Buck. My fingers gripped the table. I felt a slipping sensation, as though I might be swallowed if I didn't hang on tight. But this man's skin had a grayish tint. His profile, a weary look. No crooked grin.

"Far from a movie star," he said to the waitress. He coughed and cleared the mucus in his throat. "And your name?"

"Diane." She stuck out her hand. "Pleasure."

The cook hit the pickup bell, and the waitress went over to the food-pickup window. She stacked three plates up her arm.

The man at the counter turned his head. As if he'd felt me gauging the accuracy of my perception. Me, churning stomach, heart thumping.

"Well, as I live and breathe," he murmured. Fear flickered in his eyes. "Sheila O'Connor."

He turned his head forward again. Took a sip of coffee. Pulled a cigarette from the pack. He got up slowly, grunting as he slid into the booth. Buck had aged fifteen years. More. And in only six months. I stared at him.

"What the hell are you doing in Chula Vista?" he asked.

"Traveling." I didn't have it in me to explain why I'd left home.

"Traveling has its downsides," he said. "I got dysentery in Oaxaca." The lustrous hair that had taken my breath away outside of the Hero had turned coarse and dull. "Soon as I find a trucker to ride with I'm going back to Atlanta. Must be fate, kid. You and me here."

The infant in the next booth let out a gargled cry. The mother took the baby from the bassinette. I watched her pour formula into a bottle and insert the nipple into the baby's mouth. The baby made gulping noises as it drank.

"There's no such thing." I pretended to read the label on the ketchup bottle. I wanted him to go.

"There you go again, being wise," he said. "If I'd known half of what you know."

I thought of Our Lady, the flickering candles. I had been naïve, not wise. This was false flattery.

I waited. My heartbeat slowed to normal. This was not the Buck who'd taken my heart for a ride. He rolled the unlit cigarette on the table in front of him.

"You're a coward, Buck," I said. "I see it now in your eyes."

"You got reason to think that. I should've let you alone." He sighed. "I'm going back to Atlanta. I have responsibilities."

His eyes weren't sea-foam green but the discolored eyes of a tired man with nowhere to go but home.

"You?" My laugh sounded hollow. "Like what?"

"A son." He looked up at me. "He must be two now. Figure it's time to do the right thing."

He lit the cigarette, took a few puffs, and then extinguished it. I stared at the ham sandwich on my plate. Present company had stolen my appetite. The price of mislaid love.

Buck insisted on walking over to the Chevron station with me. The mechanic rolled a new tire over to the VW sitting inside the garage. He waved a greasy hand at me.

"I'm almost done," the mechanic called. He wiped the back of the hand across his forehead, leaving a black stripe. "About ten more minutes."

I stood with Buck, waiting. Not lusting or longing. Just waiting.

Buried under the thrill of meeting Buck had been the knowledge of him running from more than Vietnam. But running from a child was not running. He'd given into the same weakness Daddy had. The only difference between them was Buck had a chance to make it right. This didn't make him a good man.

"Be good, kid." He flinched when I refused his hand, then sighed. "All right then."

His slumped frame wandered slowly towards Sambo's. I felt neither desire nor pity. I watched him disappear into the restaurant. A bus pulled up to the stop. One man got off, another got on. I wasn't ready to leave. Not quite yet.

"Can I leave my car for a while longer?" I smiled at the mechanic.

"How long will you be?" He looked at his watch impatiently.

"Half hour," I said. "Fill the tank. I have a long drive ahead of me."

Passing the Sambo's, I caught my reflection. A bit disheveled but still pretty, tall and lanky as always, with a couple of extra inches thanks to the cowboy hat. I tipped the hat at me. Behind my reflection, Buck sat alone at the counter. He could have been anyone.

"You did it, Shee." I opened my arms wide and laughed aloud. "You made it."

I had too. I'd made it through Daddy's failures and misguided choices. Through the pain he had endured that I had mistaken as mine. Through the loss of all the people I had tried to love but had found my love wanting. The wanting I knew now had been their own. Still I had Annie. And Josh. And my mother.

Jasmine perfumed the air. I turned into the cool passageway

and heard the tinkle of chimes. I thought of the C Street garden, now under the new owner's care. As it should be.

I stepped into the sunlit courtyard. To my surprise, no chimes hung from the small olive tree with black buds. In the center of the garden sat the plain wood bench. I rested there, breathing in the scent of jasmine.

I wondered if my mother had made any progress on the new garden. I imagined Annie and the new puppy next spring, together bounding down the paths my mother planned to line in river rock. My mother shooing the dog from freshly planted beds. Her smile and Annie's giggles. I couldn't miss this. Not for my crazy on-the-road aspirations. I was ready to call my mother now.